Constable Country

By Catherine Aird

A Hole in One
Losing Ground
Past Tense
Dead Heading
Last Writes
Learning Curve
Inheritance Tracks
Constable Country

a&b

Constable Country

Catherine Aird

Allison & Busby Limited
11 Wardour Mews
London W1F 8AN
allisonandbusby.com

First published in Great Britain by Allison & Busby in 2023.
This paperback edition published by Allison & Busby in 2023.

A CIP catalogue record for this book is available from the British Library.

10 9 8 7 6 5 4 3 2 1

ISBN 978-0-7490-3085-8

Typeset in 11/16 pt Sabon LT Pro by
Allison & Busby Ltd.

By choosing this product, you help take care of the world's forests.
Learn more: www.fsc.org.

Printed and bound by
CPI Group (UK) Ltd, Croydon, CR0 4YY

For Sebastian Sharp with love
and in memory of
Theresa, Wayne, Miranda and Carol

CHAPTER ONE

Stephanie Wakefield was never to forget that day.

Ever.

The first inkling she'd had that something was wrong came when her husband had got back from work that afternoon, although she didn't appreciate quite how very wrong things were until later that evening. She had begun to suspect it, though, when Michael was late coming through from his study for their supper. She'd heard his car turn in to the Old Rectory drive at Little Missal after he'd come home rather earlier than usual but then he'd gone straight into his study – in reality it was more studio than study – as soon as he had entered the house. And that was without coming into the kitchen to deliver his customary kiss whilst she was getting their evening meal ready, which was quite unusual.

As Michael Wakefield went into his study, she had heard him shut the door behind him much more firmly and noisily than was necessary. This was always a signal that he didn't want to be disturbed whilst he was in there. And she never did. He hated to be interrupted, especially if he had brought work home with him. He was the graphic design specialist at their printing firm and sometimes needed to concentrate in peace and quiet rather than in the bustle of the workplace and its noisy machinery. Especially when there was a publishing deadline involved.

That was only the first sign that something was wrong.

The second could be seen when he finally emerged from the other room. He wasn't an old man, but his back was bent like that of one, with all his customary aplomb gone. He asked her if she'd already uncorked that evening's wine.

'Of course,' she said, surprised. She always uncorked the wine about an hour beforehand for their evening meal. 'It's a Portuguese red. You like it.'

When he groaned aloud at this, she was even more certain that something was awry. She said lightly, 'We're having a nice piece of topside tonight but you're not getting any pudding. You know what the doctor said about your substantial paunch.'

His only response was to go back into his study.

'Is your tummy all right, Mike?' she called out after him. That at least might explain his strange behaviour.

'Nothing's all right,' her husband said to her as he closed the study door behind him even more forcefully than before, 'and never will be ever again,' he added under his breath.

She took another look at him later when they were sitting at the dinner table and noticed that he did indeed look a little whey-faced round the gills. He had certainly lost his appetite, protesting when she tried to put a third slice of beef on his plate. 'We can always have it cold tomorrow,' he said, refilling his glass for the second time.

So it wasn't his tummy that was troubling him, she decided. Something was, though, and something also told her not to mention the beef casserole she was already planning for their meal the next day.

'By the way,' she remarked presently when, unusually for him, he hadn't made any effort at all at making conversation about his day, 'Christine rang this afternoon to say that they won't be coming to lunch on Sunday after all.'

Christine Forres was the wife of her husband's business partner, Malcolm, and the couple were in the habit of coming to lunch with the Wakefields at the Old Rectory on a Sunday every now and again through the year.

'They'll never be coming to lunch at this house again,' her husband responded savagely. 'Ever.'

'What on earth do you mean, Mike?' she said, surprised.

'Exactly what I said.'

Stephanie murmured, 'Actually, she didn't say anything about them being away on holiday on Sunday.'

'They aren't,' he snapped.

His wife frowned. 'Now I come to think of it, though, the telephone call did say it was an international one. That's odd, isn't it, dear, if she and Malcolm aren't on holiday?' She tried to offer him some more roast beef but he waved her hand away. 'Perhaps Malcolm's gone on a business trip and taken Christine with him. You did say something about looking for good leather abroad, didn't you?'

'It's not odd at all,' he came back quickly.

'But surely,' she persisted, puzzled, 'you'd have known at the office if they'd been going away.' The premises of the firm of Wakefield and Forres were in a business park on the outskirts of the market town of Berebury and not all that far away from the popular village of Little Missal, where they lived.

This time he came back even more smartly to what she had said. 'Running away is exactly what I would have expected of the pair of them in the circumstances.'

'Running away? What circumstances, Mike? Tell me.'

'Malcolm Forres and his precious wife, Christine, not to put too fine a point on it, Steph, have scarpered, leaving me to hold the baby.'

'What baby?'

He didn't answer this. Instead, he said thickly,

'They'll have fled the country by now, I shouldn't wonder. If you ask me, it's the only thing they could possibly have done in the circumstances.'

'Fled the country? And in what circumstances, anyway? What on earth are you talking about?'

'I expect Interpol are already looking for them by now,' he muttered into his glass.

'Interpol?' Her eyebrows shot up.

'Simon Puckle advised me to tell the police and so I did.' Simon Puckle was the senior partner of the firm of Puckle, Puckle and Nunnery, Solicitors and Notaries Public, of Berebury. Wakefield reached for the wine bottle again. 'Much good that will do to them – or us, come to that,' he added mordantly.

'The police?' She was really worried now. 'Mike,' she implored him, 'in heaven's name, whatever's the matter? You must tell me.'

'Joint and several liability, that's what's the matter, Stephanie,' he explained in a morose tone, swallowing another mouthful of wine, 'and I can't do anything at all about it. Not a single bloody thing.'

'What thing? I don't know what on earth you're talking about.'

He didn't answer her directly. Instead, he carried on. 'Simon Puckle says the government are planning to change the law introducing an option to turn it into something called an LLP, whatever that might be, but they haven't got round to it yet – governments are as slow as lawyers in actually doing anything.'

'Anything about what?' she said insistently.

He ignored this, too. 'And anyway, it's too late to do us any good now, even if they did.'

She still didn't know what he was talking about and said so now, adding firmly, 'Michael Wakefield, are you drunk?'

'No, but I'm hoping to be any minute now.'

'Why?'

'Because,' he said in a sudden burst of frankness, 'I've got to tell you something quite ghastly and I don't know how I'm going to do it. That's why.'

She looked up, suddenly stricken, blood draining instantly from her cheeks. 'Oh, Mike, not one of the children?'

He shook his head. 'No, Toby and Fiona are both all right – for the time being anyway, that is.'

She let out a long sigh of relief. 'That's all right, then.'

'No, it's not all right, Stephanie. What I meant was that their school fees are paid up to the end of the year but that's all.'

'I still don't understand.'

'What I've got to tell you, my dear,' he said, sinking his head in his hands, 'is, in a nutshell, that we're ruined. Absolutely ruined.'

She stared at him, her complexion slowly returning to normal after her fright over the children. She shook her head and said, 'I don't believe you. You're talking nonsense now.'

'No, I'm not,' he said bleakly. 'I only wish I were. We're absolutely and completely ruined.'

'Who says so?'

'Fixby and Fixby – well, actually not Herbert Fixby himself. It's their new girl who gave me the bad news today. She's called Kate Booth.' He steadied himself and reached for the wine bottle again. 'Good stuff, this,' he said, reading the label. 'Pity we shan't be having any more of it ever again.'

'Michael Wakefield,' she said, dangerously calm now that she knew their two children were safe, 'will you please tell me in the name of goodness what you're talking about. And what has somebody called Kate Booth got to do with it?' She reached across the table and removed the bottle of red wine out of his reach.

'Fixby and Fixby are our accountants, long time.'

'I do know that much, thank you,' she said crisply. 'And?'

'And old Herbert's a bit past it these days and his son, Jason, has proved to be a bit of a disappointment to the firm and so neither of them really kept an eye on the ball properly.'

'What ball?'

'Our partnership's finances.'

Stephanie didn't pretend to understand the world of business but even she knew what questions to ask. 'Isn't that what all accountants are supposed to do?'

'It is,' he said wearily. 'They took on this new girl, Kate Booth, because of Herbert's being over the hill nowadays and his son Jason being somewhat unreliable . . .'

'I heard that it was gambling,' remarked Stephanie. 'Or was it the horses?'

'Well, this Kate Booth, she spotted it as soon as she took a good look at the books.'

'Spotted what?'

'That Malcolm Forres has been robbing the firm blind for years.'

'Malcolm?' She stared at him. 'Are you mad? I don't believe it.'

His shoulders sagged. 'I didn't believe it either myself at first. Then, after this young woman Kate Booth spelt it out to me this morning, I had to.'

'Can't Simon Puckle sort it all out for you?' The firm of Puckle, Puckle and Nunnery, Solicitors and Notaries Public, had always acted for the Wakefield family as well as the firm of Forres and Wakefield.

'Not for just me, Steph – you come into this whole mess, too. It's for both of us, actually, but, no, he can't.'

'Simon's a very good lawyer. Everyone says so.'

'I know that but the answer I'm afraid is still no, he can't. Simon told me so himself this afternoon.'

Wakefield drained his glass and looked hopefully across the dining table towards the wine bottle. When she shook her head, he said, 'That's where the "jointly and severally" comes from. Simon Puckle said it was in our partnership agreement.'

'What was?'

'The words "jointly and severally",' repeated her

husband, more in sorrow than in anger now, 'which means that I'm liable for what Malcolm's taken from the firm.'

'Taken?'

'Stolen, if you like.'

'Stolen? Malcolm? I don't believe it. You're quite sure, Mike, aren't you?'

'What's more to the point, Fixby and Fixby are. I've been talking with them all morning and with Simon Puckle all afternoon, too. Simon says he'll do all he can but not to hope for anything much being left after everything's been wound up.'

'And what exactly does that mean?'

'Going broke,' he said starkly. 'Bankrupt, if you like. That's what happens when you haven't got any money and you owe everybody lots and lots.'

She looked really dismayed now. 'But being bankrupt means losing everything, doesn't it?'

'Not quite.' He gave a mirthless laugh. 'They leave you with the tools of your trade and much good that will do me because all the partnership's assets will have to be sold to pay what we owe. It seems that he's been robbing us blind for a long time.'

Stephanie stared round their comfortable dining room, taking it in as if she were seeing it for the first time. Her gaze rested on the walnut sideboard, then on the cut-glass decanter set on it and the polished dining table with its set of six matching Georgian mahogany chairs that had been her first exciting purchase at an auction ever. Her eyes finally reached the red Turkish carpet that had been a wedding present from her parents. 'Not everything?' she whispered.

He nodded, being altogether without speech now.

CHAPTER TWO

'Couldn't it all be deemed just a civil matter between business partners?' suggested Superintendent Leeyes hopefully. It was later the next morning and he was sitting comfortably at his desk in the police station in Berebury, home of 'F' Division of the Calleshire County Constabulary. Detective Inspector C. D. Sloan was in attendance, the superintendent reading the message sheet in front of him the while. 'Then their lawyers could sort the whole thing out between themselves on a commercial basis without bothering us.'

The superintendent didn't like dealing with white-collar crime, which his subordinates suspected was because he didn't understand it.

'Then in that case, Sloan,' Leeyes concluded, 'we wouldn't have to.'

The detective inspector, sitting opposite him, shook

his head regretfully. 'I'm afraid not, sir,' he said, although he was quite busy enough himself already. Being able to take no action in the case of Forres and Wakefield would have suited him very well, too.

The superintendent sighed. 'And why not, might I ask?'

'Because the complainant's solicitor had already advised the injured party to get in touch with us straight away.' The inspector was the head of the tiny Criminal Investigation Department of 'F' Division and all such crime as was committed there came within his remit.

'Oh, he had, had he?' grunted Leeyes, who didn't have a lot of time for the legal profession in any shape or form at the best of times. He considered it quite unreasonable that whilst the police always strove to uphold the law on behalf of honest citizens, defence lawyers were always seeking to find ways round it on behalf of those who had broken it. It was this last that was the rub.

'Michael Wakefield – that's the name of the victim, sir – also said to us,' went on Sloan carefully, 'that he'd been told, according to one of this man's neighbours out at Peverton village, Wakefield's business partner – that's a man called Malcolm Forres—'

'The villain of the piece, I take it,' interrupted the superintendent with a fine disregard for police impartiality and such matters that were still unproven.

'Had apparently left his residence in the village out there,' carried on Sloan, 'together with his wife in a great hurry very late indeed the night before last.'

The superintendent grunted again.

'Thus, doing what we would in other circumstances have called "a moonlight flit",' finished Sloan, distancing the move from that of a common or garden non-payment of rent to a cheated landlord.

'Do I understand you to mean, Sloan,' the superintendent came back smartly, 'that I am meant to believe that this Forres fellow actually told these neighbours that he was fleeing the country in a great hurry after dark because he'd fleeced his business partner?'

'There was a cat, sir.'

'So, he's not all bad? That's what you're trying to tell me, is it? That being an animal lover should make you exempt from police pursuit?' The superintendent was known to hold the simple view about animals that if you couldn't eat them, then you shouldn't keep them.

'No, sir. Not at all,' said Sloan hastily. 'I'm merely passing on what Michael Wakefield is reported to have been told that Malcolm Forres had said to the neighbours.' Sloan smothered a sigh. Sometimes the superintendent could be altogether too keen on chapter and verse.

'Which was?'

'That he and Forres' wife, Christine, were responding to a sudden family emergency and had to leave their home in Peverton village as quickly as possible in order that they could to get there in time and would the neighbours be kind enough to feed the cat until they got back.'

Leeyes, never an animal lover at the best of times, sniffed.

'And that they would come back home as soon as they possibly could,' finished Sloan. He planned to talk to the Forres' next-door neighbour over at Peverton himself as soon as he could.

'Which, therefore, could be said to be true as far as it went,' said Leeyes, adding sarcastically, 'I suppose it's too much to ask if they mentioned a destination to this neighbour.'

'No, sir, I'm afraid they didn't.'

'And what exactly, may I ask,' said Leeyes, as always sounding rather like Lady Bracknell, 'have you done about this man, Forres, and his wife apparently absconding after allegedly defrauding a business partner but still caring about the welfare of a cat?'

'We alerted the usual ports and aircraft terminals immediately,' said Sloan, trying not to sound too defensive, 'although I imagine it will have been a little late for that because the pair of them would almost certainly have been able to be well out of the country by the time we did so. Michael Wakefield – that's the man who's reported it to us—'

'The injured party, I take it,' said Leeyes.

'Him,' said Sloan cogently. 'This man Wakefield also seemed to think it would have been too late because he only became aware that his partner had scarpered because the man hadn't turned up at their place of work yesterday morning for an important annual accounts meeting.' Sloan glanced down at his notebook. 'That was when Fixby and Fixby, their accountants, brought Wakefield up to speed on the supposed theft.'

'Which means that this Malcolm Forres had had plenty of time to make good his disappearance,' concluded Leeyes, seizing as always on what mattered to the police. 'And to destroy any incriminating evidence as well, I suppose,' he added automatically.

'I can only assume that the meeting being arranged for the next day is what will have brought matters to a head over there at Peverton that night, sir.'

Leeyes grunted.

The detective inspector hurried on. 'It had been arranged as was customary at this time of the year by their accountants—'

'Fixby and Fixby.' Leeyes nodded.

'To take place at Forres and Wakefield's offices at the firm in the business park in Berebury at eleven o'clock the next morning.'

'Yesterday,' said Leeyes.

'Yes, sir. That meeting was presumably known by both the partners to be for the signing off, together with their accountants, of the business's annual accounts, as was normal at this time every year.'

'It's usually when a firm's accounts aren't ready to be signed off at the usual time of the year that you get real trouble,' remarked Leeyes sagely. 'It's a sure sign that something's wrong with the business.'

'Obviously,' ventured Sloan, keeping a wary eye on the expression on his superior officer's face, 'if this partner Forres is the guilty party, he wouldn't have wanted to be sitting around waiting for any denouement by the firm's accountants.'

'And at the same time, the rest of them who were there were presumably going to be told that everything wasn't hunky-dory,' concluded the superintendent. 'That's what started the whole messy caboodle off, I take it?'

'Yes, sir. There is one other rather worrying thing . . .'

The superintendent adjusted his position in his office chair for greater comfort. 'Go on.'

'The only possible conclusion that I can draw, sir, is that Malcom Forres didn't show up because he had somehow or other got wind of the fact that the balloon was about to go up that morning and therefore made very sure that he wasn't there when it did. And that his wife wasn't available either.'

'He would have known that the accounts were to be presented, surely,' objected Leeyes. 'After all, he is a partner, and if he had had anything to do with any shortfall he would have known about it anyway long before that.'

'I admit that's a bit of a puzzle, sir.'

'Doesn't make sense to me,' said Leeyes flatly.

'But he might not necessarily have known that the defalcation would come to light just then,' suggested

Sloan. The word 'defalcation' had only been mentioned once as a crime during his training and he relished the opportunity of using it now.

'Explain yourself, man.'

'For all we know he might have been getting away with robbery at a lesser level in previous years, sir.' Sloan had already made a note that this possibility had to be considered but not necessarily explored at this stage.

'How could he have done that?' Leeyes asked at once.

'I don't really know, sir. Perhaps by stealing less at a time before then. I understand he's actually taken the lot this year – if it is him,' he added hastily, mindful that nothing had yet been proven. 'But it might not have been the first time.' He paused as another uneasy thought crossed his mind. 'And if young Fixby was in dire need of money, I'm afraid that – theoretically at least – he could have been hand-in-glove with Forres in helping him in robbing the firm and then covering it up in the books. In which case Forres wouldn't have expected the annual meeting to have presented any problem to him.'

'Many a mickle makes a muckle,' observed Leeyes obscurely.

'The word on the street, I understand, sir, is that old Herbert Fixby, the accountant, is not the man he was and young Jason Fixby, his son, isn't up to it either as well as having taken to the horses.'

'The most dangerous animal known to man for money,' said Leeyes, 'and second only to polar bears for lives.'

'Really, sir?' said Sloan, trying to keep to the point. 'And in theory it's always possible that this man Malcolm Forres might not have known that Fixby and Fixby had taken a smart young cookie on the staff.' He chose not to volunteer the information that the smart young cookie was a woman, the superintendent being distinctly behind the times when it came to women's progress within the professions.

The superintendent leant back in his chair and twiddled his pen. 'So, Sloan, you're suggesting, are you, that someone in Fixby's office might have tipped the wink to Malcolm Forres that the balloon was about to go up, so that then he could make a getaway in time?'

'I'm only saying that someone might have done, sir.'

Leeyes stroked his chin. 'As you say, even young Fixby himself, perhaps. If he's strapped for cash and wanted Forres to hand over some readies in exchange for a timely tip-off, he might have done rather well.'

'Could be,' said Sloan, who had already lived long enough to know that there was some clay in the feet of all men. 'Or it could be just plain inefficiency before they took on this new employee. Lax procedures, perhaps,' he suggested, greatly daring. Keeping to long-established – not to say outdated – practices at Berebury Police Station was something the rank and file on the strength didn't like.

'Or someone in Forres and Wakefield's own firm, perhaps?' suggested Leeyes. 'They could have guessed or even known something was up, too.'

'That I don't know either at this stage, sir, not knowing yet who works there, but I shall certainly look into it.' Knowing who could have – might have – tipped the wink to the guilty party before the police got to them was always something that mattered in every investigation. At the very least it implied a disrespect for the law but more usually improper complicity, if not actual collaboration. Or even misguided sympathy, sob stories sometimes having unexpected outcomes.

'Better get on with that, then, Sloan,' said Leeyes. 'Although in my own experience, money people are usually quite cagey about what they tell other people and aren't given to letting cats out of bags before they should.' He paused and, mindful of some still unsolved cases in his patch, added thoughtfully, 'If ever.'

'What we don't know yet either, sir,' went on Sloan, 'is exactly when Forres knew that the balloon was about to go up, let alone who told him. This Michael Wakefield – as I said, he's the injured party, big time – told the solicitor that the whole debacle had been news to him until the point when their accountant spelt it all out to him at yesterday morning's annual meeting.' The Sloan family finances were kept on a rather shorter rein as their mortgage payments fell due once a month. And it would seem kept on a rather tighter rein, too, than some.

'Ah, and so in theory this man Forres shouldn't have known anything was missing before his partner, Michael Wakefield, did,' concluded the superintendent smartly. 'Or, come to that, anyone else either.'

'Exactly, sir,' said Sloan. 'No one else at all except the accountants who had no reason to talk to anyone else. Besides, it would have been quite unprofessional of them anyway if in the event they had done so.'

'But presumably this partner – Malcolm Forres, did you say he was called? – could have already worked out that this annual meeting might well be the point when the cat would be let out of the bag.'

'Could be, sir,' admitted Sloan.

'And so I suppose he had already taken off together with his wife before anything became known.' Leeyes gave a thin smile. 'Leaving their live cat behind and not in any bag.'

Sloan acknowledged this witticism with a nod. 'Presumably, sir.' He didn't like white-collar crime any more than the superintendent did: give him a simple case of assault any day. You knew where you were with physical violence and injury to real persons – that is, if you couldn't have burglars in striped shirts carrying bags labelled 'Swag' as you had done in the comics of his boyhood.

Leeyes drummed his fingers on his desk. 'Which suggests to me, Sloan, that the Forres family's absence might be going to be a prolonged one. Especially if they had already created a well-funded bolt hole in some unknown country abroad.' He scowled, foreign administrations without extradition treaties always being an anathema to him.

'Quite so, sir. And I'm afraid,' he said practically, 'it also has the effect of leaving Christine Forres unavailable for us to interview.' Wives might not in theory have to give information about their husbands to the police – and have it all discounted in court anyway if they did – but it was a very clever woman indeed who never revealed anything at all in response to skilled police questioning.

'This injured party – how injured, Sloan? What sort of scale are we talking about?'

'Mega. Simon Puckle, as I said, he's the firm's solicitor, at this stage is calling the whole affair misappropriation of the firm's assets without specifying how much has been taken or by whom.'

'Cagey blighter.'

'Yes, sir.' In Sloan's experience, solicitors usually were.

'There are a lot of fancy names for one party stealing from another,' pronounced the superintendent weightily, 'but it all comes to the same thing in the end. Larceny was a popular name for it in my day.'

'It sounds to have been grand larceny to me, sir,' said Sloan, consulting his notebook. 'For starters all the liquid assets of the firm have disappeared overnight. Working capital, bank reserves, advance payments, paper assets and so forth, all gone. We don't know exactly where yet,' he added, conscious that the police would sooner or later have to find out. He looked down at his notebook. 'Oh, and the title deeds to the firm's property are missing from the office safe.'

'An inside job, then,' concluded Leeyes.

'Possibly so, sir,' he said. 'It's too soon to say.'

'Never look a gift horse in the mouth, Sloan.'

'No, sir. Sorry, sir.'

'And what may I ask does this outfit . . .'

'Forres and Wakefield,' supplied Sloan.

'Do to earn their daily crust?'

'They're printers of top-notch illustrated books for upmarket publishing firms. Wakefield took care of the artistic element and Forres saw to the business side.'

'Which he seems to have done to his own satisfaction, if nobody else's,' observed Leeyes neatly.

'Yes, sir.' White-collar crime hadn't ever been Sloan's favourite subject either and it certainly wasn't now.

Leeyes sighed and fingered the paper on his desk. 'Well, I suppose you'd better do what you can, Sloan,' said the superintendent, offloading the message sheet and therefore the problem across his desk to his subordinate. 'You might as well take that boy Crosby with you out to the Wakefields' house at Little Missal. He's as dim as an inkle-weaver. At least if you do that it'll get him out from under everybody's feet here today and that's always something on the credit side seeing as we're talking about balance sheets.'

The sigh on the part of Detective Inspector Sloan was

unexpressed but no less heartfelt. He suppressed the thought that a chocolate teapot would have been more useful in most of the cases Crosby had had any part in in his short career in the force. Detective Constable William Edward Crosby was the youngest and most jejune policeman in 'F' Division of the Calleshire County Constabulary and prone to making faux pas in plenty.

The superintendent sniffed. 'I'm told he's been asking Inspector Harpe if he could transfer to Traffic Division because he says there's not enough excitement in the detection branch.'

Sloan said that he didn't suppose for one moment that a white-collar crime such as this one appeared to be at this stage would provide the detective constable with any excitement whatsoever.

He had seldom been so wrong.

CHAPTER THREE

Stephanie Wakefield hadn't slept any better than her husband had done the night before. They'd talked until two o'clock in the morning, Stephanie herself falling into a fitful sleep about three. When she awoke and came downstairs to make their breakfast, she found Michael already sitting at the kitchen table, cradling a mug of coffee. He had dressed for work.

'You're still going in as usual?' she said, slightly surprised. 'Somehow I didn't think that you'd be going over to the works this morning.'

'I've got to. I must be there,' he said, 'because whatever happens I've got to sign off the proofs of the Almstone Press book today. The earl will be very disappointed if his precious autobiography isn't published on time and his publishing firm will lose a lot of money and so will we.' The Earl of Ornum had recently committed to paper some reminiscences of his life and family under the title of *Muniments and their Hanapers*. 'Besides,' went on the printer, 'he's got this socking great launch party arranged at Ornum House at the weekend. Don't forget we're both invited, will you? Les Moran and his wife are still on their world cruise and so they can't go.'

Stephanie stirred her coffee mug and, forgetful for a moment of her own troubles, said, 'If the earl would only write something about those two daughters of his instead, I reckon it would sell a great deal better.'

'Very true, it would,' agreed her husband, starting to get to his feet. 'I don't know which of them causes the more trouble – Mary or Victoria.'

'Victoria,' said Stephanie promptly. 'At least that's what I heard although I must say Lady Mary runs her a close second.' The antics of the young Ornum twins were a byword in the county. 'The Twindles, they call themselves.'

'They would.' Her husband was already shovelling some papers into his briefcase and said, 'I must get going, dear. Gilbert told me that the publishers delivered the corrected page proofs to us yesterday afternoon.' He swallowed the last of his coffee, and set the mug back on the table, saying, 'At least everyone in the firm knows that that book needs seeing through the press as soon as possible no matter what.'

She did know that. Gilbert Hull was their production manager as well as being a highly skilled printer himself and responsible for getting books printed on time.

Wakefield carried on, 'And you know what they're like over there at the Almstone Press.'

Stephanie did indeed know what the private press people were like – especially the Almstone one. High-class luxury printing, fore-edge painting, gold tooling and leather casing didn't come cheap and moreover demanded highly skilled workmanship. The firm produced books that were meant to be shown off to and admired by a small coterie of learned bibliophiles or deposited in national and wealthy aristocratic libraries: something the printing experts at Forres and Wakefield were only too cognisant of. And if they hadn't been, then the publisher was usually on hand to remind them, especially when that publisher was Almstone Press, owned by the very demanding Leslie Moran.

Stephanie wanted to ask her husband who he had in mind when using the word 'us' in today's circumstances but thought better of it and only nodded. 'What will you say to Gilbert and the rest of the staff about Malcolm when you get in?' she said instead. 'Gilbert's certainly not going to be happy when he finds out what's happened to the firm.'

'I haven't decided yet. I wouldn't really want to brief him ahead of everyone else,' said Wakefield uneasily. 'You know how quickly rumours start. In fact, I'm not at all sure that Kay Harris hasn't already spotted that something's wrong. She's always in early and although I locked Malcolm's office door as soon as I realised what had happened, I can't be sure that she hadn't already been in there and spotted something was up, too. You know what she's like.'

'Inquisitive,' said Stephanie promptly. Kay Harris was their in-house layout specialist and fiendishly pernickety guardian of grammar in all their publications.

'Having the Almstone Press people breathing down our necks is quite enough on my plate already today,' said her husband, 'without my needing any more hassle.'

'I can understand that.' Stephanie nodded. 'There would be a lot of talk. Bound to be.'

Her husband went on, 'And you know what Leslie Moran over at Almstone can be like if everything isn't up to snuff. The manuscript had to be ready for us to start printing today or it wouldn't be on schedule for delivery on Friday and then there'd have been hell to pay all round.'

His wife nodded, still fearful of saying the wrong thing, but glad that Mike was still concentrating on his work.

'And that book's going to be a real winner, Steph.'

'Good,' she said warmly.

'From the earl's point of view, anyway, if nobody else's. He's very pleased with it so far and so he should be.' Wakefield always took the view that the contents of the books they printed were none of his concern. It was the physical book that mattered to him.

'Good,' she said again.

'I must say Forres and Wakefield have made a thoroughly good job of it.' Wakefield had vowed never to mention Malcolm Forres' name ever again and so he went on hastily, 'Gilbert's done exceptionally well with all the illustrations.' Gilbert Hull was a dab hand at dealing with those. And with photographs.

'But did you get it past Kay all right?'

She knew that Mrs Kay Harris was also their proofreader par excellence, quite prepared to hold up production over a semi-colon and ready to deliver her renowned disquisition on the Oxford comma at any time.

He managed a half-smile and a nod.

'Will you still be able to start printing it today, though?' Stephanie asked dubiously. 'That's if the firm isn't yours any longer? Technically, I mean, of course,' she added hurriedly, catching sight of the expression on his face.

'I think so since it's work in progress. Leslie Moran'll be pretty upset if we can't,' her husband replied. 'Seeing as the Ornums have got this enormous launch party lined up for it over at Ornum House with the local press and all coming, to say nothing of the great and the good of the whole county.'

'And the twins,' pointed out Stephanie.

He grimaced. 'It does mean, though, that I'll have to come to some arrangement with the bank pretty smartly so that we can keep going on a day-to-day basis. I'm going to go and see them as soon as I possibly can. We'll need the money for the wages by the end of the month. And more paper, too.' He downed the last of his coffee as he shrugged his shoulders into his coat. 'Luckily, we'd just paid the ink people.'

'Then you haven't told the staff anything at all?' she persisted.

'Not yet,' he said. 'I don't want to risk anyone walking out on us – I mean, me – before this book gets printed.'

CHAPTER FOUR

Breakfast at Ornum House was more traditional than that which was usually eaten elsewhere in the county of Calleshire. Nothing out of cardboard boxes graced the table there. Serving dishes at Ornum were still laid out in the old-fashioned way on the long sideboard in the dining room with the family helping themselves to whatever they wanted as and when they appeared downstairs.

'Now that damn printer, Michael Wakefield, won't even let me have marble endpapers in my book,' complained Jonas Augustus Bonamy Cremond, 15th Earl of Ornum, casting an opened letter down on the breakfast table with a gesture of disdain.

His wife, Letitia, murmured, 'How tiresome of him, dear,' but didn't look up from her study of the Births, Marriages and Deaths columns in the daily newspaper.

'The man seems to forget who's paying the bill for

printing my book.' The earl puffed his chest out and said, 'After all, I am the author.'

'And how,' muttered his daughter Victoria under her breath.

'What's marbling?' asked his other daughter, Mary, her twin.

'A nice design inside both the front and back covers of a book,' said her father. 'The endpapers, they call them.'

'Wavy lines,' pronounced Victoria.

'In colour,' added her father.

'Usually just shades of dark blue,' said Victoria. She was the elder twin and inclined to make much of it. 'Mixed with red.'

'Blue and red is mauve,' said Mary.

'T'isn't,' said her sister.

'Blue with a touch of red, then,' came back Mary.

'Don't argue,' said her mother automatically. 'By the way, darlings, who's coming for the weekend?'

'Simon,' said Victoria immediately. 'He dances divinely. Unless, that is,' she added, 'he's in today's hatches, matches and dispatches.'

'His what?' asked her father.

'Oh, Daddy, don't be such an old fogey,' said Mary. 'Victoria means the births, marriages and deaths column that Mummy always reads in the newspaper first thing every morning.'

'To see who's been born, got married or died,' supplemented Victoria.

'He isn't there,' said her mother, looking up from her paper. 'There's nobody in there called Simon today. What about you, Mary? Who are you going to invite?'

'Charles,' said Mary dreamily. 'At least I think I will.' She frowned. 'Or perhaps not. Daniel's really much more fun.'

'May I remind you both,' said their father sternly, 'that the occasion is the launch of my book and not a jolly for you two.'

'Simon, did you say, Victoria?' echoed Mary, taking no notice of what her father had said. 'Why not Roderick?'

'Don't tease your sister, Mary,' said their mother, aware of a blush rising on her other daughter's cheek.

'That's if Simon's very good,' said Victoria as if she hadn't heard her twin mention Roderick, 'and only if he brings his car.'

'You could have used yours if you hadn't bashed it about so much,' pointed out her father, helping himself to a plate of kedgeree from a still-warm chafing dish laid out on the long sideboard. He soon put his fork down so that he could riffle about among his post again. 'I've had the estimate for repairing your car this morning. "Making good" is what they call it at the garage. I wish you'd do a bit of that, too, Victoria.'

Victoria pouted. 'Don't be like that, Daddy. I wasn't going all that fast.'

'That, my dear girl, is a matter of fact, not opinion,

and incidentally not what the police had to say on the matter at the time.'

'Inspector Harpe is always so sweet,' she murmured. 'He understands that a girl has the urge to put her foot down sometimes.'

'The police also said, if I remember rightly,' carried on her father, 'that you should expect to receive a summons from them in due course for exceeding the speed limit in a built-up area.'

'Oh, that's all right, Daddy,' she said airily. 'I've had that already and I've sent it on to that nice Mr Puckle at the solicitors', like always.'

Her mother lowered her newspaper. 'Oh, Victoria, do try to speak the Queen's English. Saying "like always" is not grammatical.'

'But everyone knows what I mean and that's all that matters, isn't it?'

'Not quite,' said her father.

'Besides,' said Victoria, 'Mr Puckle always takes care of that sort of thing.'

'Whilst I take care of his fees, I suppose,' grumbled the Earl of Ornum.

'Well, someone has to,' pointed out his daughter practically, 'and I can't since I don't have any money.'

'You would have if you spent your allowance more carefully.'

She rolled her eyes. 'A girl has to have clothes.'

'She doesn't have to have quite so many,' countered her father.

Adept at defusing family conflicts and with a skill born of long practice, Letitia Ornum judged this the right moment to bring their argument to a close. Lifting her head again from her study of the newspaper, she said, 'You won't forget to collect the silver from the bank this morning, Jonas, will you? We'll need it for the party.'

'Couldn't the caterers just bring their own stuff?' he objected. 'They usually supply eating irons along with everything else.' Time was when everything needed for a celebration party would have been on hand in their own kitchens at Ornum House, but those days of the pre-war amplitude of entertaining with plenty of staff on hand were long gone. Now they managed with the help of one woman, Mrs Bennett, who came in from the village every day.

'The silver needs an airing, Jonas,' pointed out his wife. 'And it won't get another one until one of the girls gets married.'

'Married?' said Mary scornfully. 'I'm not going to get married. Matrimony is soooo old-fashioned these days.'

'I'm going to live in sin, too,' said Victoria. 'Much more fun.'

'Ornums only do that if they don't mind being disinherited,' said their mother, herself comfortable in the knowledge that young Lord Cremond, the Ornum son and heir, was still a schoolboy and contemplating nothing more important than being picked for the first cricket eleven the following Saturday. 'So, I hope that whoever eventually takes you off your father's hands can afford to keep you in the style to which you are accustomed.'

'And provide you with endless motor transport,' her father reminded them. 'Remember that we Ornums don't do sins-in-law. They don't go down well in the stud book.'

'He means the *Peerage*,' explained Victoria unnecessarily. 'I'm going to live in sin, too, Daddy, especially as Daniel couldn't afford to keep me in toothpaste let alone anything else.'

'Roderick could,' said her twin unhelpfully.

'Don't be so beastly,' said Victoria. 'Daniel says he hasn't even got any money to buy a proper shirt for the party and that he'll have to come as he is.'

'As long as Daniel can afford to buy a copy of my book, he can come,' said His Lordship, afflicted by an anxiety about sales figures common to all new authors.

'Daddy, he won't even understand the title, let alone what's in the book,' declared Victoria.

'I don't suppose anyone else will either,' chimed in Mary.

'What on earth are muniments and hanapers anyway, for heaven's sake?' asked Victoria. 'It's not exactly what you could call a catchy title, is it?'

'Muniments are all the deeds and documents about this house and our family, and hanapers are what you keep them in,' explained her father.

'Roderick's got plenty of money, even if Daniel hasn't,' remarked Mary. 'Oodles of it.'

'I'm not marrying either Daniel or Roderick,' said Victoria with dignity.

'I'm glad to hear it,' said her father. 'You're much too young, both of you.'

'What you are both doing, you girls, like it or not,' said their mother firmly, 'is cleaning the silver when it comes back from the bank.'

CHAPTER FIVE

Detective Constable Crosby had already brought the car round to the police station door and was waiting for Sloan at the ready. 'Where to, sir?' he asked.

'The Old Rectory, Church Street, at Little Missal,' said Sloan, adding swiftly that there was absolutely no urgency at all about their visit there this morning. Crosby's driving tended towards the fastest legal, if not rather more than that when out of town and more importantly when out of range of any speed cameras or any other police cars.

'Right posh village, that, sir,' the constable informed him, quite soon peeling off the main road and taking a minor one in a westerly direction.

Sloan nodded. 'So I've heard. And I may say that the Old Rectory that we're heading for now sounds like it's quite a posh address, too. Old rectories usually are both old and large, which is presumably why the church got rid of them in the first place.'

'Big families in those days,' observed the constable. 'Not like now.'

Detective Inspector Sloan resisted the temptation to say that nothing was like it used to be any more: there was no phrase that sounded more ageist – or, come to that, more like their own superintendent's oft-repeated sentiments. 'But I'm very much afraid that the Wakefields' current home address isn't likely to be a posh one for very much longer,' he said instead, having seen only too often what those compelled to downsize by death or divorce – let alone bankruptcy – had to resort to after the dust had settled on their shattered lives.

The constable changed gear and asked with interest if that was because someone was going to go to prison. 'It usually is, isn't it, sir?'

'I very much hope that someone is, Crosby, when we get him – or her, that is – but if I know the ways of the Crown Prosecution Service, it won't be until long after the Wakefields have lost their house and home. And I can tell you one thing for certain and that's that their next address won't be in the same league as any old rectory anywhere or in a village half as good as Little Missal.'

'Really, sir?'

Sloan went on to explain that it appeared that the owner of the house they were heading for, one Michael

Wakefield, had had all his money filched from him under his very nose: the firm's money, that is. 'I don't know about his own resources yet,' he said. 'But those'll have to go, too, unless they've already been put in his wife's name to be on the safe side in case of trouble.'

'Not all of it?' was the young constable's first wide-eyed reaction.

'All of it, Crosby,' said Sloan with some solemnity. There had been, he knew, those known as Names at the famous insurers, Lloyd's of London, who had also lost everything 'right down to their back-collar stud' as the old saying went, but that had been very different. Those people called Names had invested in the insurance market with their eyes wide open – or at the very least, they should have done – but the Wakefields' loss was somehow different, somehow sadder.

'Bad luck them losing everything,' said the constable, struggling to comprehend the enormity of such a loss.

'And moreover,' he added heavily, 'what is worse is that it would seem to have been brought about by someone Wakefield knew well.'

'An inside job, then,' decided the constable immediately, glancing in the rear-view mirror in case there were traffic cars about.

'In the sense that there hasn't been an actual break-in at the works, yes.' It was one of the aspects of white-collar crime that in Sloan's book made it worse – much worse – than a smash-and-grab raid. 'Betrayal' was the word that came first to his mind, and it was one guaranteed not to endear the perpetrator to anyone at all, no matter his or her gain. Treason was a crime high in most people's personal *Newgate Calendar*.

And in history.

And why the executioner at the Tower of London had been kept so busy. Traitors had no friends.

'How come?' asked the constable, changing down a gear for a tight bend.

'That is something we have yet to find out, which is why we're on our way out to Little Missal now.'

'I see, sir,' said Crosby, coming out of the bend, straightening up and taking a sudden left fork at a speed not quite commensurate with the camber of the narrow country road.

'In the meantime, Crosby, you might keep your speed down,' said Sloan, bracing his feet on the floor in front of his seat where he would have liked the brakes to be. 'And your eyes on the road, not on your rear-view mirror, please.'

'Very good, sir,' promised the constable, taking another swift turn down a road that led even further into the countryside. The police car next breasted a little hill, a pleasant rural valley then coming into view. The village of Little Missal was about half a mile further ahead on the other side of a lively-looking stream. As they drove over a small bridge and into its main street, Detective Inspector Sloan, the part owner (with the mortgage company, that is) of a small semi-detached house in suburban Berebury, decided that the village was in no danger of being described as 'twee'. This was by virtue of having at least two prosperous-looking farms in view and no imitation Tudor houses at all. What looked like a Tudor building in Little Missal was clearly a Tudor building whilst the enclosed courtyard adjacent to the nearby Royal Oak public house still spoke of the days of horses and stagecoaches, if not of good King Charles himself.

Sloan scanned the village street for a church and soon spotted the square tower of a Norman one and then saw the Old Rectory not far beyond it. Crosby drew the police car to a stop in front of the house, a pleasant Georgian building notable for the regularity of its features.

'And,' Sloan reminded Crosby as he released his seat belt, 'in the proper pursuit of our enquiries, we have also got to make quite sure that the man said to be the injured party—'

'Michael Wakefield?'

'Him,' agreed Sloan, 'isn't himself involved in any malfeasance connected with the disappearance of the firm's money?' He added drily, 'It has been known.'

'That he wasn't getting a bit of elbow for himself, you mean, sir?'

'Exactly. And don't forget the fact, either, that insurance fraud has also been known to happen in the best of circles. Some losses can be entirely fictitious.' He got out of the car and added sententiously, conscious of his duties as a mentor of the young, the superintendent's favourite mantra, '"Remember in all criminal cases, every avenue has to be explored without any preconceptions on the part of the investigating officers".'

'Yes, sir.' Crosby clambered out of the car and surveyed the building in front of them. 'Bit plain, isn't it, sir?' he said, viewing a perfectly ordered Georgian building, correct down to its last string course and alignment of doors and windows. He sniffed. 'It doesn't melt my butter.'

'I'm sorry about that,' said Sloan. 'Tell me, what sort of houses do – er – melt your butter?'

The constable grinned. 'Big stone ones, sir, with those holes in them at the top for firing out of.'

'Loopholes?' asked Sloan. 'Ah, yes.' He should have remembered that when Crosby had first joined the police force the constable had applied to be a member of the firearms squad, the idea of being strapped up appealing to him. The verbal and quite explicit reaction of the officer in charge of that section of 'F' Division had been the stuff of canteen gossip for several days.

'That's them, sir. You fired on people through them.'

'Or did something nasty with boiling oil down a handy murder hole behind the portcullis,' Sloan reminded him, advancing to the front door, and ringing the brass doorbell of the Old Rectory.

CHAPTER SIX

Michael Wakefield gave a deep sigh as he pushed open the double doors and entered his firm's works. He was trying hard not to think that one of these fine days it would be for the last time. The sight of his beloved antique handset printing machines – the famous Heidelberg Platen Press and the 1950s Vicobold one – standing opposite it in the entrance hall did nothing to cheer him today. All he could think was that those two ancient hot metal presses would have to go in the end to pay the business's debts. It would be like losing old friends.

'Morning, Mike.' Gilbert Hull, their production manager, looked up when he saw him come in and jerked his head in welcome. 'So, do you want the bad news or the bad news?'

'I'd better have them both,' said Wakefield evenly,

less bothered about talk of bad news today than he might once upon a time have been. He knew now that whatever it was, it couldn't possibly be worse than that which he had been told the day before. Michael Wakefield, master printer, businessman and husband and father, had only just begun to realise that even bad news had its own hierarchy of despair. 'What's wrong now?'

'Someone over in their office at Luston Printing Inks says there's something wrong with the cheque the firm gave them the other day.'

'Really? I'll ring them soonest,' promised Wakefield, 'and see what's up.'

Gilbert sniffed. 'There's no sign of Malcolm coming in again this morning so I couldn't ask him. It's his department, really, money. He wasn't in yesterday either. And another thing, Mike, he's gone and left his mobile phone behind when he left. He must have forgotten it although I can only say that it's not at all like him.'

'He must,' agreed Wakefield, 'and as you say, not at all like him.' Mobile phones, he knew – and he supposed Malcolm Forres knew, too – whether switched on or not, could be traced and reveal their whereabouts. Leaving it behind, he was sure, was no slip of his partner's memory: more likely to be a deliberate precaution against being traced and found by it.

'Probably why he hasn't been in touch,' said the production manager.

'Could be,' agreed Wakefield. 'And the other thing?'

'I've had that idiot Leslie Moran from the Almstone Press on to me from his cruise ship. He wants us to change the font on this famous production of his for old man Ornum. I ask you, Mike! We were absolutely ready for an all systems go first thing this morning and now he wants to change all the text from Baskerville to Garamond.' He swore gently. 'And that's not all he wants.'

'No? Go on.'

'He's wondering whether there's time to have some fore-edge printing done on his customer's precious new book.' He grinned sardonically. 'Or do I really mean his precious customer's new book?'

'No way,' pronounced Wakefield immediately. 'There isn't time for any of that nonsense. Not if he wants it printed this side of Christmas, that is.'

'That's what I told him. Thank God he didn't want a carpet page too although I wouldn't put it past him.'

'Nor would I,' said Wakefield. 'At least we're not dealing with an illuminated manuscript. That's something to be grateful for.'

Gilbert grimaced. 'Remember when we did?'

'A total nightmare.'

'Besides, we'd already done all the casting off for the Ornum book yesterday.'

Wakefield nodded. 'I know. At least you got it past Kay Harris. That's something to be happy about.'

'Even so, Les Moran wasn't happy, and he wants to talk to you.'

'For one thing,' said Wakefield, more to himself than to his production manager, 'Moran'll have to pay us a darn sight more quickly than he did for the last book we did for him and for another . . .'

He broke off as his telephone rang. He answered it and said, 'Yes? Who? Oh, good morning.' He listened carefully, thanked the caller at the other end of the line and said that he would visit their premises later that day.

'Sounds like I've got to go out presently, Gilbert,' said Wakefield, putting down the telephone. 'You'll have to deal with Moran when he rings again, I'm afraid. Thank God he's in Timbuktu or wherever and can't get to the office.'

The production manager gave a short laugh. 'Thanks a bundle.'

'You know that Les Moran usually calms down in the end. Besides, there are very few other people who do our sort of work these days for him to take his business to.' As soon as he had said this, Wakefield regretted it. The last thing he wanted to do was to remind his production manager that there wouldn't be any other firms around likely to take him on when Forres and Wakefield went out of business. Certainly not at his age.

'And as I told you, Mike, not only isn't Malcolm in today,' Gilbert reminded him pointedly, 'but he wasn't in yesterday either.'

'No,' agreed Wakefield, unwilling to say any more. 'He wasn't.'

'And for another thing . . .'

'Yes?'

'That boy was late again this morning.'

Wakefield knew without being told that when the production manager said 'That boy' he was referring to their apprentice, young Lenny Datchet. The lad was a real printer's imp if ever there was one, and an employer's nightmare into the bargain.

'Do you know what he said to me when I spoke to him about it?' asked an aggrieved Hull.

Wakefield had too much on his mind to think about idle apprentices. They were the same the world over and as they always had been throughout the ages. He shook his head whilst at the same time remembering the contract that he had signed, committing the firm to the apprenticeship of Lenny Datchet and to the boy's time off at the local college. What would happen to that now? he wondered to himself. He knew that death was said to cancel all contracts, but could the living do the same if they were bankrupt?

Hull was still talking. 'Do you know that Lenny had the cheek to tell me that punctuality wasn't his thing. His thing, indeed! I ask you!'

'He'll grow up one day,' murmured Mike absently, his mind on the telephone call he had just had.

'Mind you' – Hull gave a twisted grin – 'I was very nearly late in myself this morning. My wife's away at her mother's and I overslept.'

'Bad luck,' said Wakefield, who had hardly slept at

all himself the night before. 'Lenny's got a motorbike, hasn't he?' he said, hit by a sudden thought. 'So, he can take a copy of the earl's new book over to Ornum House as soon as it's printed. That'll keep the old man happy for a bit and get Datchet out from under.'

'Good thinking,' said Hull appreciatively. 'By the way, Mike . . .' He produced an envelope and handed it over. 'Two tickets for Sharon's next production for you both. It's a week on Saturday, remember? She's really into amateur dramatics these days.'

'I thought it was family history that she'd last gone overboard with?' Sharon was the man's daughter and a great enthusiast for whatever she took up next.

Gilbert sighed. 'Not any more. This time it's for the Berebury Amateur Dramatic Society's production of *The Importance of Being Earnest*.'

'And is Sharon in it herself?' asked Wakefield, one half of his mind elsewhere.

'Definitely not. Wardrobe mistress and that's keeping her busy enough as it is and so,' he added, 'our house is full of posh clothes. If you ask me, it's just as well my wife's gone to her mother's.'

Thanking him gravely for the two tickets, Michael thought that of all the punishments inflicted on the human race, obligatory attendance at an amateur dramatic performance of uncertain merit ranked high. 'Tell her we'll be there,' he said.

The production manager acknowledged this with a jerk of his head and said, 'So, what shall we do about this book of the earl's now that the timing's got so critical?'

Michael Wakefield, master printer and potential bankrupt, took a deep breath and said, 'To hell with the lot of them. Get started with printing it straight away. Let the presses run.'

'If you say so, Mike.'

'I do, Gilbert. So go ahead and print and be damned.'

CHAPTER SEVEN

Stephanie had sent her husband off to work with a wave of her hand and then had sat down again herself on the chair in front of the kitchen table, pulling a mug of coffee towards her as she did so. She didn't really feel like eating any breakfast this morning. She glanced at the clock. Ordinarily by now she would have begun to set about telephoning around her friends for their usual morning chat but today wasn't ordinary.

Oddly enough, her immediate problem was whether or not to put in an appearance at the fundraising coffee morning held in their village hall every week. Attendance at this function was *de rigueur* among her friends and neighbours, some of whom regularly contributed homemade cakes and jams to the stalls. She herself had knocked up a couple of lemon drizzle cakes the day before to take with her this morning and found herself now wondering whether she could afford to give them away. This thought, though, served only to delay making the much trickier decision of whether to attend herself.

If she went as usual, she reasoned, there would be nothing to show that all was not well at the Old Rectory in Little Missal. The only action she would have to take then would be to parry any invitations for future hospitality that she and Mike couldn't possibly afford to repay any more. Or even want to. But if she didn't go to the village hall today bearing her usual weekly contribution to the coffee morning and pleaded a headache instead, there would be a barrage of telephone calls later in the day making sure everything was all right at the Old Rectory. These would be calls that she wasn't quite ready to handle just yet.

That everything wasn't all right at the Old Rectory was something she didn't want the whole world to know about just yet either. Not until she and Mike had worked out how to leave Little Missal quietly with their dignity intact and in their own good time. And with well-prepared statements making it clear that they'd left with their heads held high and their reputations intact.

In the long watches of the night, Michael had spelt out to her some – but not all – of the fine details of how bad things were with the business. He had made it even clearer that they would have to sell the Old Rectory as soon as possible and find somewhere less expensive – she refused to use the word 'cheap', even in her mind

– to live instead. That it wasn't likely be in Little Missal wasn't something she wanted to contemplate either. That they would have to make even bigger changes to their entire way of life was something her husband had chosen not to specify to her just yet.

Stephanie's dilemma about attending the coffee morning was put on hold by the unexpected ringing of their front doorbell and the even more unexpected arrival of two plain-clothes policemen.

'Mrs Wakefield?' said Detective Inspector Sloan, producing his warrant card. 'We'd like a word with your husband if we may.'

'He's gone in to work,' she said.

'I'm sorry. We thought he'd be at home,' said Sloan. 'You'll understand that in the circumstances we would like to talk to him about his business partner, Malcolm Forres.'

'And I would like to talk to Malcolm Forres in person,' she said, barely suppressing her unaccustomed fury. 'Very much indeed.'

'Quite so, madam,' said the older of the two policemen, tugging a notebook out of his pocket.

'And,' she said firmly, 'I would also like to know what the pair of them have done with all the money that they've taken from the firm.'

'Quite so,' said Sloan, who wouldn't have minded knowing that himself too. How exactly the police were going to track the missing money down was something he hadn't worked out yet. It was all very well that one of the superintendent's favourite admonitions was to 'follow the money' but he could see that wasn't going to be easy in this case.

'Christine Forres certainly didn't spend it on clothes.' Stephanie sniffed. 'That woman couldn't look well-dressed if she tried.'

'My wife,' offered Sloan tentatively, but nevertheless making a note the while, 'always insists that money hasn't got a lot to do with dressing well. She says the ability to dress well is a gift.'

'And they don't seem to have spent it on their house either,' went on Stephanie, not listening to this piece of sartorial wisdom. 'The one they live in wasn't up to much in the first place and it's been needing painting for ages. It's in Peverton, if you didn't know.'

'Stubblefield jumpers,' said Crosby dismissively about the village of Peverton. 'A load of caravans with roofs on, mostly.' The detective constable looked appreciatively round the Old Rectory kitchen, modelled, had he known it, on that of a French peasant, even down to a bunch of fresh herbs from Buis-les-Baronnies hanging from the ceiling. 'This room is very nice,' he said naively. Crosby's landlady didn't let him into her kitchen.

'Which is just as well if we're going to have to sell it,' she said, her shoulders drooping. 'Which my husband says is what looks like is going to have to happen now.'

'People choose to spend money on different things,' said Sloan prosaically, hoping to keep her talking. And deliberately refraining from offering her false comfort. That didn't ever do anyone any good.

'My husband, Inspector, says we shan't even be able do that any more,' said Stephanie. 'Spend money, I mean.'

Detective Inspector Sloan resorted to the practical. 'We have been told that in the first instance, madam, a voluntary petition in bankruptcy is likely to be put in train by Mr Wakefield's own solicitors rather than waiting for a creditor to do so. That's with a view to bankruptcy proceedings being brought in early.'

'What does that mean?' she asked shakily.

It was the young detective constable with Sloan who enlightened her. 'To try to keep the show on the road,' he said.

Detective Inspector Sloan intervened. 'To deal with the firm's creditors in an orderly manner,' he said instead.

'Creditors?' she echoed. 'Michael doesn't have any creditors.'

'He will have now,' said Crosby.

She shook her head, protesting, 'But they've always taken great care not to get overdrawn or owe our suppliers at Forres and Wakefield. Michael always said that they were well known for it and that Malcolm always saw to it.'

'I'm very much afraid, madam,' said Sloan, 'that this may not be the case just now. And furthermore, you must understand that there is a distinct possibility that some time in the future your husband might not be allowed on the premises.'

'Michael not allowed in his own firm?' she responded angrily. 'But it's his – well, half of it, anyway.' Belatedly she remembered that his missing partner, Malcom Forres, had always owned half of the business and presumably, bizarre as it might seem, still did.

'Not that it's under your husband's control any longer,' Crosby informed her in what Sloan thought was much too chatty a tone in the circumstances. 'Only half ever was his if they were full partners, and they say that that half's now gone walkabout too.'

Detective Inspector Sloan stepped in to explain that legal restrictions applied to running a business whilst about to be declared bankrupt, but it was for their solicitor to advise them.

'But we're the victims, not the villains,' she protested, tears beginning to well up in her eyes.

They were interrupted by the telephone ringing. Detective Inspector Sloan ostentatiously folded his notebook and started to put it away as if the call were of no consequence to him whilst Detective Constable Crosby, taking his cue from Sloan, gathered himself up as if preparing for departure, too.

The call was Sloan's concern, though.

But not until later. Much later.

Stephanie's dilemma about attending the coffee morning in the church hall that day with her lemon drizzle cakes was resolved by the caller. She didn't need to worry any longer about what to tell her friends in Little Missal.

They told her.

At least one of them did. That was her nearest neighbour, Meg.

'My dear,' she said to Stephanie down the telephone, 'I'm so very sorry. You poor things, you!' she exclaimed sympathetically. 'What very bad luck for you and Mike.'

'What have you heard?' Steph asked her warily, dry-mouthed.

'Everything, Steph. About the robbery, or rather about Mike's partner absconding with all your money. And the firm most likely having to close down. Everything,' she repeated, adding for good measure, 'all of it.'

'But how did you hear?' Stephanie managed a reproachful look in Sloan's direction, raising her eyebrows at him in query as she did so. 'Not from the police, surely?'

The detective inspector shook his head.

'What have they told you, Meg?' Stephanie Wakefield persisted despite seeing Sloan's head shaking in denial.

'No, no, it wasn't the police telling me. I don't know how it got there but I read all about it myself. It's all over the front page of this morning's *Berebury Chronicle*. It's Thursday, remember? The local paper's publication day.'

CHAPTER EIGHT

'Where to now, sir?' asked Crosby as they left a stricken Stephanie Wakefield at the Old Rectory at Little Missal doing her very best to stop her friend Meg coming straight round to her house. Whether this was to give her a hug or glean more gossip, Steph didn't know.

Or care.

'Peverton village, please, Crosby, before the trail gets too cold,' said Sloan. 'If it hasn't already,' he added pessimistically, conscious that their most likely suspect was probably already out of their reach.

'You want to know about Malcolm and Christine Forres, Inspector?' said the man out at Peverton as he greeted the two policemen. He was tall and rangy and sported important-looking spectacles. His tweed jacket, which he was wearing over a soft shirt and knitted jersey, had brown leather patches on the elbows. Sloan was not surprised to learn that he was a schoolmaster. 'Come along in, Inspector. I'm Halstead, by the way, David Halstead, and I live next door.'

'Just a routine enquiry that's come in from someone about Mr and Mrs Forres' sudden absence, who was worried that they weren't answering their phone,' murmured Sloan easily. That the someone in question was a police superintendent he didn't see fit to mention.

The man nodded knowledgably. 'Oh, I've heard all about that sort of thing before, Inspector. It's what you people call a welfare visit, isn't it?'

'In a manner of speaking,' said Sloan, hoping that Crosby wouldn't say anything at all. 'You say you know them?'

'I do, indeed, Inspector. Both Malcolm and Christine. We've lived next door to them for a long time and we couldn't have asked for better neighbours. They didn't have any children, either, which helps a lot.'

'I'm sure,' said Sloan, confident that not many children would dare to play 'knock down ginger' on this man's front door anyway. He went on, 'Only, you see, Mr and Mrs Forres weren't answering their telephone, so we thought we'd better come round and just check if they were both all right.' As far as Sloan was concerned, both individual statements were true in themselves although the juxtaposition of the two of them might have aroused suspicion in a less self-assured man than the one talking to them now.

'Oh, they're quite all right, Inspector,' Halstead

assured them. 'It's Christine's poor mother who isn't. Sounded to me as if she was sinking fast. A stroke, I think, it was. Christine was very upset at having to leave the house in such a hurry.'

Detective Constable Crosby stirred and said he could quite understand that.

'They hardly had time to get properly packed,' said David Halstead. 'Christine just flung some clothes into suitcases whilst Malcolm got some papers out of his safe – it seems he held the old lady's power of attorney and thought he might need it in the circumstances, then they took off.'

Detective Constable Crosby said that he could understand that, too, adding, 'In the circumstances.'

'And then there was Podge,' went on the schoolmaster.

'Podge?' queried Sloan.

'Their cat. No doubt named after Dr Samuel Johnson's Hodge.'

'Really, sir?' Sloan didn't know of any doctor in these parts called Johnson and said so.

'Author of the famous diction—oh, I'm sorry, I see you haven't made the connection. Silly of me.' Halstead gave a thin smile. 'So, of course we promised to look after Podge. Not too difficult since, as you gentlemen will know, all cats are *obligato carnivorous*.'

Detective Inspector Sloan, educated at Berebury Grammar School and proud of it, didn't like being patronised. Crosby, on the other hand, wasn't aware that he was being and said all he knew was that cats liked mice. It was his landlady who didn't.

'And they just asked you to look after the cat?' said Sloan. 'That all?'

'Yes, indeed. And Podge is no problem,' said the schoolteacher instantly. 'Not since he became a confirmed bachelor, that is.'

'Come again?' said Crosby.

Brown twisted his lips. 'Before that I often had to hurl a shoe at him in the middle of the night. That's before Malcolm took him to the vet.'

Crosby's brow cleared. 'Oh, you mean the cat's been done.'

'These people . . .' began Sloan hastily, notebook to hand, before the man could speak.

'Malcolm and Christine Forres,' supplied the schoolmaster.

'Did they give you any indication at all as to where they were going, sir?'

Halstead shook his head. 'None at all, although Malcolm did keep looking at his watch even though he had told me they were going wherever it was by car. I think he was just very anxious to be off.'

Or just very anxious to catch a continental ferry, thought Sloan to himself.

'Besides, it was getting late,' went on Halstead, 'and I had to be at school the next morning, so I didn't stay around.'

CHAPTER NINE

'A short-term loan, Mr Wakefield?' echoed Mr Thomas Parker from behind his pseudo-walnut-topped desk, tapping his pen on the pad there in front of him the while. Because the manager of the Berebury branch of the Calleford and County Bank had specially requested an early meeting with him that day, Michael Wakefield had made an extra effort to get the presses running again before leaving Gilbert Hull in charge and heading for the bank. Perhaps, he thought as he had walked through the banking hall to the manager's office, he was still a valued customer after all.

It was soon very apparent that, on the contrary, he was no such thing. He should have taken note of the fact that this morning he hadn't had his usual cheery wave from his favourite cashier as he walked across the bank's floor to the manager's office.

'A short-term loan?' repeated Tom Parker, the manager, shooting his cuffs in an old-fashioned way. He enjoyed a reputation at the local chamber of trade as being the last man in the town of Berebury to stop wearing spats. Less respectful commentators in the Coach and Horses public house declared him to be the second-best-dressed person at any funeral, the best one being in his winding sheet in the coffin.

'Just until we get this terrible business sorted out,' explained Wakefield.

'Let me see now,' said Parker, making a great show of appearing to consult a printed statement on his desk. 'Your firm's business account appears already to be significantly overdrawn.'

'Overdrawn?' responded Wakefield, alarmed. 'Surely not so soon?'

'Overdrawn two days ago, Mr Wakefield,' said the manager, regarding him severely over the top of his glasses, 'overdrawn, moreover, without any pre-existing arrangement.' It was not entirely clear to Wakefield whether it was the fact of being overdrawn or of not having made any pre-existing arrangement for it to so be that was the more heinous offence in the world of banking.

'Both of which actions,' Parker went on, 'I am sure you will already be aware can be quite expensive.'

'I knew that most of the money had been taken from the firm's business account, but I didn't know it was so completely overdrawn,' stumbled Wakefield apologetically.

'It's all in the red,' said the banker in his own language.

'I swear that there was plenty of money in there at the beginning of the week.'

'Since when,' continued the bank manager, noticeably even less cordial now, 'as I said, the entire contents of the account were withdrawn on the instructions of Malcolm Forres, a duly authorised signatory of the business account, whom I understand is your partner . . .'

'Was my partner,' growled Wakefield.

'As you know,' went on Parker, 'you are both individual signatories of the business account. Jointly and severally, so to speak.'

'Were,' snapped Wakefield.

'Subsequently,' Parker said, tapping the paper again, 'your business account was then made overdrawn by a normal monthly direct debit for the insurance cover on the works building, which is what drew our attention to the matter.'

Wakefield ran a finger round the inside of a collar that seemed to have suddenly tightened. 'What I would like to know is where exactly all the money has gone.'

'Which, unfortunately, is something I am unable to tell you save that the withdrawals were all made in favour of Malcolm Forres himself, in cash.' He paused and then repeated portentously, 'In cash.'

Wakefield groaned aloud.

'And since,' went on the banker, 'it would appear that as there are now no further funds immediately available to put the account back into credit, I'm afraid we have had no option but to suspend the partnership account, unless, that is, there is some collateral in, say, your premises.'

'But the wages will be due at the end of the month.'

'Besides which . . .' Parker paused significantly.

'Besides what?' Wakefield noted the man's use of the royal 'we' with wry detachment. He could have been referring to the gnomes of Zurich for all he knew.

'Besides which, there is the whole question of what I hear is to be your impending application for bankruptcy.' He looked over the top of his glasses and gave Wakefield a thin smile. 'Oh, yes, Mr Wakefield, we do know all about that. Word does get about in Berebury, you know. It's a small town.'

'That is what is worrying my wife more than anything,' said Wakefield feelingly. 'What you might call the social consequences.'

At this, Parker's manner mellowed slightly and for a moment he sounded quite human. 'And with good reason, Mr Wakefield. I'm very much afraid that you will find that some of those whom you formerly considered good friends of yours or sound business colleagues will no longer be so keen to associate with you following public bankruptcy proceedings. Some of them will even ignore you or go out of their way not to have to acknowledge you.' He gave a little professional cough. 'I'm told by former customers of the bank who have found themselves in similar situations – Names at Lloyd's and so forth – that the first thing that your wife will notice is that you are no longer *persona grata* in some quarters and thus not always included in invitations to important social events.'

'Stephanie will mind about that a lot,' he admitted. 'She likes meeting people.'

'I'm afraid *schadenfreude* is an unpleasant but common reaction to a fall from financial grace,' pronounced Parker. 'This is because so many people fear it might happen to them.'

Michael Wakefield, unsure of what the word meant, said nothing.

'It's a human characteristic but not a particularly pleasant one. Taking pleasure in the troubles of others has nothing to commend it,' said the banker, immediately resuming ploughing his own furrow. 'It is important, Mr Wakefield, that you remember that a person who is insolvent or has reason to suppose that he is about to become bankrupt may not borrow money or incur further debts or undertake future financial commitments, or indeed become or remain the director of a company, public or private.' He gave him another of his meaningless small smiles. 'Unlike our American cousins, we don't have a Chapter 11 system working in this country, which might be preferable for you.'

Wakefield nodded. He'd already worked that all out now for himself.

'Nor may a person who has been declared bankrupt enter into contracts that are not approved by the official receivers in the bankruptcy section.'

Wakefield nodded again.

Parker leant back in his chair and steepled his fingers. 'And there is also the wider question of what is known as wrongful trading whilst bankrupt. This is something about which you will have to be very careful from now on.'

Wakefield moistened his lips. 'We – that is, the police – do not appear to know where all this money has gone, other than in the direction of Malcolm Forres.'

'That,' the other man said stiffly, 'is something that I am quite unable to help you with. Quite apart from the matter of customer confidentiality, I can only tell you that Malcolm Forres was not a personal customer of this bank.'

Wakefield, unsurprised, acknowledged this with a nod.

Parker forged on. 'You will appreciate, however, that since your business account was without pre-arranged overdraft facilities to meet it, your recent cheque to Luston Printing Inks Ltd. has been referred back to the drawer.'

'And the short-term loan that I came in about?' persisted Wakefield gamely.

'Out of the question,' Parker came back instantly. 'If what I have been advised about your impending situation is in fact the case, then you may not legally be able to borrow any money at all on any terms whatsoever from the bank or indeed from anyone else.'

'I suppose that means that it would cost more if I could,' said the businessman wryly.

Tom Parker rose above this slur on the banking world with practised fluency. 'And I, as an employee of the Calleford and County Bank, and to whom I owe my primary fiduciary duty, am certainly not empowered to accommodate your request for further funds.'

'Don't you have a duty of care to your customers, too?' demanded Wakefield, tight-lipped now.

Parker swept on regardless. 'And in any case, the bank would require some form of surety against any future business loan' – he tapped the pad on his desk once again and added in a studiously neutral tone – 'which I understand you would not be in a position to supply at this time, quite apart from the question of preferential creditors taking priority.' He gave a little cough and went on, 'I fear Her Majesty's Commissioners of Inland Revenue are not always helpful in this respect.'

'And my personal account?' Wakefield asked desperately, a man clutching at straws now.

'That appears to be in order,' said Parker, sounding a little surprised, 'as of the present, that is. The usual domestic payments are being processed from that – for the time being, anyway.'

Wakefield hardly had time to breathe a sigh of relief before the banker went on, 'You will appreciate, however, that we have not been able to process your recent cheque to Luston Printing Inks Ltd., which has been returned to sender. It's a matter with which you will now have to deal yourself.' He bestowed a thin, professional smile on him and went on, 'It's not only death that cancels contracts, Mr Wakefield. Bankruptcy can do, too.'

His favourite teller didn't give him a cheery wave as he made his way out across the bank floor either.

And it was only when he was back in the car park and getting into his car that Michael Wakefield remembered something else. It had been when Tom Parker had told him about some other people who had been customers of his there whom he knew and with whom he, as manager, had had dealings at the bank. They were customers of his who had also lost a lot of money.

What he remembered now as a shiver ran down his back was that the manager had referred to them as 'former customers'.

CHAPTER TEN

'Come along in, gentlemen.' It was Kate Booth, the new young accountant at Fixby and Fixby, who welcomed Detective Inspector Sloan and Detective Constable Crosby to her firm's offices when they got back from Peverton. These were in the High Street and thus not very far from the police station at Berebury. 'And take a seat,' she said.

Crosby had wanted to head straight off to Forres and Wakefield's works on the grounds that it was where the action had been. Sloan's advice that it was better to gather all the information they could first had not gone down well.

Nor had Sloan's next comment been at all well received either.

'Walk?' Crosby had echoed mutinously when Sloan had suggested the accountants' buildings were too near to take the car.

'Walk as in putting one foot in front of the other, Crosby, and repeating the process as often as necessary,' went on Sloan solemnly. 'It's known as shoe-leather policing. You can get lot of detection done that way. Remember,' he added, 'that cars, fast as some of them can be driven' – here he cast a meaningful glance in Crosby's direction – 'are not the only means of human locomotion.'

'But Fixby's won't know who we are if we turn up on foot in plain clothes,' protested Crosby, a last-ditcher by nature.

'I'm so sorry, Inspector,' apologised Kate Booth, who quite clearly did know exactly who the two detectives were, 'but Mr Herbert Fixby, our senior partner, isn't in today to talk to you two gentlemen himself.'

'What about your junior partner, then?' asked Crosby, before Sloan could speak.

'And I'm afraid,' responded Kate Booth swiftly, 'our young Mr Jason Fixby is not in the office today either. He's visiting a client over at Calleford.'

'The three o'clock race there this afternoon,' remarked Detective Constable Crosby to nobody in particular, his eyes firmly fixed on the ceiling, 'is the famous Calleshire Cup. Everyone'll be there for sure.'

'We've come in the matter of Forres and Wakefield Ltd., miss,' Sloan interrupted him firmly, his notebook open in front of him.

The woman shook her head, ignoring what both

policemen had said. 'No, gentlemen.'

'No?'

'The whole trouble, Inspector, is that Forres and Wakefield weren't ever a limited liability company.'

'No? But I thought . . .'

'Theirs was just a simple old-fashioned partnership agreement between two businessmen.' She opened her hands in a gesture of despair and said, 'I'm afraid that their relationship wasn't even just a gentlemen's agreement either, which might conceivably in certain circumstances have made things easier.'

Sloan sat up. He had once heard a gentlemen's agreement described in court somewhere as one that was an unenforceable verbal pact between two men, neither of whom was a gentleman.

Crosby wrinkled his nose. His interpretation of this was rather different. 'Honour among thieves, you mean, miss?'

'I mean, Constable, that in that case, then, there's nothing in writing,' she said, going on to explain to the two policemen exactly the same situation that Simon Puckle, the solicitor, had spelt out to Michael Wakefield the day before. 'Which means, I'm afraid, that your Michael Wakefield's personal liabilities are unlimited.'

'Sounds nasty,' remarked Crosby.

'Theft always is,' said Sloan, an old nursery rhyme about the Knave of Hearts who stole some tarts coming into his mind from his childhood. He had gone on to meet quite a lot of knaves since then: real ones and not on the backs of playing cards, either. He had had to meet some tarts in his time on the beat, too, but that had been a different ball game altogether.

'No.' Booth shook her head again. 'What happened at Forres and Wakefield, Inspector, wasn't theft, either.'

'Not theft, miss?' Sloan frowned. 'But it would seem to us – and to Simon Puckle, too, let alone Michael Wakefield – that a crime has been committed all right . . .' Sloan started to pick his way delicately through the verbal minefield that constituted an injury to someone else's property as opposed to that on their person. 'What is it, then?'

'Embezzlement,' replied Booth promptly. 'It would appear to me – at first sight anyway – that Michael Wakefield has been the victim of embezzlement.'

'Which is what?' asked Detective Constable Crosby colloquially, suddenly sitting up and taking an interest in a word that was new to him.

'You can't steal something that has previously been entrusted to you,' explained the accountant. 'And as a partner of Michael Wakefield's, that situation definitely applies to Malcolm Forres. It is agreed that although the man was a perfectly competent printer himself, he was, as it worked out, also in business control of all the finances of the partnership.'

Detective Constable Crosby looked puzzled. 'I still don't get it, miss.' He added, grinning at his own joke after saying, 'He did, though, didn't he? Get it, I mean. All of it from what we've heard.'

Kate Booth ran her hands through her mop of curly hair and started again. 'If, Constable, I were to ask you to look after my wages for me and instead of your putting them into – say – the bank and keeping them safe, you spent them on something you wanted for yourself or on something risky . . .'

'The favourite for the Calleshire Cup this afternoon is odds-on,' remarked Crosby, catching on rather more quickly than Booth, the newest member of the firm of Fixby and Fixby, quite liked.

'I gathered that Wakefield isn't much of a business-person,' intervened Sloan to try to keep the peace. 'I believe that it's said in the firm that the man's not really interested in anything except the craft side of fine printing.'

'And then, Constable, instead of looking after my wages properly and keeping them safe for me,' Kate ploughed on, regardless of them both, 'you would have been committing the crime of embezzlement, which,' she added, 'is what would appear to have happened to the unfortunate Michael Wakefield with his partner.'

Somewhere at the back of his mind, Detective Inspector Christopher Dennis Sloan, dutiful son of a church-going mother, was trying to remember the parable of all the talents. It was one of those he had never really understood since the servant who had played it safe in the Bible with his talents had been judged a failure. He was just about to ask the accountant exactly where one stood if the bank into which you'd put the money failed when you had trusted it with someone else's money, when he realised that she was still going on talking.

'Sorry, miss, what was that you said?' He wasn't here to discuss either the finer points of criminal law or those of stewardship as set out in St Matthew's Gospel in the Bible. He was conscious that Superintendent Leeyes would have been the first to agree with him there.

'It was when I – we, that is – at Fixby's discovered that matters weren't as they should be at Forres and Wakefield that we – that is, I – realised that the partnership's annual accounts could not be signed off this year as had been usual in previous years.'

'Who had done the audit the year before?' asked Detective Inspector Sloan pertinently.

'As far as I could establish,' said the accountant, 'the work was partly done by Mr Herbert Fixby, the senior partner . . .'

Detective Inspector Sloan decided that this was a coded message, if ever there was one, the word 'senior' being capable of several interpretations. One of these was age-related.

'He lost his driving licence last year, too,' Crosby informed them. 'Didn't see a red light. Didn't pass the eyesight test afterwards, either.'

'So, miss,' said Sloan quickly, 'who else did the Forres and Wakefield accounts last year instead then?'

'I was given to understand that it was Jason Fixby,' she said with visible reluctance.

'Chip off the old block?' asked Crosby.

Sloan thought – only thought – that he heard Crosby add something under his breath about really meaning 'blockhead', but he chose to press on. This was neither the time nor the place for upbraiding the constable.

'Presumably on the Forres and Wakefield side,' Sloan said instead, 'it would have been Malcolm Forres presenting the accounts for audit.'

'Presumably,' she said cautiously, 'but I think in all fairness that it should be said that Jason lacks experience. He's very young still.'

And, sighed Sloan to himself, because of all this Michael Wakefield was now personally heading for bankruptcy, and all its attendant miseries.

'I can see all that, miss,' said Detective Inspector Sloan, police officer and not accountant. He was still working his way round to what he really wanted to know. 'So . . .'

'So naturally we started going back through the firm's records as quickly as we could,' said Kate.

'Naturally,' echoed Crosby, to whom the ins and the outs of a balance sheet were a closed book. He was very sound, though, on making sure that the cashier in the police canteen gave him the right change.

'And?' said Sloan, whose family finances he left in the capable hands of his wife.

'And I duly went back over the six years that, if they were so minded, HMRC could in the first instance look back into someone's affairs,' said the young accountant. 'To take a look at the books, that is. Earlier than that, the Revenue would have to have had just cause.'

'Is that what they call "the seven-year itch", miss?' asked Crosby.

'Not exactly, Constable,' she said, hiding a smile.

'And?' repeated Sloan as Kate Booth's voice had trailed away into an uneasy silence.

'And I came across a number of matters that didn't seem to quite add up,' she said obliquely.

Detective Inspector Sloan returned to his notebook.

'Which neither Herbert nor Jason would seem to have noticed?' asked Crosby with the air of one just seeking clarification. 'That right?'

'Which must have escaped their attention,' agreed the woman with some reluctance.

'Funny, that,' remarked Crosby, at last sitting up and taking notice.

'Go on, miss,' said Sloan. Escaping the attention of a pair of accountants seemed to him to be far-fetched, to say the least. But not if that pair comprised an ageing one with failing eyesight and a young and inexperienced one with his mind on horse-racing.

'Fingers in the till?' suggested Crosby.

'Only in a manner of speaking,' said Kate Booth, flushing a little.

'By what other name, then . . .' began Crosby.

'If you would let me put it another way, gentlemen, it might help,' she said. 'It would appear from my preliminary examination of the accounts and ledgers that money had been being taken out of the firm for quite some time. Small amounts to begin with, but then more – much more – as time went by when the original thefts went undetected.'

'The usual pattern,' observed Sloan sagely. It was a great argument for not letting malefactors get away with sweating the small stuff. It was not, though, always a popular one with those victims with a penchant for the quiet life. Or for the naïve or the charitable but especially not for those who had been scammed and who were ashamed to admit that they had been caught out.

'In the books that I have looked at so far, the amount missing has risen noticeably each year,' she admitted.

'Noticeably but unnoticed?' asked Sloan.

She bowed her head. 'It would seem so.'

'Until now,' said Sloan significantly.

'That is indeed the case, Inspector.' She nodded.

'And was there any indication, miss, where this money had been going?'

'None at all, I'm afraid, that I could find. A really detailed audit might help. Since Malcolm Forres did not attend the partnership's annual meeting this year, I had no means of knowing what his procedures were in respect of money coming in. All I could establish was that there was no evidence of teeming and lading.'

'What's teeming and lading?' asked Crosby inevitably.

'Some other time, Constable,' said Sloan, at last feeling able to put the question to Kate Booth that he had really come about. 'Tell me, miss, who in your firm here knew before this annual meeting that you had made this discovery in the accounts about the regular abstraction of the firm's money – besides yourself, that is?' He sat back, pleased with his careful choice of words.

She sighed audibly, having clearly got the message. 'Only Jason Fixby, I'm afraid, Inspector. You see, he'd helped me with the ledger work this year as I was so new here. And as your constable here has told us, Mr Herbert's eyesight isn't up to much work with figures these days.'

'I'm beginning to get the picture,' said Sloan.

'Me, too,' chimed in Crosby, unasked.

'But,' she said, smiling now and adding unexpectedly, 'Jason's a young man and he's very much in love.'

'Mind not on the job?' suggested Sloan, old enough now to know a bit about the effects of Cupid's darts.

'Head over heels?' suggested Crosby, not yet having felt their piercings . . .

'You could put it like that,' she said, sounding as indulgent as most women are when true romance comes into the picture. 'He's even got the nickname of Sheep's Eyes.'

CHAPTER ELEVEN

'Now that we are more in the picture, Crosby,' said Inspector Sloan, as the two policemen left the accountants' office in Berebury and walked back to the police garage, 'I think that a visit to the works of the late lamented partnership of Forres and Wakefield, high-quality printers, is called for next.' Detective Inspector Sloan carefully stowed his notebook away in an inside jacket pocket. That done, he fastened his seat belt and sat back in the passenger seat, prepared to interview Michael Wakefield with an open mind.

Crosby grinned. 'The scene of the crime, you might say, sir, their works.' He didn't mind where he was going to, only that it was somewhere by car.

'You might,' agreed Sloan cautiously, Crosby being just as quick to jump to a conclusion – right or wrong – as Superintendent Leeyes. 'On the other hand, remember that you might not. I only wish that I were sure. Making up one's mind too soon is a snare and delusion in all detective investigations and you would do well to remember the fact.' He was, after all, supposed to be mentoring the jejune constable.

As they arrived at Berebury's modest business park, Detective Inspector Sloan noted automatically that the works of the printing firm still bore the name of Forres and Wakefield above its front door. It was the firm's youthful apprentice, Lenny Datchet, sporting a green baize apron, who answered Detective Constable Crosby's knock. His rolled-up sleeves revealed unattractive tattoos climbing up both his arms from wrist to shoulder.

'Full sleeve tribal,' pronounced Crosby in an appreciative way, pointing at it. 'Very fashionable tattoo, that.'

Datchet sniffed. 'I don't know who you two want to see in here, mate, but you'll be unlucky. They're all too busy to see anybody at all today.'

'They'll see us,' declared Detective Constable Crosby, also now a man with a grievance. He muttered under his breath that they weren't used to being told to call back later – not them, they weren't.

'No, they won't,' retorted Datchet combatively. 'They're all running around the works like headless chickens.'

Detective Inspector Sloan, who had a well-honed professional instinct for any unusual activity, stepped inside the small entrance hall and started to look around the place, taking in the old printing presses standing there. At the county constabulary's spanking new headquarters in Calleford, they displayed a set of old truncheons in a glass case in their entrance. He supposed it came to the same thing: a yearning for a simpler past. Or an inability to throw anything out of date away. 'We'd like a word with Mr Wakefield himself, please,' he said.

'If you was to ask me,' said the youth, tossing a lock of hair back out of his eye, 'I'd say to come back later. Like next week.'

'What's up, then?' asked Crosby, following Sloan through the double doors leading to the working printing presses. They were immediately assailed by the loud clatter of machinery and soon became aware of a hive of human activity round them. The nearest machine was churning out pages and pages of text, disgorging them first onto a tray and then into piles that grew at a great rate even as they watched the presses working.

'Big trouble,' said Datchet succinctly.

'Tough,' said Crosby, whose usual idea of big trouble encompassed attacks on his own person first and on those of other persons well after that.

'I'll say,' declared the youth. 'They've gone and promised this new book for tomorrow or whatever.'

'So?'

'Bit of a panic on here in case it can't be done.' He sniffed. 'Myself, I don't think it can.'

'Panic over what?' asked Detective Inspector Sloan, policeman first, last and all the time. Panic in crowds was dangerous, panic in escaping villains very helpful to the pursuers.

'There's this urgent printing job needed to be finished soonest,' explained Datchet, waving one of his arms in the direction of the presses and revealing the tattoo even further. 'Dead important job. Top priority and all that.'

'And?' asked Crosby. Even in his limited experience, police priorities were usually rather different.

Datchet sucked his teeth. 'They've gone and found a river, haven't they?'

'A what?' The constable started to look round for signs of water.

'Don't be daft, man. Not a real river. A river of white colour running down the middle of the type. And so,' he added importantly, 'they had to stop the presses whilst they sorted it.'

'And what might your river be when it's at home, then?' asked Crosby.

'A long, empty space starting at the top of the page and working its way down through the paragraphs between all the sentences on the page like a white snake,' he chanted, an earlier lesson well learnt. 'Sticks out like a sore thumb if you're in the business of being the best printers in Calleshire, which they say they are, so they won't let it go, will they? Oh, no, not them. They won't let anything go here. Not with old Mother Harris breathing down their necks anyway.'

'Who is she?' asked Crosby.

'The lady round here who says what's what on the pages before they get printed.' He sniffed. 'They're all frightened of her.'

'Why?' asked the constable simply.

'I dunno but whatever she says goes,' said Datchet, putting in a nutshell a world of power versus anti-authoritarianism.

'And so what exactly are they doing about this river?' asked Detective Inspector Sloan. The problems in his own world were rather different, too.

'They got old Mother Harris to look at it first. She's the expert and nothing printed ever gets past her.' He thought for a moment and added, 'And nothing much else either, come to think about it. She's as sharp as a tack.'

'And what else?' asked Sloan.

'Search me,' said Lenny, pushing back the overlong lock of hair from his forehead again. 'I'm only the apprentice here and all I know is that I've got to take the first copy of this new book over to a posh customer's posh place at Ornum on my motorbike the minute it comes off the presses and gets itself bound. Which, I may say, it hasn't done yet and if you was to ask me, at this rate it isn't likely to be any time soon.'

'Got a motorbike, have you?' asked Crosby, whose dream it was to bestride a powerful police model in pursuit of some important malefactor – come to that, any malefactor would do.

The youth leant back. 'I'll say. A beauty. A 750 steel-blue Suzuki GSXF.' Seeing the look on Crosby's face, he added swiftly, 'Used, of course.'

'I get you,' said Crosby sarcastically. 'One careful lady owner.'

'Nevertheless,' interrupted Detective Inspector Sloan, sticking to the business in hand as was his wont, 'we would still like to talk to Mr Wakefield.'

'And Mr Hull says I've to mind how I behave when I get there with the book,' went on Lenny Datchet, clearly a man with a grudge, let alone a one-track mind, 'because his nibs is someone important and he doesn't half know it.'

Crosby, with the members of the local magistrates' bench in mind, said that people like that usually did.

'Mr Hull says the man's just like Uriah Heep's mother, whoever she is, and knows his place all right only it's a much better place.'

'Mr Wakefield . . .' Sloan tried again, vainly trying to remember who Mrs Heep was.

'In there somewhere if you can find him.' Datchet scowled. 'I'm supposed to be here to learn the business of fine printing, but nobody'll even talk to me today so they're not likely to talk to anyone else either, are they?' He sniffed. 'Stands to reason.'

'Something must be up,' said Crosby, still struggling to resist the temptation to announce that they were policemen and weren't used to being kept from those whom they wished to see.

'I'll say there is, mate,' Lenny shrugged his shoulders, 'but all I know is to my mind that though they say it's about this flipping river, there's something else up, too.'

'What's that?' said Crosby.

'I don't know, do I?' said Datchet in an aggrieved voice. 'Nobody here'll tell me anything. All I know is that one of the partners hasn't shown since Tuesday and nobody seems to know why. They've kept his room locked.' He brightened suddenly and said, 'Perhaps he's lying in there dead with his head bashed in.'

'It looks as if they're carrying on all right without him,' remarked Sloan, ignoring this tempting thought and pointing to the whirring machines.

'Huh, it's like that "missing man" flying formation that the Air Force goes in for,' said the apprentice. 'He was here and now he isn't, but they carry on flying just as if he was, leaving a gap to show where he had been. A big pretend if you ask me.'

'Not here?' said Crosby.

'One of the partners has gone AWOL but I don't know exactly why or where he is now.' He smirked with some satisfaction and added, 'And neither does anyone else here. Or say they don't.'

'Really?' said Sloan before Crosby could speak.

'All I know is that he hasn't been seen since Tuesday and he hasn't been in touch either. Not that I know about, anyway, and it's him that does the wages so it's important.'

'Funny, that,' agreed Crosby.

'And Mr Hull, he's the foreman here although he likes to call himself the production manager, he says it's nothing to do with me where anyone is except me and him and if I'm late again, there'll be big trouble.'

'Well, I never,' said Crosby unsympathetically.

Datchet sniffed. 'They say they're all too busy to talk to me, the lot of 'em. What I say is that that isn't right.'

As Crosby drew breath to argue, Detective Inspector Sloan cut short this unpromising dialogue between the young. 'Perhaps, all the same, you'd just tell Mr Wakefield that we'd like a word.'

Lenny Datchet jerked his head. 'Sure thing. I'll go find him. Who wants him, anyway?'

'Tell him we've been sent by Mr Simon Puckle,' said Sloan with perfect truth.

Lenny Datchet wasn't the only one in his shirtsleeves. So was Michael Wakefield, visibly preoccupied by the machine over which he was hovering with the solicitude of a mother hen protecting her chicks. 'Ah,' he said when he saw them, divining their identity, 'come this way.' Wakefield led them to a locked room, tidy but empty. 'If there was any evidence of anything here,' he said wearily, 'it's gone now.' He swung open the door of the safe in the corner of the office and pointed to its empty interior. 'So has everything else that was in here.'

Detective Inspector Sloan had hardly got his notebook out and assured Wakefield that he would be sending in a forensic team as soon as possible when the double doors of the workshop burst open and a distraught woman crashed in. He had difficulty in recognising her as the same one he had left barely more than an hour before over at Little Missal.

Stephanie Wakefield, her face mottled and highly flushed, looked like a clownish parody of her former self. 'I shan't be able to show my face anywhere ever again,' she shrieked at her husband in a high shrill voice, quite unlike her own usual one. 'Ever.'

'My dear,' began Wakefield, advancing hastily across the workshop floor towards her and trying to take her arm whilst William Edward Crosby, detective constable, and Leonard Datchet, printer's apprentice, both stood transfixed, their mouths agape at the sight quite unfamiliar to them of a woman in such a distressed condition. She was oblivious of their presence and now quite beside herself, all normal restraint gone. The other workers there either attended assiduously to feeding the presses or melted quietly away in the direction of their staffroom.

Stephanie Wakefield's loud keening, audible even above the clatter of the printing presses, produced a middle-aged woman from a door that suddenly shot open at the far end of the workshop. 'What on earth's going on out here? Stephanie, whatever's wrong?'

'You tell him, Kay,' shouted Stephanie at her across the room. 'You tell Mike that I'm never going to be able to show my face outside the house ever again.'

'Kay,' said Wakefield, 'I'm afraid Steph's a bit upset.'

Detective Inspector Sloan, no stranger to observing violent passion in others, considered this a considerable understatement and watched whilst she angrily shook off her husband's arm.

'We've had some bad news, you see,' Mike went on.

The woman called Kay responded quickly enough with an offer of a nice cup of tea.

'Tea!' wailed Stephanie. 'I don't want a cup of tea. What I want is to go back to before all this happened.'

'Nobody can ever do that, my dear,' said Kay calmly. 'Nobody at all. The only thing is to go forward after bad news, whatever it is. Not backwards.'

Stephanie, having shaken her husband's arm away, continued moaning. 'Oh, Mike, why didn't you tell me?'

'Tell you what?' he asked as Kay Harris steered his wife to a nearby chair.

'That the whole thing was going to be splashed all over this week's *Berebury Chronicle*?'

'Because I didn't know it was going to be, that's why.' He looked across at Hull. 'Did you see it, Gilbert?'

'What story?' asked the man.

An enquiring glance, too, in Sloan's direction produced only a shake of that policeman's head. 'Not police policy, sir,' said the detective inspector, mentally crossing his fingers behind his back because it was sometimes.

Gilbert Hull also shook his head. 'I don't ever see the local paper until I get home, Thursdays.'

'How could you, Mike?' Stephanie sobbed.

'So what's gone wrong, Mike?' asked Gilbert quietly. 'Should we know?'

Michael Wakefield took a deep breath and braced himself. 'I'm afraid it looks as if Malcolm Forres has walked away with all the firm's money.'

This important exchange was quite lost on the hysterical woman. Her voice still shaking, and her face a travesty of its usual amiable appearance, Stephanie said, 'And I won't be able to hold my head up ever again in the village – not now that everyone knows that we're bankrupt.'

Gilbert asked if what she had said about the bankruptcy was true.

'I'm afraid it looks like it'll come to that in the end, Gilbert, unless the police can recover the money pretty soon,' admitted Mike. He hung his head like a mediaeval penitent. 'I'm very sorry.'

Stephanie wasn't listening to either of them. 'I don't care who told the paper,' she cried, 'but let me tell you this, Michael Wakefield, we're not going to the launch party at Ornum House on Saturday night – either of us. I'm not having everyone there staring at me and talking about us behind our backs.'

'They won't be – there'll be too many people there for anyone to see anyone.' Wakefield passed a hand over his damp brow.

'I don't care about that,' she said wildly. 'I'm not going out anywhere ever again.'

'I think I'd better get Kay to take you home, Steph,' he said, 'because Gilbert's got a big job to do printing off this book as fast as he can and binding a sample copy for the earl to have tomorrow.' He managed to cast a meaningful glance at the production manager over his wife's head. 'And then I can stay here to give him a hand.'

'Home!' she echoed richly in tones that rang round the works. 'We haven't got a home any more, have we?'

CHAPTER TWELVE

The two policemen were unusually silent after they left the printing works, Detective Inspector Sloan because he was thinking and Detective Constable Crosby because he was still trying to process that which he had just witnessed. It was a far cry from what he had imagined being in the police force would mean. Where was the excitement of the tracking down of a criminal followed by the brisk chasing of said subject culminating in the making of a resisted arrest and the swift snapping on of handcuffs?

When he did speak it was to remark that he wouldn't want to get on the wrong side of that Mrs Harris.

'Me neither,' said Sloan thoughtfully. 'Did you notice that she didn't bother with asking any questions? Unusual, that, for a woman in those circumstances.' He looked up. 'You may slow down, Crosby. We're very nearly there now.'

The editor of the *Berebury Chronicle* welcomed them both without delay, insisting that he was pleased to talk to the police at any time. 'Always willing to help the boys in blue, Inspector,' he said as the two policemen were shown into his office. Actually, he often had to rely on their goodwill in commenting on a number of his stories – strictly off the record, of course.

'I'm sure you are,' said Sloan untruthfully, explaining what it was that he had come about.

'Ah, yes, the Forres and Wakefield debacle,' said the newspaper man, leaning back in his chair. 'We covered it rather well, I thought. I'm told it has aroused quite a lot of interest in the town.'

'I can see that it might,' said Sloan acidly, knowing full well that the newspaper editor never had any scruples about running stories that frequently ruined reputations and sometimes lives, too, in the process.

'Bad luck, poor Wakefield losing everything like that,' remarked the editor perfunctorily. 'I did hear on the grapevine that he was in the running to be the next chairman of the Berebury Chamber of Trade. That won't happen now for sure. They like their members to be solvent even if some of 'em are hanging on by their fingertips.' He gave a little smile. 'You know that saying about nobody knowing that you're swimming naked until the tide goes out.'

'And then having the news of it plastered all over your front page,' Sloan reminded him, ignoring this last and adding heavily, 'Unsubstantiated and without warning.'

It was the inspector who then had to settle back in the visitors' chair whilst the editor went through his usual spiel of explaining why he was truly sorry that he couldn't help the police any further with their enquiries in this particular instance.

Detective Constable Crosby rolled his eyes at this but did not speak.

The editor began his litany by making it abundantly clear to the police and anybody else prepared to listen that he was ready to go to the stake rather than disclose his sources of this or any other story he published, but in this instance he couldn't anyway.

'Pull the other one,' muttered Crosby under his breath.

The expression 'press freedom' cropped up more than once, which Sloan immediately countered with 'an uncalled-for invasion of personal privacy'. The editor gamely came back with the fact that anyone can photograph the front of someone else's house from the street without let or hindrance or, come to that, their permission either, it being a free country still. Not for long, he conceded, things being what they were. This last he solemnly pronounced, echoing the views also held by Superintendent Leeyes.

'Rather a good picture, I thought myself,' he said shamelessly. 'And the photograph of Michael Wakefield himself we had on file anyway. Something from some function or other in aid of the funds of the Bowls Club, I think it was.'

'An old man's game,' pronounced Crosby, who favoured football and excitement.

The editor did agree in the end that the coverage of the story had tended towards the sensational but that was what sold newspapers, wasn't it? And the circulation figures were up this week, he was happy to say. Besides, he added, with a vulpine smile, you had to let cub reporters learn their craft, hadn't you? 'Like constables,' he said unkindly, casting a glance in Crosby's direction.

That constable was lounging in the other visitors' chair, manifestly uninterested in what was going on. The editor opened his hands in an age-old gesture, adding, 'And, Inspector, you know how it always is with the police and the press.'

'A symbiotic relationship,' said Detective Inspector Sloan shortly. It wasn't one he liked. 'And, I may say, one always to be handled with extreme care.'

Since Crosby didn't know what a symbiotic relationship was, he had to have it explained to him. 'I get you,' he said, sitting up. 'You scratch my back and I'll scratch yours.'

'No, Crosby,' Sloan protested. 'Certainly not.'

'Yes, Constable,' said the editor. 'When you lot want something or someone to crawl out of the woodwork or to be shown up by neighbourhood witnesses, you ask us to spread the word for you.'

'But what you don't always do,' insisted Sloan, 'is lay off when we would like you to. And sometimes you reveal matters we would prefer not to be made public at that juncture.'

'We like to speak truth to power,' said the editor sententiously.

'What we want to know,' said Sloan, getting down to business and leaving more dubious connections to one side, 'is who fed you the story about Forres and Wakefield's bankruptcy in the first place. It's quite important that you tell us as it hadn't been made public before you splashed it all over your front page.'

'I can't tell you that because I don't know.'

'And,' said Sloan, 'in exactly what form did the information about Forres and Wakefield reach you?'

'Telephone call,' said the editor promptly.

'Who took it?'

'Our Tracy. She takes them all.'

Our Tracy, when summoned, remembered that one well. 'The caller made me write down exactly what he said.' She sniffed. 'As if I couldn't remember or get it right the first time.'

'His name?'

'He wouldn't give me that, Inspector. All he did was call himself a friend of the *Chronicle*. Then he said that if we didn't publish the whole story, he would offer it to the *Berebury Independent*.' She sniffed again. 'Some friend.'

'Your deadly rivals,' observed Sloan. The *Berebury Independent* was a struggling little paper, only just keeping its head above water, but nevertheless a thorn in the editorial flesh of the *Berebury Chronicle*.

'They can't stand the competition,' said the editor.

Crosby sat up, interested at last. 'You got a turf war, then?'

'More your *Pickwick Papers* and the two Eatanswill newspapers in that,' said the editor.

Detective Inspector Sloan had reached an age when he didn't mind admitting his ignorance. It was a sign of maturity: something that he already knew. 'You will have to fill me in on that,' he said now.

'One of Charles Dickens's more inspired creations, Inspector.'

'Whatever it was, you went ahead and printed the story.' Literary allusions would have to wait.

'True.'

'Presumably after first checking the information.'

'Naturally,' said the editor glibly. 'As far as we could, obviously. Sometimes people are not available for comment at the time and the presses won't wait.'

'A likely tale,' muttered Crosby.

'Might I ask where you checked?'

'Here and there,' he replied airily. 'The matter not being *sub judice*—'

'Yet,' put in Crosby, who enjoyed making arrests.

'—which does make everything so much easier, naturally,' said the editor, who seemed fond of the word.

'Naturally,' echoed Crosby, not under his breath this time.

'Then,' expanded the editor, 'all you have to worry about if you do go ahead and publish is libel and if what you're writing is fact then you're in the clear and nobody can touch you.'

'But you can touch other people,' pointed out Sloan, remembering Stephanie Wakefield's stricken face.

'Their problem, not mine. I take it, Inspector,' he said, here casting a sideways glance at Sloan, 'the fact that there has been no charge of theft is still the case?'

'Embezzlement, you mean,' put in Crosby. 'Get it right.'

'There has been no charge as yet,' said Sloan briefly. 'Tell me, this story that you've printed – gospel, is it?'

'It's based on all the information we were able to ascertain before going to press,' said the editor with dignity.

'Sort of confirmed,' put in Tracy, who had been standing by, 'by the fact that one of Forres and Wakefield's cheques bounced, yesterday. We'd heard that someone was making a fuss about it in the Dog and Duck at dinnertime and our reporter asked him about it.'

Crosby muttered something about the Dog and Duck pub being a good place to do your research, which the editor chose not to hear.

'Luston Inks,' said the editor. 'That was so unlike Forres and Wakefield's firm that we decided that the story had merit.'

'Merit!' snorted Crosby, more audibly this time.

'And then when our reporter started asking around at the places where the story might have been confirmed or denied, everyone started shutting up like clams.' The editor waved a hand. 'That, Inspector, take it from me, is when you know you're on to something.'

'We noticed that you quoted them all as not available for comment.'

'Code, Inspector. That is code for something going on, but we don't know exactly what or think it better not to say at that stage.' He looked across his desk and said, 'I don't suppose you'd like to tell me where that chap Forres is hiding out these days, would you?'

'No,' said Sloan flatly.

'Worth an ask,' said the editor. 'But believe you me, we're on to something and you must know it.'

'What you are also on to,' said Sloan, getting up to go, 'is causing a great deal of collateral damage. Come along, Crosby. We're going now.'

CHAPTER THIRTEEN

'Kay? Is that you?'

'It is,' replied Kay Harris with her customary brevity.

'Mike here. Sorry to ring you so early in the morning but I've got a favour to ask you.'

'Go ahead.'

'I don't know what you were planning to do at the works today . . .'

'If that's a question then the answer is I was planning to work on the woodcuts for the Calleshire Art History Society's next book. There's some quite tricky collagen stuff to go in it, too.' She paused and then said, 'I would have thought you would have remembered that, Mike, since we went into it all so carefully only on Tuesday morning.'

'Sorry.' He dismissed the highly skilled – not to say elegant – work Kay had on hand and got straight to the point. 'Do you think that instead of going into the works today you could come over to Little Missal and keep an eye on poor old Steph for me? Dr Browne says that she shouldn't be left alone, not in the state she's in.'

'Still in?'

'I'm afraid so. She hardly slept last night even though the doctor gave her a hefty dose of sleeping pills – she spent it pacing up and down the bedroom and so I didn't get much sleep either. She's obviously not fit to be left in the house on her own today and I've just got to get the earl's book finished and out to Ornum House in time for tomorrow evening's launch party there or we'll be absolutely sunk.'

'It sounds to me, Mike,' said Kay astringently, 'that you are absolutely sunk already. Or have I misunderstood the situation?'

'No, of course you haven't. I only wish you had. You're quite right, I know, but in spite of everything I'd still like to get the book out in time.' He drew breath and added heavily, 'Whatever else happens.'

'Come hell and high water?' she asked him ironically.

'We promised the author that the book would be printed on time,' he said a trifle stiffly. 'And it will be.'

'Professional pride coming before a domestic fall?'

'Very possibly, but the book itself is a lovely piece of work and if it's going to be the last one I ever do, then I want it to be perfect although I say it as shouldn't.'

'What you should be saying,' she said crisply, 'is

what on earth was Malcolm about by making you broke.'

'I don't know,' he admitted, 'and I can't even begin to imagine although I've been doing nothing but think why ever since he took off with every penny in the business.'

There was a noticeable pause before Kay said, 'Me, too. Think and wonder.'

'And all that the police will say to me is that they will be pursuing their enquiries today.'

'They'll have to be getting on with it, then, before the trail goes cold. I expect,' added their in-house grammarian, 'that they have ways and means that we know not of. Passenger lists if they've gone abroad, witnesses perhaps, credit cards, mobile phones and so forth.'

'Not mobile phones. Malcolm left his at the works.'

'Did he indeed?' Nobody had ever called Kay Harris slow. 'That's interesting and it means all of this was premeditated.'

'I'm afraid so. What I can't begin to think is why. It can't have just been for the money, surely?'

'I shouldn't be too sure about that.'

'But we've always had equal shares in the business and we've neither of us done too badly.'

'Other people's money can be a closed book, just like other people's marriages,' she said.

'That's true,' he agreed. He knew almost nothing about Kay's late husband or her life before she came to

Forres and Wakefield, although he had never been in any doubt about her skill. 'But even so, in my opinion what the police should be doing now is pursuing Malcom Forres before it's too late,' said the printer.

'And Christine.'

'Why do you say that?'

'She's his wife, isn't she?' said Kay enigmatically. 'Perhaps she's had a shock, too.'

'All I can say is that Steph's certainly had a very nasty one.'

'So have you, Mike. Riches to rags practically overnight – it's the other way round that's the stuff of fairy stories. Have you any idea at all about what got into Malcolm to make him commit robbery – as he would seem to have done?'

'None. It's the last thing in the world I would have expected of the man. We've been working together for years, and I would have thought he cared about the business itself as much as I did, let alone his share of the profit. I would have been the first person to have said it was not like him at all.'

Kay said, 'You do realise, don't you, that the staff aren't going to be very happy?'

'I know. I'm just so very sorry for letting them all down, including you.'

She gave a short, mirthless laugh. 'You don't need to worry about me, Mike. I can always go back to teaching English, but the others won't be able to find work like they do with you unless a similar outfit takes over before you have to have a fire sale.'

'You don't mince words, do you?' he said bleakly.

'No point,' said Kay.

'I know that none of this is my fault, but I still feel very guilty all the same.'

'If it's not your fault then you've got no call to feel guilty,' she came back logically. 'Not that that helps,' she added, mellowing slightly.

Itching to be off, he said, 'Please do tell me that you can cope with Steph today,' adding persuasively, 'Dr Browne did say he would call again this morning. And after all, Steph did let you take her home after that nightmare scene at the works yesterday.'

'It was a near thing when we reached your house,' said Kay. 'She got quite hysterical again.'

'I'm afraid she's taken it all quite badly.'

'I don't blame her for that,' said Kay, adding in quite a different tone, 'I take it that it must have been a big shock to you, too.'

'Of course it has.' She sensed his voice stiffen and then he said, 'What makes you think that it wasn't, Kay?'

'Because none of this makes any sense to me, that's why, Mike. Nothing at all and I don't like it one little bit.'

CHAPTER FOURTEEN

Lenny Datchet was very disappointed in the size of the road from Berebury to Ornum House. Charged with delivering the first copy of *Muniments and Their Hanapers* with all possible speed to the Earl of Ornum, he had set out with every hope of reaching his destination very speedily by doing a ton-up on the way. Literally hot off the press and bound with haste, the earl's book was packed safely in one of the panniers of his motorcycle. Lenny had planned to place it without delay into the waiting hands of its expectant author and then immediately return to Berebury for an evening out with his mates. What was delaying the process was the intricate network of minor roads out in the wilds of the Calleshire countryside that eventually led to the village of Ornum and its stately home.

What Lenny enjoyed doing most of all was to open

the throttle of his powerful machine and then to surge ahead on a clear road, frightening any bystanders in sight and not constantly to have to lower his speed to dead slow whilst he tried to figure out which way to go. Reading signposts whilst standing astride his heavy motorbike took every ounce of his strength. He had made reasonable progress to begin with through a confused maze of little lanes, passing one farmstead after another on his way, until he came to a dead stop in front of a signpost, two of whose three arms read 'Ornum'. The third one pointed to the way he had come so was unhelpful from his point of view since it was labelled 'Berebury'.

Eventually, having chosen the more promising opening of the two routes, he came across Ornum House and was genuinely awed for the first time in his young life. He'd never seen a house as large or so old as this one before. Instinctively making for the back door, he knocked on it quite timidly for him. It was answered by a very pretty teenage girl with noticeably dirty hands. These she wiped on an equally dirty apron before grasping the parcel.

'It's for the earl,' he said awkwardly, handing it over. 'From the printer's. Can you give it to his nibs, please, miss?'

The girl shouted out, 'Daddy, your book! It's just come!'

'Come in, my boy, come in,' said a man appearing behind her from a room beyond. He was also wearing an apron, his hands far from clean too. The earl grasped the parcel, displaying more excitement now than he had shown as a young subaltern when yomping across the Falklands Islands in the war there. 'This calls for a celebration all round, everyone.'

Lenny advanced warily into the largest kitchen he had ever seen. Seated round the scrubbed wooden table, there was a living replica of the young woman who had opened the door to him and an older woman, not unlike them both. On the table was a great collection of silver, some clean and shining, some dull and tarnished. Cans of silver polish and piles of rags and dusters were heaped in the middle of the table.

'Mind you wash your hands before you open the book, Jonas,' warned the older woman. 'They're very dirty.'

The man in the apron said, 'Yes, dear,' and disappeared through a distant door, through which the sound of splashing water could soon be heard.

The woman smiled kindly at Lenny and, pointing at the silver, said, 'We've got a party here tomorrow night, you see.'

Lenny nodded speechlessly. He knew nothing whatsoever about silver but to him what it spelt was money – a lot of it.

'And a crowd of people are coming to stay for the book launch,' put in one of the young women, waving an arm over the assembled silverware. 'It's going to be a great party.'

'Not Richard, though, Mary,' said the other girl. 'He can't make it now.'

'Perhaps Roderick will come instead,' suggested her sister slyly.

Lenny watched as a blush crept up her face whilst the older woman said, 'Now, girls . . .'

'And Roderick wears such beautiful pyjamas,' went on Mary. 'You know that.'

'But how do you know?' challenged her sister, Victoria, immediately. 'He's not your friend. He's mine.'

'What about Sheep's Eyes? Is he coming too?' asked Mary.

Lenny stared at each girl in turn, quite bemused.

'Jason Fixby? He's coming, all right.' Victoria smirked and said, 'He told me he'd kill himself if he couldn't come.'

'Jason shouldn't talk like that, Victoria,' remonstrated the twins' mother. 'Nobody should.'

'And he put all of his money on a horse yesterday at Calleford so that he could buy a new suit for the party,' announced Victoria.

'Did he win?' asked Mary.

'I don't know yet, do I?' said her twin blithely. 'He won't tell me.'

'That means he lost his shirt,' said Mary.

'He's not coming here if he has,' growled her father, coming back into the kitchen with clean hands and carefully unwrapping the parcel with his book in it. 'It's lovely, quite lovely,' he crooned, stroking the gold-tooled binding. He turned to Lenny as he continued to handle it. 'Tell me, who in your firm did all the work on this?'

'Mr Wakefield and Mr Hull,' stammered Lenny, finding his voice at long last.

'I must thank them,' said the author, feeling in his back pocket, 'and thank you, too, my boy, for bringing it over in time for the party.'

A small currency note exchanged hands and Lenny was ready for off, his engine soon started and with its throttle at hand ready for a good twist. He always liked to take off with a full-throated roar and he was primed for take-off now.

But he didn't attempt to leave before he had made a careful study of the exterior of Ornum House in the gathering dusk.

And he didn't even go then, being waylaid as he was outside the house by the Ornum twins, both pleading for a ride on his pillion before he left.

CHAPTER FIFTEEN

'Ah, Sloan, I see you've arrived this morning at last,' said Leeyes, looking up from his desk on the Saturday morning. The superintendent himself always made a point of coming into the police station on Saturday mornings to ensure that he didn't have to do so on Sunday mornings. These were sacrosanct to his playing the game of golf, what religious obeisance he made on Sundays being confined to bending down to insert a tee in the grass or kneeling to retrieve a ball out of the hole. 'I told them I wanted to see you in my office first thing.'

'Yes, sir,' said the detective inspector, marvelling, as always, at the superintendent's capacity for wrong-footing his subordinates. Someone wiser than he had once advised someone else to 'Never apologise, never explain,' so he did neither today.

'So, tell me, what exactly do you have to report after your investigations into the Forres case, then?'

Detective Constable Crosby had last been seen heading for the police canteen, whose all-day breakfast had always had a lot to be said for it. Sloan had had his own breakfast in his own home and hadn't been late in although he didn't say so. It wouldn't have been worth it. You could be wrong for being right with the superintendent: something that had taken him quite some learning.

'We began our enquiries at Little Missal on the first morning, sir,' temporised the detective inspector, taking a policy decision not to mention the word 'embezzlement' to the superintendent. 'If you remember, sir, that was the home of the injured party.'

'And then?' demanded Leeyes on the instant.

'Michael Wakefield wasn't at his home, so we set out to interview him at his works here in Berebury instead but weren't able to do so properly on account of his being in the middle of a pretty nasty domestic just as we arrived. He had to have his wife taken away by a member of his staff in the end because she became quite hysterical.'

As excuses went with the superintendent, this one was bomb-proof. There wasn't a man on the force who didn't run the proverbial mile from attending domestic disturbances if he possibly could. There was only one situation that was worse, and that was a hotly contested allegation of attempted rape. There was always the lurking danger in both cases then that couples engaged in bitter disputes between themselves would unite briefly to attack the officer attending. Therefore, trying to defuse such situations carried its own risks and both policemen already knew this from hard experience when on the beat.

'No use interviewing a man with something like that on his mind,' agreed Leeyes sagely. 'Waste of time.'

'I really should have liked to talk to his staff at the same time but in view of this development, sir, I deemed it better to try to get a clearer picture of the set-up of Wakefield's business first. After all, it is what in some ways you might call a white-collar crime rather than simple theft.'

Leeyes grudgingly said that he got his drift.

'And then, sir, after visiting the printing works, we went out to the home of the man we are seeking to interview in connection with the missing money at the Berebury firm.'

'Come over a bit cautious in quite how you put it, haven't you, Sloan?' Leeyes sniffed. 'It sounds like an open and shut case to me.'

'Malcolm Forres and his wife live at Peverton,' said Sloan, nobly rising above any question of early police partiality in a new case.

'That isn't one of those villages for the old and rich that they call a cemetery with the lights on, is it?'

'No, sir.' The worry about those, both policemen knew, was that they posed an open invitation to burglary and worse. 'On the contrary, sir, it's an ordinary working one.'

'That makes a change,' commented Leeyes, the invasion of the countryside by the well-to-do retired being one of his hobbyhorses. 'Now, about this Malcolm Forres – his present whereabouts still unknown, I take it?'

'I'm afraid so, sir.' Sloan pulled out his notebook. 'And since the neighbour said that the last time he saw the couple they appeared to be in hurry to get away from their home . . .'

'This was the night before the firm's annual meeting and presumably thus with a showdown in prospect, I take it?'

'Yes, indeed, sir.' He took breath and carried on. 'So, we've done a few calculations.' That wasn't strictly true since Crosby usually had difficulty in working out from the timetable when to catch the next bus back to his lodgings and so had made no significant contribution to them.

'Go on.'

'Given the time that the couple left Peverton and the distance involved – to say nothing of the hurry Malcom Forres was said to have been in at the time by the neighbour – we felt that they were most likely to be aiming to catch the ferry scheduled to leave Newhaven at one o'clock in the morning.'

'Heading for where?' The police superintendent's view of Europe was best summed up in the old xenophobic saying 'Fog in Channel, Continent isolated'.

'Dieppe.'

'Does arriving there get you anywhere special?'

'France is a big country, sir,' said Sloan, aware that his superior officer would never admit to knowing the location of anywhere abroad, 'but Dieppe would be as good a starting point as any for going places without leaving too much of a trail. We have been trying to find out if the pair had repeatedly visited anywhere in that direction before – on holiday, say.'

'In order to set up a bolthole, you mean?'

'It is a possibility that we shall obviously take into consideration in due course.' Every now and then Sloan found that police speak fitted the bill.

Or the Old Bill.

Leeyes grunted. 'I suppose it may come down in the end to asking Interpol although I bet they won't act unless someone has been charged.' His relations with international policing could never have been described as cordial and especially not *cordiale*.

'And after that, sir,' pressed on Sloan, 'we interviewed the new accountant at Fixby and Fixby.' Sloan hesitated whether to tell him that a woman called Kate Booth was the new accountant in question, since his attitude to women in any of the professions was uncertain to say the least.

'Not young Jason Fixby?'

'No, sir, not him. I was told by Fixby's that he wasn't

in the office there at the time.' He coughed. 'I was given to understand by Constable Crosby that there was a big meeting that afternoon over at Calleford racecourse in which he was likely to have been interested.'

'And was the Fixby boy over there at the race? Is that what you're trying to say?'

'We assume so, sir, seeing as his firm mentioned that was where he had gone that day when we called. Not that they said so in so many words, naturally.'

'The honour of the regiment always leads to a lot of trouble,' remarked the superintendent ambiguously. 'In every setting.'

'Yes, sir, I'm sure,' said Sloan, although he had no idea what his superior officer meant by it.

'Except the police force, Sloan. We don't go in for protecting our own for the sake of our reputation.'

'No, sir. I'm sure not.'

'Rotten apples do do a lot of damage all the same,' declared Leeyes. 'Can't be doing with them.'

'It's the *Monilinia fructigena*,' said Sloan, taking this literally. In his spare time, Detective Inspector Sloan was a keen gardener.

Leeyes ignored his reply and instead sighed and said, 'To be realistic, I suppose if it wasn't the gees-gees with the Fixby boy it would be something else. Weaknesses in families will out.'

Detective Inspector Sloan, model husband and father, agreed. The superintendent was never other than realistic.

'And if he'd taken to drink instead of the horses, he might have killed someone on the road,' said Leeyes, 'which would be worse.'

'Very true, sir.'

'And if he had been dealing in drugs then he would be putting us all here to a lot of trouble,' went on Leeyes. 'As well as other people.'

In Sloan's view it was quite possible that young Jason Fixby was about to put the police to a lot of trouble anyway, especially if he had been getting his hand in the till at Fixby's or – come to that – at the printer's. Or, more difficult to prove, being the conduit for information from one firm to the other. For a price, of course. That he probably needed the money went without saying if he was a betting man.

'I hope, Sloan,' said Leeyes, 'that you haven't lost that man Forres entirely.'

'Europe's a big place,' temporised Sloan, only too aware that the chances of finding Malcolm and Christine Forres were pretty low, Interpol notwithstanding.

'And Britain's only a small one,' interrupted Leeyes, 'and yet, do you know, in the second century AD the Romans managed to lose upwards of four thousand men in it?'

'No, sir, I didn't know. Four thousand, did you say? That's a lot of men to lose.'

'The Ninth Hispanic Legion, the lot of them. The Missing Ninth,' he said, 'they were called.'

'How come, sir?' The ploy of keeping his superior

officer talking off the subject was an old one and well-practised by all his underlings. It was better than having to tell him how little progress had been made in a case.

Any case.

'Nobody knows for sure. Marched north from York one day towards Scotland and were never seen again.'

The detective inspector sat back in his chair at this and relaxed, relishing a memory as it slowly came back to him. That of an evening course attended by Superintendent Leeyes one winter on the history of the Romans in Britain, that was it. The superintendent's encounter with Roman Britain had foundered when he discovered that as far as Rome was concerned, the country of Britannica – his own country, that is – had been known to the Romans merely as the Western Province. This he took as a personal affront.

Hearing at one of the talks that an entire Roman legion had disappeared without trace was something else. It aroused all Leeyes' police instincts and he had left the lecturer to his own devices shortly afterwards, murmuring darkly about Roman incompetence. The lecturer, not knowing him well, had ventured to suggest that we owed the Romans sanitation, roads, good buildings, law, theatres and peace – the latter, though, only after a fashion.

The superintendent had retaliated, saying that since the legion had set out from York, it should have been easy to find four thousand men – or was it six – or their bodies. Either would do, as far as he was concerned.

'Unresolved infamy – that's what I called it, Sloan,' trumpeted Leeyes.

'There's a lot of that about still,' murmured Sloan, mindful of a number of unsolved crimes on their own patch.

'I'd call it plain inefficiency myself,' snorted Leeyes.

Detective Inspector Sloan brought him back to the present by saying that he had already interviewed the editor of the local weekly paper about their story.

'No joy, I suppose,' his superior officer grumbled. 'Not that anyone could touch the man if he's got his facts right.'

'It's not that so much as knowing who gave him the story that matters, sir, which of course he wouldn't tell me.'

'But why?' added the superintendent. 'Funny thing to do. Makes it personal. Someone else wanting to maximise the damage, perhaps?'

'Perhaps, sir. So I've arranged to interview Michael Wakefield after work today instead over at Little Missal. I gather, sir, he's a bit uneasy at leaving his wife alone at home just now.'

Leeyes grunted.

'Apparently she's so upset at the prospect of being penniless and everyone knowing about it that she'd said something about burning the house down rather than let anyone else have it.'

Superintendent Leeyes sat back in his own chair and

said reflectively, 'We haven't had a case of arson for a long time, have we?'

Detective Inspector Sloan said as repressively as he dared that he was of the opinion that the force could do without one now and took his leave.

CHAPTER SIXTEEN

'But, sir, it's Saturday afternoon,' protested Detective Constable Crosby.

'So I am given to understand,' said Sloan astringently. He had been tempted to say instead, 'God bless my soul, so it is,' in tones of great surprise at being made aware of the fact. In the end he decided against it. There was always the lurking danger that humour – or was it irony? – might confuse the detective constable, which wouldn't do at all in the middle of an investigation.

Certainly not in a case like this.

The house they visited at Little Missal that afternoon was in every respect outwardly the same as the one that they had first visited. It was still Georgian, still restrained and still – nearly – in impeccable condition. In fact, the physical scene at the Old Rectory at Little Missal was quite unchanged. It was the human atmosphere in the house that was totally different from that prevailing when they had made their original visit there.

On that first occasion, Stephanie Wakefield had been sitting at the same table in the same kitchen. She had been quite alert then, really spirited – militant, even – and fighting back against what the absent Malcolm Forres had done. But she was a different woman this afternoon. Now she was as silent as a wraith and as still and as expressionless as a monument. The floor beside her, though, was now covered in debris from two lemon drizzle cakes that had been smashed on it and then ground down on the floor tiles with the heel of a woman's shoe.

A haggard-looking Michael Wakefield had admitted the two policemen to the house, apologising as he did so for the mental state his wife was in. 'I don't know quite what to do, Inspector,' he said, leading the way through to the kitchen. 'I've never seen my wife behave like this before.' He shook his head. 'It was seeing the front page of the local paper that did it, I know.'

'We've seen it, too,' Sloan said briefly, forbearing to say that they had already talked to the paper's editor.

'It was all her friends ringing up that did it, Inspector,' said Wakefield savagely. 'Every one of them went on to tell her how sorry they were about our being made bankrupt.'

'That was nice of them,' began Crosby naively.

'No, it wasn't, Constable.' Wakefield turned and stared at him, saying, 'But really what all of them only wanted was to get the low-down on what had happened to us before anyone else did so that they could carry on gossiping about it all behind Stephanie's back.'

'Ghouls, then,' offered Crosby instead.

Detective Inspector Sloan, experienced police officer that he was, did not attempt to deny this as more than likely. The best moment to approach someone dealing with great loss required a sensitivity not possessed by everybody, so did breaking that news. His own mentor in his police training school used to cite, as a warning of the worst possible way of bringing bad news, the old chestnut of one who asked where Widow Jones lived and on receiving the reply that no one called Widow Jones lived there, had said, 'They do now.'

Wakefield was still talking. 'In the end, Steph just stopped answering the telephone. I had to get Dr Browne out to give her something to calm her down. He advised me not to leave her here alone.' He added simply, 'I'd be afraid to, anyway, with her in the state she's in.'

Detective Inspector Sloan could see for himself the effects of what the woman had been prescribed in her dull appearance and the slow-mannered way – not unlike the careful actions of a drunkard – in which she made any movements.

This was confirmed by a whisper from Crosby to Sloan, as he spotted her unfocussed eyes as well.

'No, Crosby. Acting like a drunk, yes, but drugged, not drunk,' said Sloan, starting to feel in his pocket for his notebook. 'Always a great worry for doctors trying to sort them out in hospital – get it wrong and you've let someone die.'

'She didn't take it too badly at first,' Wakefield was going on. 'I was hoping in the beginning that we might ride the difficulties out together.'

'Coping too well to begin with, perhaps,' murmured Sloan, looking at the tableau before him. 'It never does.' He opened his notebook and asked the printer if he had had any reason to suspect that anything was wrong at the firm before his partner, Forres, had departed so precipitously.

'Taking the dibs with him,' muttered Crosby, beginning to get bored.

Wakefield shot a glance in the direction of his wife and said, 'I think I'd rather talk about this in another room, Inspector, if you don't mind.' He led the way through to a well-furnished sitting room, a good Georgian mirror set over the fireplace being the centrepiece. Prominent on the mantelpiece were two tickets to a performance by the Berebury Amateur Dramatic Society the following week of *The Importance of Being Earnest*.

Sloan spotted them and was immediately transported back to the Year Twelve form play. A gruff-voiced boy had made a meal of playing Lady Bracknell but it was the one in the true Shakespearean tradition of a boy playing a girl who had brought the house down as Cecily Cardew, sweet Cecily. Catcalls heralded his every entrance whilst the boy being Algernon had had his wolf whistles in plenty.

The fireplace was flanked by two matching polished period tables, one on either side of the hearth. Catching Sloan's gaze, Wakefield said, 'Steph was always so houseproud. She enjoyed searching for genuine period stuff to go with the house and it's been almost more than she can bear to know that all this will have to be sold.' He shook his head. 'Perhaps she cares too much.'

'You'll get a very good price for it all the same, I shouldn't wonder,' observed Detective Constable Crosby sedulously. 'Bound to.'

Detective Inspector Sloan reminded himself to explain to Crosby in the privacy of the police station that uncalled-for remarks like that should not be made to or in front of witnesses. He also reminded himself that although Wakefield was technically a witness – and a victim, even – he might possibly also be no such thing. Businessmen the world over had been known to conspire to leave firms with heavy losses for others to bear – sometimes, but not always, insurance companies.

Wakefield pointed the policemen to a deep sofa and then settled himself in a Georgian library chair built for a man who had eaten well all his life. 'My wife's very attached to this place,' he said by way of explanation of the finely furnished room, 'and naturally she – we – that is, aren't happy at the prospect of losing everything we've ever worked for.'

'Quite so,' said Sloan, not unsympathetically.

'And moving somewhere downmarket,' added Crosby superfluously.

'Somewhere that with the best will in the world she won't like, I'm afraid,' said Wakefield, shaking his head. 'Not after living here. How could anyone?'

'Disaster takes people differently,' observed Sloan moderately, this being something that every policeman learnt very quickly early in their career. What was one man's sore trial and tribulation was shrugged off by another one more resilient or more used to dealing with trouble. He tried to get back to police business. 'Tell me about your partner.'

'Malcolm Forres? I've known him ever since we were being taught printing together. I would have trusted him anywhere.'

'You did trust him,' pointed out Crosby egregiously. 'Everywhere, like you said.'

Wakefield added, 'He was good with figures, too.'

'Sounds to me like he was too good,' said Crosby, sotto voce this time.

Wakefield waved a hand round the well-appointed sitting room. 'We wouldn't have been living here like this if he hadn't been. Money isn't my line. I'm a printer, not a chartered accountant.'

'And a very good one from all accounts,' said Sloan. Not that that was relevant now. Nor was the fact that the man had a sensitive face and the finely tapered hands of the true craftsman. So far nobody had managed to lay hands on a photograph of Malcom Forres to check, among several other things, his artistic credentials. He made a mental note to also check whether the absence of photographs was accidental or premeditated.

'We were just a couple of young lads starting from nothing and nowhere at first,' said Wakefield. 'In an old garage, actually.'

Sloan nodded. There had been another couple of young lads who'd started out in an old garage, too, and now would seem to own half the world.

Wakefield gave a little laugh. 'Gilbert Hull's daughter was into family history research before she took up amateur dramatics, but she couldn't find any printers in either my family or Malcolm's.'

Sloan hadn't any plans for his own son's career although he was sure he would be able to conquer the world.

'Malcolm always kept his hand in with my side of things, too,' explained Wakefield. 'We were both in love with what we were doing, you see, and he was a still a good printer at heart for all that.'

'That's worth a lot,' said Sloan. 'Enjoying your job.' And he meant it. If anyone ever asked him about his own work and whether he liked it or not, he usually gave some seemingly judicious reply about liking some but not all of it. In his own mind, though, he thought about what he did quite differently. There was never anything to compare with the deep satisfaction of bringing a killer – or worse, and he'd been a policeman long enough to know that there were worse than killers about – to justice, that is, to trial. At least as far as trial anyway, he was wont to add cynically to himself.

And though he would never admit it, not even to his wife, Margaret, who would have upbraided him for it, there was always the excitement of the chase. 'Daddy's gone a-hunting' was something he chanted to his young son after telling him his bedtime story that always reminded him of this feeling. Men and hounds had been programmed for it, cats too. He wasn't sure about horses.

'You can get quite addicted to fonts, Inspector, you know,' said Wakefield, who had naturally not been privy to his thoughts.

'I can well understand that,' said Sloan hastily, before Crosby enquired what baptism had got to do with it. He turned to Wakefield and asked again whether he had had any reason to suspect that Malcolm Forres was about to rob him.

'Blind,' added Crosby.

'No, Inspector, but perhaps I was being a bit stupid about that because we always get a bit of stirring among the workers when the bonuses are due and it's infectious. We used to announce them each year after our meeting with Fixby and Fixby, you see.'

'Not this year,' interjected Crosby.

They didn't have bonuses in the police force. You did your job to somebody else's satisfaction and got paid what everyone else in that rank got paid. And took an examination to move further up the career ladder. It wasn't ever a case of who you know rather than what you know in their upward progress.

'Thinking back now, Inspector, I suppose there might have been something going on – a groundswell, perhaps, that I couldn't quite put my finger on. Nothing more definite than a feeling, though.'

'I'm going to need a list of everyone who works for you, please,' said Sloan, sitting back and steadying his notebook on his knee, 'and anything else you think I ought to know about them.'

Sitting by his own fireside last thing that evening, Sloan asked his wife how she would view their being made bankrupt.

'Losing everything, you mean, Chris?' Margaret asked, nursing a mug of coffee.

He who was known at work as Detective Inspector C. D. Sloan and to his friends there as 'Seedy' from his initials, answered to the names of Christopher Dennis in his own home. He nodded in reply now. 'Lock, stock and barrel,' he said, grinning, 'And probably your pin money, too.'

She pointed to the ceiling above. 'But not our boy, though, or you?'

'No, no, just the house – well, that bit of it that's ours and doesn't still belong to the mortgage people – and all our money and possessions. We'd be left with just enough to live on.' This, after all, was what was probably going to happen soon to the Wakefields.

Margaret set her mug of cocoa down, thought for a while and then said seriously, 'I shouldn't like it at all, but as long as you two were both all right then it would be bearable.'

He went to bed a strangely happy man.

He didn't stay that way for long.

Not after the duty sergeant at the police station had rung him to say that a body had been found at Ornum House.

CHAPTER SEVENTEEN

'But, Sloan,' howled Superintendent Leeyes down the telephone, 'don't you know it's Sunday morning?'

'I'm very sorry, sir . . .' he began. He hadn't been planning to make any smart response to his superior officer anyway. He had learnt better than to do that already.

'And I'm already in the clubhouse, man, ready to go out any minute now.'

'I'm very sorry, sir,' he said again, 'but we've been called to Ornum House. The earl says they've found a body there.'

Slightly mollified by the name-dropping, the superintendent said, 'Then whatever you do, don't take that young idiot Crosby with you. He's bound to let us down in that sort of company.'

'I'm afraid, sir,' said Sloan stiffly, 'that there just

isn't anyone else in the division available this morning.' He was tempted to add that everyone else was playing golf, too, but having his pension to think of, he didn't give way to temptation. Instead, he said truthfully, 'There's been a major incident over at Kinnisport and 'E' Division have asked us for assistance.'

In the ordinary way Leeyes would have grumbled about that, too, but Sloan heard someone call out in the distance, 'Hurry up, Leeyes, we're due on the first tee next.' And the line went dead.

Jonas Cremond, Earl of Ornum, had known death when he saw it. And had known exactly what to do when he did. Taking a numbered key off a hook, he'd led the way through the long corridors of Ornum House and up two flights of stairs to the second floor.

'Place was very full last night, Inspector, especially of youngsters,' he said as they turned a corner and went down yet another corridor. 'It was supposed to be my party to launch a book I'd just written but the twins asked all their friends to come too and made what they were pleased to call a "proper bash" of it.'

'I can see that, my lord,' said Sloan, hoping that this was the right way of addressing the middle-aged man ahead of them. The police were by no means unfamiliar with the detritus left after a party, after almost every party they had attended. Sometimes this amounted to a rollcall of injuries, sometimes the sequestration of illegal substances, sometimes dealing with those who had drink taken in unwise quantity and quality. Just normal debris was something to be grateful for in these days of the vogue for fatal stabbings.

'And so, he – whoever he is – must have been one of my daughters' friends, not mine. Many of the people here last night were at the twins' invitation and they had all been cavorting everywhere over the house practically all night long. My own friends had more sense and went back home for a good noggin in their own houses.'

'Nightcap,' translated Sloan for the benefit of Crosby, standing one step behind him, clearly puzzled.

'The lord-lieutenant left early, thank God, Inspector,' said the Earl of Ornum, 'and Miss Meadows did her usual Cinderella act and went home before midnight.'

'Needs her beauty sleep,' commented Crosby under his breath.

Since this was undeniably true of Miss Henrietta Meadows, the redoubtable lady chairman of the Berebury Bench of Magistrates, Sloan held his peace.

'I'm afraid that my daughter Victoria found him and she's very upset. She'd actually gone upstairs to look for another boy who hadn't turned up for his oats this morning either.'

'I don't like porridge,' announced Crosby from the sidelines. 'Bacon and eggs for me, please.'

'He?' queried Sloan. 'It's a male, this body?'

'Oh, yes.' The earl nodded. 'The deceased. Young and unknown to me. My daughter Vicky – Victoria, that is – didn't recognise him either as it happens, not that that means anything these days. It was because his face was a nasty colour and distorted and she didn't look at him twice.' He sighed. 'These days the young issue blanket invitations to all their friends over what they are pleased to call the social media.'

'So I am given to understand, sir – I mean, Your Lordship.' Something that always made policing difficult was not knowing who had been where at the material time. And, in this case, who had invited whom to a house party in the depths of the Calleshire countryside.

'My wife, Inspector,' said Jonas Cremond, 'decided at eleven o'clock this morning that she wasn't going to go on serving their breakfasts to anyone who came down after that.'

'Very sensible of her, if I may say so.'

'Unfortunately, though, she sent both our two daughters – the twins – upstairs to rootle out anyone who hadn't come down for breakfast by then.' He grunted. 'If there was more than one person in a bed, I told them I didn't want to know, and they told me I was out of touch with the modern world.' Cremond fished the key out of his pocket and let the two policemen into a small bedroom. Lying in the bed was a figure with only its head visible above a counterpane that had been drawn up well under its chin.

'Vicky knew that one fellow hadn't come down yet and had gone off to find him.' He waved a hand towards the bed. 'But she says this wasn't the one she was looking for, he must have been someone's guest because he's in his pyjamas.'

The notebook of Detective Inspector Sloan was in his hand in a flash. 'A name would be a great help, Your Lordship.'

'Got to start somewhere,' muttered Crosby.

'I don't know this one's name,' said the peer, pointing to the bed. 'And all I know about the other one – the one Vicky was looking for – is that my daughters always called him Sheep's Eyes.'

'Sweet on one of them, was he?' asked Crosby conversationally.

'Victoria.' Victoria's father grimaced. 'Besotted with her, or so they told me, and couldn't take his eyes off her. I expect she led him on.' He sighed. 'Heartless creatures, young women in search of the right man.'

'And have they found the other one yet?' asked Sloan urgently. 'This fellow Sheep's Eyes?' That he wasn't the right man for the girl was open to question at this stage, but he thought probably not.

The earl jerked his head. 'Good thinking, Inspector. I don't know and I think I'd better go and see if we can find this other man straight away.'

'It might be important,' said Sloan. 'You never know. And you, Crosby,' he added, 'can feel if the bed is still warm.'

The detective constable put his hand under the bedclothes and shook his head. 'No, sir, it isn't. It's quite cold.'

'There is something called "sudden adult death syndrome", Crosby, that you ought to know about, which might account for his dying like this in the night whilst lying in bed,' said Sloan, always conscious of his duty to instruct young constables, 'although I don't know that that would account for those little red blotches on his face.' An illness might, he realised. Meningitis perhaps. He didn't know.

'Nothing catching, sir, I hope,' said Crosby, backing away and wiping the hand that had been in the bed on his trousers.

'Too soon to say,' said Sloan, advancing towards the bed and carefully pulling back the counterpane a little. He regarded the pale, spotty face of the dead man for a moment and then gently lifted the corpse's chin. He covered up the pale, spotty face pretty smartly with the counterpane and said, 'Sudden adult death for sure, Crosby, but there's not a syndrome in sight. He's been strangled.'

CHAPTER EIGHTEEN

'Not strangled, Sloan,' Dr Hector Smithson Dabbe, consultant pathologist to the Berebury District General Hospital, corrected the policeman immediately he arrived in the bedroom.

'Really, Doctor?' Whatever it was, the manner of death of the man in the bed patently not being from natural causes had just opened up a whole new scenario for the small Criminal Investigation Department of 'F' Division of the County of Calleshire Constabulary and its head, Detective Inspector Sloan – and he knew it.

At the back of Sloan's mind there was something else to worry about, too. The earl hadn't returned yet with news of he whom his daughters had chosen to call Sheep's Eyes and who – if Kate Booth was right – Sloan feared could be really called Jason Fixby. By now he was beginning to be worried about the Fixby boy on other grounds as well. For all he knew there could be a serial killer loose in the house.

That, thought Sloan, as he opened his notebook, would open yet another can of worms by any policeman's standards.

'No, Inspector,' said the pathologist, pointing a bony finger at the bed, 'this man, whoever he is, hasn't been strangled. He's been garrotted, which is technically quite different.'

'He's still dead,' pointed out Crosby, sotto voce.

'Quite a popular cause of death still, I understand, in some countries,' remarked Dabbe conversationally.

'If you can't afford a gun,' murmured Crosby.

'Do you know, gentlemen,' said Dabbe, ignoring this and giving way to reminiscence instead, 'I haven't seen a case of true garrotting in years.'

Sloan wasn't at all sure that he had ever seen one and he certainly wasn't enjoying seeing this one now. The bloated, spotted face of the man in the bed did not present a pretty picture. 'And I'm afraid, Doctor,' he apologised, 'that we don't even know who he is yet.'

'If you ask me,' muttered Crosby, 'his own mother wouldn't even know him now either.'

'Your problem, that, Sloan, not mine.' Dr Dabbe was not interested in names, only in bodies. He'd arrived at Ornum House in record time because although he usually spent his Sunday mornings sailing his Albacore off the coast of Calleshire, he hadn't been able to put to sea today. 'Did you know that Kinnisport's been blockaded?'

The question of what plans the doctor's taciturn assistant, Burns, who had come with him, had had for his Sunday morning didn't arise.

'There's big trouble over on the coast today,' continued Dr Dabbe, explaining his prompt arrival at the scene. 'They've closed the place down completely. It seems some foreign tanker has been taken over at gunpoint out at sea and was last seen sailing towards the harbour there. I don't know what they have in mind.'

'I saw a pirate in a pantomime once,' Crosby remarked to nobody in particular. 'He had a skull and crossbones painted on his hat and he was called Captain Hook.'

Still talking, the pathologist bent over the bed to examine the neck of the dead man more closely. He drew back the counterpane a little further and said, 'The tissue is too engorged for me to tell you much more about any ligature here just yet. You'll have to wait until I get him on the table, Sloan, and get a good look at his back as well before we can know exactly what it was that did the trick.'

'Yes, Doctor,' said Sloan whilst the perennially silent Burns set about taking a reading of the ambient temperature and that of the body, too, before starting to take notes for the pathologist.

'A precaution against garrotting was why your early Metropolitan policemen used to have those high uniform collars in the old days, remember, Sloan? It stopped your villain coming up behind you with a bit of rope whilst you weren't looking. Did you know that?'

'Look behind you,' quoted Crosby in a credible imitation of a stage whisper, still with pantomime on his mind.

Detective Inspector Sloan, a more modern policeman, gave unspoken thanks for a comfortable collar and tie: he was less grateful for a constable with the attention span of a butterfly.

Dr Dabbe continued ploughing his own forensic furrow regardless of them both. 'And once you'd got the rope or whatever it was round the man's neck all you had to do was pull it towards you, and upwards a little, then give it a quick jerk and a twist and the job was done.'

'And quite quietly,' added Sloan soberly. Not that anyone in a great well-built old house such as this was likely to have heard anything at all. Even so, that was one of the things that would have to be checked as soon as possible. That and a great many other things as well. 'He'd have had no time to talk for long, whoever he is, poor fellow.'

'Or have anyone around to say anything to,' suggested Crosby, who added after a moment's thought, 'except whoever did it, that is.'

'We don't know that yet either, Crosby,' pointed out Sloan. 'Too early to say.'

'Or having any breath left to talk with,' said the pathologist, adding mordantly, 'and if you can't breathe, you can't struggle for very long, let alone say anything.' He turned and started to dictate to Burns. 'Body of a young man, age unknown, lying supine in a single bed, bedclothes apparently undisturbed, and wearing old-fashioned striped pyjamas . . .' The doctor pulled the counterpane down a little further and said, 'Hullo, hullo, Sloan, what have we here?'

'We know, Doctor.' Sloan saw at once what it was that Dr Dabbe had found and said quickly, 'It's a real conundrum, that is. You don't have to tell me.'

'It's very odd, all the same.' The pathologist plucked at the edge of the body's sleeve. 'This man's wearing a black top under his pyjama jacket.' He was already carefully pulling back the sheets lower down. 'And black trousers and shoes under the lower half of his pyjamas.'

'He died with his boots on, then,' concluded Crosby, sometime armchair cowboy and still a man not above watching old Westerns.

'Therefore, someone's put the pyjamas on him after he was killed,' began Sloan.

'Or he had been wearing them in the first place,' concluded Dr Dabbe neatly, 'over his other clothes.'

'Funny, that,' said Crosby.

'And very significant,' sighed Sloan, conscious of there being yet another imponderable to add to an already lengthy list.

'Got all that down, Burns, have you?' asked the pathologist. 'We'll have to move him over a bit now, before I can tell you anything more. I need to get a proper look at the back of his neck. Ready, Burns . . . Ah, what did I say, gentlemen?'

'Garrotting,' said Crosby, taking this literally.

Sloan had been meticulous in not disturbing the body but since he was now able to look closely at the back of the man's neck, the mode of murder was clearly revealed. It became immediately apparent to them all what it was that had been used in the garrotting of the victim.

'Well, I'll be damned,' said the pathologist, regarding with detached professional interest two short, thin, circular lengths of wood now clearly visible lying either side of the neck of the deceased. These two little handles were fixed at each end of a piece of thin wire coming round from both sides of the front of the dead man's throat. 'What we have here, I can tell you straight away, Sloan, is an old-fashioned cheese-cutter.'

'A cheese-cutter!' echoed Detective Inspector Sloan, who had thought he had been a policeman long enough not to have been surprised by anything ever again.

'That's new,' observed Crosby.

A fleeting memory carried Sloan's thoughts straight back to an English lesson with a schoolmaster quoting somebody – he couldn't any longer remember who it had been – who had written something about death having ten thousand doors. This case looked like it was a death going through one of those ten thousand doors but also through a door that was not opened all that often. Like, he thought involuntarily, the original death's door in a monastery church, one only opened to let the body of a dead brother through on his way to the establishment's own burial ground.

'You only find proper cheese-cutters in the better stores these days, of course,' qualified the pathologist, who had been thinking along other, quite different lines. 'Those good old-fashioned shops that don't sell the more ordinary cheeses sold wrapped in plastic packets but carve exactly how much you want out of some great truckle of the best stuff.'

'The upmarket ones,' said Sloan. They were in an upmarket house here with a vengeance so that, at least, made sense even if nothing else had done so far today.

'Your real grocer develops a good eye for cutting the right weight,' said Dabbe, who had a good eye himself for judging anything to do with a dead body.

'There's tricks in every trade,' said Crosby, staring fascinated at this unusual agent of death.

'And there's nowhere much for any fingerprints even if the assailant wasn't wearing gloves,' pointed out Sloan, his mind totally on the job now.

'Which he will have been, sir, surely,' said Crosby, 'seeing as he must have meant to do it.'

'Good point, Crosby,' said Sloan generously, although he knew already that this was no spur-of-the-moment killing.

'Thank you, sir,' said the constable.

'You don't find cheese-cutters everywhere,' agreed

Sloan gravely, although he wasn't so sure about Ornum House being just everywhere. For all he knew, in an ancient dwelling like this they might have them in the kitchen by the bucketful – you could never tell what the occupants owned – had owned – for ever. A family such as the Ornums didn't move house and home and jettison what it didn't need at the time as most ordinary families had to do. This was something else that he would have to look into, he noted, as he made yet another entry in his casebook.

'Going equipped, you might say,' added Crosby eagerly. 'That's an offence, too, sir, isn't it?'

'But an offence not quite in the same league as murder,' Sloan reminded him. There were some policemen on the strength in 'F' Division who took a delight in 'throwing the book' at all miscreants – especially motorists – and he didn't want Crosby to turn out like one of them. They didn't do the force any good. He turned to the doctor and asked him if he could help with estimating the time of death.

'I'd hazard a guess at the best part of ten hours myself but as you know, the timing of a death is not an exact science. Last seen alive and first seen dead are the most reliable parameters you can be sure of. Let me know if the time of death is of the essence and I'll do what I can for you.' The pathologist straightened up and said, 'You've noted the petechiae on the face, I'm sure.'

'Well . . .' the detective inspector began cautiously.

'I can tell you that those little red spots that you

can see there demonstrate the presence of subcutaneous haemorrhages.'

'Yes, Doctor,' said Sloan, who had certainly noted them but equally certainly had not known what they were called. 'What does that mean to a simple policeman?'

'Blood leaking from the capillaries into the adjacent tissues, which is a characteristic of both strangulation and garrotting,' replied the pathologist, starting to close his bag.

'Thank you, Doctor,' he said, making a note. Perhaps translation was really the true function of the medical profession: telling the owner of a body what had gone wrong with it. And that action hopefully before offering any nostrums to the patient: guaranteeing the efficacy of these was a whole new ballgame, and not for your amateur, ambiguously put as it usually was.

The pathologist, unaware of this subversive train of thought, said, 'Right, Sloan, then you can get your friend Ted York to send him round to me when you're done with him, and Burns here will let you know when I'll be doing the post-mortem. I don't think I'll be able to tell you – or the coroner – much more about the cause of death until then, I'm afraid, but you never can tell in my world.' He snapped his bag shut and said, 'Come along now, Burns.'

Police Constable Edward York was the division's coroner's officer and thus responsible for the removal of all dead bodies with history – that is, those without a certificate of death from natural causes signed by a duly authorised medical practitioner. Before Sloan could invoke York's help, though, there were other specialists that he needed at Ornum House.

Already alerted by Crosby, it wasn't long before the next specialists in sudden death arrived on the scene in the shape of the two police photographers. Where the scenes of crime people had got to, he didn't yet know.

'Nice little place you've got here, Inspector,' said Williams, shedding his equipment as he came through the bedroom door. He was followed by his mate Dyson, carrying a tripod. Both men were quite cheerful about having had their Sunday mornings disrupted.

'No problem, Inspector,' said Dyson when Sloan apologised for this. 'I was trying to find a way of getting out of the house anyway.' He pointed to Williams. 'And it got him over there out of collecting the kids from Sunday school, it did.'

'And we spotted this promising little old pub in the village on the way,' said Williams, hefting a collection of heavy cameras around and beginning to set them up.

'The Cremond Inn,' said Dyson. 'It looked a bit of an all right so we thought we'd give it a try on our way back.'

'Some people have all the luck,' said Crosby.

'It's a hard life on the detective side, is it, then?' asked Dyson, lining up the tripod.

'It can be a very hard one,' interrupted Detective

Inspector Sloan, suddenly assailed by an unwelcome thought: that he didn't know how long a round of golf lasted. Or the round in the clubhouse bar afterwards that they called the nineteenth hole.

One thing was certain, though, and that was that it wasn't going to be anything like long enough to keep Superintendent Leeyes off his back.

CHAPTER NINETEEN

Michael Wakefield wasn't a religious man. He was undoubtedly an excellent craftsman in his own field, though, as well as being more than something of an artist. This was a characteristic the printer knew that often went hand in hand with good craftsmanship. Over the years these attributes had led him to believe – no, not truly believe, perhaps only just to have become aware – that there were moments when something other than his skills and artistry came from outside himself. This was a feeling, he knew, that transcended rational explanation. This wasn't something that he had ever attempted to put into words. Indeed, he would have had some difficulty in finding the right ones to explain what he had experienced.

Or to find anyone who would know what it was he was trying to convey to them.

This awareness, he would have been the first to admit – that is, if he had ever talked about it, which he never did – had nothing whatsoever to do with his weekly attendance at morning service at the village church at Little Missal. He and his wife, Stephanie, went to church on Sunday mornings as members of the community in which they lived. Just as Stephanie went to the coffee mornings in the church hall on Thursdays with her weekly contribution, homemade and tailored for quick, easy purchase by those there. It was part of the routine of living in the village of Little Missal, that was all. That and including the rector and his wife in their social circle.

This Sunday morning was different. So aware of this was Wakefield that he hadn't even bothered to put on the tidy dark suit and tie that he habitually wore to church on Sundays. Dr Browne had stressed that Stephanie was not to be left alone and as she was patently unfit to go anywhere at all today, he was going to stay at home too.

Stephanie hadn't attempted to get dressed at all today, merely having flung an old dressing-gown over a crumpled nightdress before coming downstairs. She hadn't done her hair this morning either. This now hung unbrushed and straggling around her ears. Her husband had watched her as she had made her way, crab-like, slowly down the stairs, clinging to the banister and taking each step as if calling upon a different set of muscles in turn to make sure of every separate move.

He breathed a sigh of relief as she reached the bottom step and then the ground floor. Now at last she was safely sitting in a chair at their kitchen table.

'Coffee, Steph?' he suggested. He got no answer to the question, but he slid a mug of it in front of her all the same.

She sat quite still in a frozen, zombie-like state, at first making no response to him. Whether it was the aroma of the newly brewed coffee that eventually started to get through to her or the sight of her husband watching her, patently worried, he couldn't decide, but after a little whilst she clasped both her hands round the mug and slowly lifted it to her lips. She held it there against them for a while as if she couldn't quite remember what to do with the mug next.

'Who is it who hates us so much, Michael?' she whispered at last.

'Nobody hates us,' he said.

'Someone does,' she said, beginning to show signs of her old spirit.

'Try to have a drink,' he urged her, unsure of what to say next without upsetting her.

'It must be someone we know,' she said, putting the coffee mug to her lips, then opening them wide like an obedient child being fed by its mother. 'Or someone who knows us, anyway,' she added, conscious thought beginning to return, too. 'It stands to reason.'

'Surely not,' he said. Whatever Malcolm and Christine Forres had done to them, he was pretty sure it hadn't been from personal animus. Greed, perhaps, but not personal hatred. Wakefield wasn't a man insensitive to the feelings of others and he would surely have known – well, suspected at the very least, anyway – if that had been the case. You can't work alongside a man daily for week after week, year after year, as he had done, without being aware of that.

Malcolm's wife was a different matter: Christine Forres was no chatterer; in fact, she was consistently rather reserved although never ever in the least unfriendly. Malcolm had met her years ago when he had been on holiday somewhere in the north of England – much more than that, Wakefield didn't really know about her. He had an idea that she'd once worked with children although she never spoke about it and she and Malcolm were childless. They never spoke about that either and he and Stephanie had in consequence tended to moderate their references to their own two children.

'Yes,' Stephanie said flatly, all intonation missing from her speech. 'It must be someone we know.' She took a sip of coffee but set the mug down on the table almost immediately and started to look round the kitchen in wonderment as if she'd never seen it before. Then she suddenly began to pluck at her clothes and tug at her hair.

Her husband, alarmed now, nearly reached out to stop her. His hand was stayed by a memory of having seen such behaviour once before somewhere. He searched in his mind for where it could have been –

that is, witnessing a woman in a distress too severe to manage. It couldn't have been in real life, or he surely would have remembered it more clearly. But he'd witnessed the scenario before somewhere, he was sure about that. It might have been in a film or a play, he thought now, searching his memory until it came to him. In a play, that was where it had been.

It had been on stage, he decided after a moment's thought. In happier days – could they have been as recent as they were, those days before their descent into chaos? – both he and Steph had often gone on trips to the theatre at Stratford-upon-Avon with the Berebury Theatre Society.

Lady Macbeth came first to his mind, endlessly trying to wash the guilt from her hands. He metaphorically shook his head. It hadn't been Lady Macbeth. Unlike Lady Macbeth, his Stephanie hadn't done anything to feel guilty about – nothing to wring her hands about over and over again – he was sure about that.

'That makes it all much worse,' Stephanie insisted, her face still an immobile mask.

'What does?' He stared at her, his mind still dwelling back to Stratford. As far as he was concerned, nothing could make anything worse than it was at present – losing everything they owned and now, it would seem, his poor wife losing her sanity, too.

'Knowing that someone we know hates us so much.'

He couldn't find an answer to that.

Rousing out of her torpor at last, she said, 'And then

telling the newspaper so soon about our being made bankrupt. It couldn't possibly be as quick as that.'

It had been at Stratford, he remembered now, where he had first seen a woman so very distressed. Granted, the occasion had only been in a performance on stage but it had been no less memorable for that. Not Lady Macbeth, then, but still Shakespeare. Then it came back to him in a rush. It had been the behaviour of Ophelia in *Hamlet*. That was where he'd seen a woman with a mind completely changed by stress just like poor Stephanie's now.

'They didn't need to know yet,' she said painfully.

'No,' he agreed.

She went on plucking at the edges of her dressing-gown and then wailed, 'We should have had time to hide.'

'So we should,' he said pacifically.

But he didn't mean it.

All he himself could think was that someone was gunning for them.

Or Forres and Wakefield, master printers of Berebury.

What he couldn't think for the life of him was who it could be.

And more importantly, why?

That was the moment when his thoughts were disturbed by a ring on the front door of the Old Rectory.

CHAPTER TWENTY

Police instruction manuals always advised that the interviewing of witnesses should be conducted as soon as possible after the event seen by them and preferably alone, alone that is save for another member of the force, taking notes. That it was also preferably not in the presence of a member of the legal profession was not spelt out – only implied, although the manual reminded the reader sternly this could not always be counted on.

Sitting now, his notebook well to the fore, in the crowded kitchen of Ornum House at one end of the long wooden table next to a young woman did not, in the opinion of Detective Inspector Sloan, constitute ideal surroundings for the taking of a witness statement.

Nor was she anything like alone. Close by on Lady Victoria's other side was her twin sister, Lady Mary, and hovering protectively not far away were both their parents. Reminding himself firmly that this witness could in no way be described as an unaccompanied minor within the meaning of the regulations, not even by the most defensive of defence counsel, he turned over a new page in his notebook and tried to begin the interview.

This was when another stumbling block loomed: one not envisaged in any of the police instruction manuals. This was the fact that – detective inspector or not – he didn't by any manner of means have the full attention of his witness.

'Roderick?' She looked round anxiously, her words tumbling out in a rush. 'Where is Roderick, Daddy? Haven't you found him yet? He's all right, isn't he?'

Her father nodded. 'Don't worry, Vicky. He's quite all right. It's another boy we just can't seem to find anywhere just at the moment and it's rather important.'

'That's Sheep's Eyes,' Lady Mary informed everyone. 'Isn't it?'

'Then where is Roderick?' Victoria demanded breathlessly, ignoring any mention of the missing Sheep's Eyes. 'Tell me, Daddy! Why isn't he down here with all the others over there?' She turned great saucer-like eyes on her father and pointed to the opposite end of the great kitchen table, scrubbed white for generations, where a cohort of distinctly hungover youngsters was clustered. They were drinking coffee and sharing gruesome rumours about the dead man upstairs. She started to cry. 'I can't see Roderick there and I must talk to him. I must, Daddy, I really must.'

'He's all right, Vicky.'

'Really and truly all right?'

'It's only that he wouldn't come down from his room,' explained her father. 'He just turned over in bed and said he was going to go back to sleep again. And to tell you that it had been the bestest party ever and he didn't want it to end.'

'Did Roderick really say that?' Victoria, her tears beginning to dry up, sat up straight and brightened immediately.

'He said he didn't want it to end ever,' embellished her father with the best of intentions. He turned to Sloan. 'But I'm afraid we can't find the other lad anywhere, Inspector.'

'That's Jason Fixby,' Letitia Ornum called out. The countess had gone back to the giant cooking range on the other side of the kitchen. It was still giving off a tantalising smell of fried bacon, even though another woman in an apron working beside her was starting to prepare lunch on it. 'That's who the one they call Sheep's Eyes is, Inspector,' she went on. 'He was meant to be going home last night.' She turned to her assistant and said, 'You carry on here, Mrs Bennett, whilst I go and show the inspector which room he might have just been in. There were a couple spare.'

'He could have been,' said Lady Mary, 'but he isn't in either there now.'

'How do you know?' demanded the Countess of

Ornum, turning her attention away from Sloan to her daughter.

'He isn't there now, Mummy, because we've looked in those rooms,' said her daughter Mary. 'I went to see myself instead of Victoria in case he was there and grabbed her.'

'Not so likely as all that, Vicky. I should say if he's like all the other lads here last night that he would have been too hungover the morning after to do any such thing,' murmured the earl, still able to remember his own youth.

'Even so, Daddy, you know how Sheep's Eyes feels about Vicky,' persisted her twin. 'He's head over heels in love with her.'

'Whoever he is,' said Jonas Cremond, his literary venture long out of mind, 'I can tell you, Inspector, that he's not in any of the other upper rooms because we've checked them all too. That's right, Toby, isn't it?'

A beefy boy standing among those hungover ones sinking their coffees said, 'Yes, Your Lordship. We've looked in all of them . . . well, all of them but one, if you know what I mean.'

The Earl of Ornum turned to Sloan and said apologetically, 'I'm afraid there are a great many other places in the house where someone might be.'

As far as Sloan was concerned, this was a considerable understatement. Ornum House was enormous. It would take a lot of searching and as of this moment there were no spare men on the strength of 'F' Division available to do it. They all had even more pressing things at

Kinnisport than murder on their plate this morning.

'My grandfather sealed off the dungeons long ago but that still leaves plenty of other places for anyone else to be in. He hadn't got up and gone home,' added the earl, 'because I've checked with his father that he's not there either.'

The policeman offered up silent thanks for a former serviceman, and one who could still think straight at a difficult time.

'I'm sorry, my lord, but nevertheless I really must have a word with Lady Victoria.' The inspector had left Crosby to await the arrival of the scenes of crime team and had come down to the kitchen in search of her. 'I'm afraid we're not dealing with a death from natural causes.'

'Thought not,' said the Earl of Ornum, a man who had been in action himself once upon a time.

'You're not dealing with Sheep's Eyes, either,' said Victoria's twin sister, Mary, sitting on her other side. 'Vicky said he wouldn't have killed anyone.'

'And that man in the bed definitely isn't him,' asserted Victoria, manifestly upset but quite sure. 'I don't know who he is, either, not with a ghastly swollen spotted face like that. He looked horrible.'

'What I need to know, all of you, is where he who you call Sheep's Eyes is now,' said Sloan. 'It's very important.'

'I don't know where he is but he's really nice,' said Mary, proceeding to damn the absent young man with faint praise. 'In his own way, that is.'

'Naughty but nice,' chimed in a now more cheerful Victoria.

Detective Inspector Sloan, who hadn't wanted a character assessment just at this moment, suddenly stopped his proposed interrogation. Instead, he changed course as another idea came to him. 'Before I talk to you, Lady Victoria, I'm afraid I must make an urgent phone call.'

'The flower room is best for a good signal,' sang out the Countess of Ornum, someone else who could think straight. 'Show him where it is, Jonas.'

The number that Sloan dialled was that of Kate Booth of the firm of Fixby and Fixby. He hoped her Sunday mornings weren't spent out of telephone contact.

'Good morning, Inspector,' she answered him at once. 'You've caught me just in time. I'm standing at the top of Gaskell Ghyll all kitted up and ready to go.'

'Go where?' he asked stupidly. He thought he could hear the bleating of a sheep in the background.

'Go down the cave here.'

'Sorry.' He'd quite forgotten that the accountant's hobby – no, not hobby, passion probably – was caving. Caving couldn't be like climbing, then, when you reckoned to reach your destination by noon. 'Listen, can you tell me what car Jason Fixby drives?'

'Sure. It's a small Audi.'

He held his breath. 'And do you happen by any chance to know the number?'

He heard a gurgling laugh at the other end of the

telephone. 'Of course I do, Inspector. I'm an accountant, remember? I think in numbers.'

Detective Inspector Sloan didn't know what line of business it was that he thought in – not numbers, certainly, mug shots probably. Putting aside this interesting thought for further consideration at a more suitable moment, he got back to current detective work. Standing surrounded by all the paraphernalia of flower arranging, he made a hasty note, thanked her and went back to the kitchen.

CHAPTER TWENTY-ONE

Detective Inspector Sloan, ever the realist, had temporarily abandoned his attempt to get any further with his questioning of the Lady Victoria Cremond about her finding of the body.

That would have to wait now.

Finding Jason Fixby couldn't – mustn't on any account – wait. Nor could finding out who it was who had killed the man in the second-floor bedroom. Nor could establishing the identity of that same dead man wait either. That last ranked high, too, in his mental triage of police priorities.

So instead of carrying on trying to interview Lady Victoria, Sloan singled out the beefy lad called Toby from amongst the covey of youngsters still sobering up in the kitchen. He had chosen the one who had earlier shown some signs of leadership and said to him, 'Go out to the car park here and take this number with you, you and your mates, will you, and bring me back a list of the registration numbers of all the other vehicles still out there, pronto.' He handed him over a slip of paper and said, 'Including this one of Jason Fixby's. That's if it's still there.'

He devoutly hoped that it wasn't, that Jason Fixby had woken early and gone for a spin in the Calleshire countryside to clear his head before going back home after what had sounded to him like a very good party.

After that, all he could do was the most difficult thing of all and wait.

He didn't have to do it for very long. The boy Toby soon came back with a list of car numbers. 'There're eight cars still out there, sir. That's including a small Audi with the number you gave me that Pete here says belongs to a chap called Fixby because he knows him.'

'I was afraid it might,' said Sloan.

'He's still here, then,' concluded Toby.

'You couldn't walk anywhere from here,' agreed a youth called Pete, one who from childhood onwards had in all his life never been without having vehicular transport available. 'We're absolutely in the middle of nowhere out here.'

'So he's around somewhere,' chimed in Toby, who could obviously think too. 'Must be.'

'That's Sheep's Eyes' car,' sang out Lady Victoria from the other end of the great table.

'Trust Vicky to know that,' murmured her sister.

'Don't be beastly,' said Vicky.

'Now, girls . . .' began their mother.

'What about these numbers, then?' asked Sloan, calling out the other ones in turn.

One after another, all the car registration numbers were identified as owned by guests at the party who had stayed the night at Ornum House and were staying on to luncheon.

All, that is, save one.

Sloan crossed his fingers and devoutly hoped that learning its ownership would lead him to the name of the body in the bed. 'Jason's car is still here, then,' he agreed, pointing to a registration number, although he was even more worried about him now, *pour cause*. 'But what I need to know about now, sharpish, is this other one. The car that you don't know who it belongs to.'

'Whose car is still here, too,' pointed out Toby, quickly catching on.

'Exactly,' said Sloan, deciding that the boy would do well in the force. He would keep in touch with him when this case was over and done with and talk about police cadets.

'Here somewhere, that is,' said Toby. 'He must be.'

'But first of all we need to find someone called Jason Fixby, wherever he is in the building.' If the owner of the unknown car was the dead man in the bed, there was no hurry about identifying it. Dead men couldn't drive their cars away.

Toby offered to lead a search party. Cremond, who had been sitting quietly at the table near his daughters, got to his feet and said, 'It won't be easy here, Inspector. I'll come with you and show you round the house.'

'We're coming, too,' sang out the twins in unison.

'No, you aren't,' said their father. But the wishes of Jonas Cremond, who in his day had had half a regiment obedient to his every command, held no sway over his two daughters. They were on their feet in seconds.

Sloan sighed. The joining of a search party by a material witness wasn't something that was mentioned in the rule book on interviews either and wouldn't have been condoned if it had been, thought Sloan to himself, as Lady Victoria disappeared along with the others.

There was more than one member of the Calleshire Force who had been severely reprimanded for making unauthorised use of the Police National Computer. This number was usually illegally sought by friends of someone in the force in order quite improperly to come to their aid after having a set-to in their car and wanting to know the name and address of the other driver in an accident that had not been officially reported to the police.

Or even worse, the name and address of the other party's insurance company or, much worse still, the owner of a car parked too often outside the home of a jealous husband.

Detective Inspector Sloan had never been one of

those who agreed to do this for either friendship or reward and always gave the same reply to anyone who approached him in this way: 'Sorry, chum, but it's just not worth my pension.' Since his pension was something that ranked only second after their mortgage, he was never asked twice.

Today, he just fished out the number of the unidentified car and without a qualm rang and asked the man on duty at the police station to punch it into the Police National Computer. The answer came back in minutes, but it wasn't the one he had been hoping for. That had been the name and address of the dead man in the bed.

The registration number, announced Sloan to them all, related to a small, elderly Ford Ka.

'An old push-rod manual,' said one of the boys, who enjoyed the nickname of Wheels.

'Only a 1.4,' said another lad scornfully.

'The owner's name is Mrs Winifred Bennett of 2, Orchard Cottages, Church Lane, in Ornum village,' read out Sloan.

'That's me,' called out the middle-aged woman in an apron who was standing over the kitchen range at the other end of the room, helping the Countess of Ornum prepare the luncheon. 'And that's my car.' She turned towards Sloan, a large ladle in her hand. 'If that's the police asking, you can tell them that I'm having that broken rear light fixed on Monday.'

CHAPTER TWENTY-TWO

In the event, the superintendent's round of golf hadn't taken anything like long enough for the detective.

'That you, Sloan?' demanded a voice down the inspector's mobile phone.

'Yes, sir,' he had answered him, almost, but not quite, automatically coming to a halt, and standing to attention in the grand entrance hall of Ornum House as soon as he recognised his superior officer's voice. He had been on his way back from the kitchen to the bedroom on the second floor to check if the people from scenes of crime had arrived.

'Well?' barked Superintendent Leeyes.

'It was murder all right, sir. Young male from the looks of him. Dr Dabbe's not long been gone and that's what he said.'

The superintendent grunted. He automatically

rejected the opinion of any professional in the first instance.

'But I'm afraid there's not a lot to report otherwise at this early stage,' said Sloan, falling back on police speak and taking a policy decision not to mention the missing Jason Fixby just at this moment.

'By the way, Sloan, the ACC texted me this morning to say that he was at that launch party at Ornum House last night.'

'Really, sir?' Sloan had long ago abandoned the idea of getting any reliable guest list of those at the party. There might well have been a proper one in the capable hands of that experienced hostess, Letitia, Countess of Ornum, but the tendency of her daughters to invite any young men who took their fancy negated its value to a working policeman.

'Yes, and he asked if we needed any help with our investigation.'

Helpful intentions he might have, but the assistant chief constable of the Calleshire County Constabulary wasn't, in Sloan's opinion, your ordinary policeman and thus not likely to be of any help in a routine homicide investigation. He had been a classical scholar somewhere or other and this was inclined to show. Murder in ancient Greece wasn't a lot of help in today's world.

'He was at school with the earl,' amplified Leeyes.

Detective Inspector Sloan wasn't in the least bit surprised to hear it. 'I'll bear that in mind, sir,' he said, mentally crossing his fingers behind his back. 'Very kind of him, I'm sure.' He quickly seized on a sure-fire diversionary tactic and asked the superintendent if he had had a good game that morning.

'Very, Sloan, thank you. I had a birdie at the second but then I went and got into the rough at the fourth.'

'Bad luck,' murmured Sloan. Not as bad luck as the bloke dead in the bed had had. Whether young Jason Fixby had been as unlucky, as well, it was much too soon to say.

Leeyes wasn't listening. 'Lost my ball there and had to play a provisional.'

'Tough,' said Sloan, hoping it was the right response.

'But I had a nice shot after that and then got really near the pin on the eleventh.'

'That's good,' said Sloan. That was something easier to understand. Getting near the pin if not actually in the hole yet seemed to be one of the objects of the exercise. That exercise was the object of the game he did understand.

'It's a tricky little hole – uphill work, you might say – and I don't always do as well on it. It's basin-shaped and the ball's inclined to drift downwards away from the pin if you're not lucky.'

'Sounds as if you had had a good round, sir, all the same,' said Sloan. 'Uphill work' described his own problems here very well, too, and the top of the metaphorical detection hill at Ornum House wasn't even in sight. He presumed that the green at the eleventh, wherever that might be, was in clearer view.

This genuine plaudit didn't stem the superintendent's flow. Still sounding quite ebullient, the Sunday morning golfer carried on. 'I even managed quite well at the twelfth, all things considered.'

What Detective Inspector Sloan, head of the tiny Criminal Investigation Department of 'F' Division, wanted to do more than anything else now was to get down to considering all things at Ornum. Finding Jason Fixby ranked high among them.

'The twelfth is the devil of a hole, Sloan. You need a good long carry to get onto the fairway there from the men's tee.'

'I'm sure,' said Sloan mendaciously. He hadn't the faintest idea what the man was talking about.

'But I managed to get a bogey there after all.'

'Well done, sir,' he said since appreciation seemed to be called for.

'Then I had a really straight drive at the thirteenth and cleared the stream and the rough with it.'

Sloan could understand this. 'That's good, sir,' he said. He didn't know the game at all well, but he thought he knew now what to say about it.

'Moreover, my ball didn't end up in the rough, which is good going at that hole.'

'It certainly sounds like it, sir,' he said, although he didn't suppose that the superintendent would be listening.

'And then I had another birdie on the fourteenth.

That meant that we had won our match, of course.'

'I'm pleased to hear it, sir,' said Sloan warmly, pleased himself too that the recital was coming to an end.

'It wasn't quite over, Sloan. Not then.'

'Really, sir? How come?' It was quite over for the body in the bed, bar the shouting, that is. Whether it was all over for Jason Fixby was not yet clear. Sloan mentally borrowed a metaphor from the game of golf. The young Fixby was not out of the rough yet.

Not until he was found and perhaps not even then.

'You know that man who owns the brewery down by the river, don't you, name of Wilkins?'

'Yes, sir.' Detective Inspector Sloan was not the only one to know Wilkins and his beer. Most of the neighbourhood drunks did, too.

'Well, poor Wilkins had a hole-in-one on the seventeenth.' Superintendent Leeyes positively chortled. 'He had to buy us all a drink when he came in and the clubhouse was absolutely packed, it being a Sunday morning.'

'What you might call a mixed blessing, then, sir, winning.'

'Exactly. The fellow very nearly had a sense of humour failure.'

'I can understand he might,' agreed Sloan. Sudden calls on the Sloan finances never went down very well either, especially towards the end of the month.

'He was playing in a four-ball so he couldn't even

shut them all up and get out of paying up that way,' said the superintendent, automatically putting a police spin on this as he always did with everything else.

'Witnesses can be very helpful,' said Sloan prosaically before resuming his way up to the second floor. He could well have done with one in Ornum House last night but there was no use saying so to the superintendent.

CHAPTER TWENTY-THREE

Detective Inspector Sloan had left the countess and her assistant preparing food for their family and guests' luncheons, just as he supposed all other chatelaines at Ornum House had gone on doing throughout history, come what may.

The earls of Ornum would have provided for Yorkists (or Lancastrians, as the case might have been), Royalists (or Cavaliers – but he thought Royalists), billeted troops, evacuees, passing companies of prisoners from several different wars, air raid wardens, firewatchers, the Home Guard, a handful of special auxiliary units and would have also catered for generation after generation of harvest suppers and parish teas, to say nothing of visiting cricket teams. A murder there would be something that he was confident that they would take in their stride at Ornum House, which, he added to himself, in the circumstances was just as well.

Like the countess, he also had work to do.

He made his way slowly and thoughtfully up to a second-floor bedroom. He found it more crowded than he liked.

'Scenes of crime are here now, sir,' explained Crosby unnecessarily.

One of the men there clothed in white nodded to Sloan. 'We won't be long now, Inspector,' he said, 'and then Ted York can take the deceased over to the mortuary. That's if he's not over at Kinnisport, too, like all the other uniform.'

'Any fingerprints?' asked Sloan not very hopefully but keeping to the matter in hand.

The SOCO shook his head. ''Fraid not. We've been over everything here without finding anything very much in the way of evidence at all.' He qualified this by saying, 'Not at first sight, anyway.'

As far as Detective Inspector Sloan was concerned, second sight would have been considerably more helpful at this stage. A little bit of precognition would have come in very handy.

The scenes of crime specialist pointed to the carpet and carried on. 'We did find a few signs on the back of his heels of his having been scuffed along the carpet, though.'

'So not killed in here, then,' concluded Detective Constable Crosby, anxious to be helpful.

'Not necessarily. More likely just dragged into the

room on his heels from somewhere nearby,' said the scenes of crime man more precisely.

'Walking wounded, then,' muttered Crosby, who had heard the phrase somewhere but not known that it came from an army after combat.

'I'll only be able to tell you that for certain, of course, when we've managed to have a proper look at the backs of his shoes,' countered the SOCO.

Sloan was glad he himself had remembered to come into the room carefully, keeping to the edges of it and well inside the yellow and black evidence tape on the floor that Crosby had laid down, which outlined the common entrance to be used by all who entered the murder scene. Spare-time gardener that he was, Sloan was always reminded by the tape that the combination of yellow and black spelt danger in the natural world, too.

'We'll be having his shoes off in a minute anyway,' the SOCO said. 'We need samples of the fibres from his clothing as well as from the sheets and the rest of the bedding. Got to bag it up nice and tidy for forensics.' He jerked his head in the direction of the body in the bed. 'Does he have a name?'

'Not yet,' said Sloan temperately. 'A. N. Other will have to do for the time being.'

'Not a pretty sight, is he, Inspector?' said another of the men there.

'I reckon his own mother wouldn't know him now,' opined the SOCO.

Sloan nodded his head in agreement with this and said, 'In my experience, murder is never a pretty sight.' Until the middle of the nineteenth century, homicide used to be called an offence against the Queen's peace and he could quite see why. Looking across at the engorged and bespotted face of the man in the bed now, he thought murder was an offence against humanity, too.

The SOCO motioned to one of his assistants and together they lifted the counterpane off the bed, looked it over and then placed it carefully in a large evidence bag, which they proceeded to label. 'Same again with the sheets,' he commanded.

There were two of these, top and bottom.

'That's funny,' said Crosby, peering over their shoulders at the top sheet. 'Look at that corner. There's something stitched on the sheet there.'

'A laundry mark?' suggested one of the scenes of crime men hopefully. 'From before they had washing machines, do you think?'

Detective Inspector Sloan took a long look at the sheet for himself. 'Looks to me more like the Ornum family crest.'

Crosby brightened. 'Better than what they call personalised, then.'

'Better even than top-of-the-shop,' chimed in one of the SOCOs, whose wife couldn't be trusted with a credit card.

'Can we get on?' said Sloan.

'Now for the blankets,' said the man quickly. 'And the shoes.'

It wasn't long before they had the pyjamas off the corpse, too, which exposed the outdoor clothing that the man had been wearing under them. 'Strange ways they have in posh places like this, isn't it, Inspector? That party that they said had been held here last night must have been a right carry-on. Fancy dress, was it?'

'Only up to a point,' said Sloan. 'You might call this man as being in disguise rather than fancy dress.'

'Same difference,' said Detective Constable Crosby. 'Anyway, sir, why should he be wearing disguise here?'

'To better facilitate a burglary,' said Sloan. 'What would you think if you saw a man wandering around in a place like this in the middle of the night in his pyjamas?'

The scenes of crime man gave a leer. 'I know what I would think, Inspector. Naughty, naughty.'

'Especially in a place like this,' said another of the men, whose ideas of how the other half lived were taken entirely from the popular press. 'Orgies, that's what they have in these big houses.'

'What I'm afraid that they have in houses like this,' said Detective Inspector Sloan, a very experienced policeman, 'are burglaries. Now, carry on.'

The pyjamas, having been duly bagged and labelled, the men turned their attention to the outdoor clothing. That, too, was equally carefully dealt with, exposing the scruffy wear favoured by all young men, rich or poor, everywhere in accordance with current fashion.

'Not up to much, is it, sir?' Crosby sniffed disparagingly.

'Burglars aren't usually rich,' said Sloan. This nugget of wisdom was something else he had gleaned in the course of his career and had heard often enough in mitigation – as if that was any excuse for frightening old ladies out of their wits and stealing their money. 'Not the young ones, anyway.'

'It's coming off in any case,' said the scenes of crime man in a businesslike way. He and his assistant proceeded to remove the rest of the deceased's clothing, exposing the top of his torso first. They paused as it was stripped bare.

'Strewth,' exclaimed Detective Constable Crosby as soon as he saw what had been revealed. 'A full sleeve tribal tattoo,' he pronounced, pointing to the man's arm.

'Forres and Wakefield's apprentice,' said Detective Inspector Sloan. He turned to the SOCO. 'My apologies, I was wrong earlier. We do have a name for the deceased.'

'Lenny Datchet as ever was,' breathed Crosby.

CHAPTER TWENTY-FOUR

There had been no question of the young man called Toby taking charge of the search of Ornum House for the missing Jason Fixby. It was Jonas Cremond himself, sometime soldier, who took over and organised the posse of searchers to fan out through the ancient building looking for he whom his daughters called Sheep's Eyes.

'Victoria, you can do the attics,' he said. 'You know your way round up there.'

That young lady's immediate response was to survey the eager little crowd on the other side of the kitchen, pick on the first likely-looking lad that took her fancy and peel off upstairs with him in tow.

'And Mary, you can take a couple of these boys with you and see what you can find in the cellars.'

'Guy Fawkes and gunpowder, most probably,' said

one of the pair she had selected. 'To say nothing of treason and plot.'

'Certainly not,' said Cremond stiffly. 'Our family's total commitment to the regime in power at the material time has never been questioned.' He was tempted to give the young man his usual lecture on why the family had prospered for so long – by putting policy before principle, as someone had once remarked unkindly – but this was not the moment for his talk on the subject or to remind them of Aesop's fable of the oak and the reed, otherwise known as bending before the storm. 'Off you go,' he said instead. 'Quickly, now.'

'Yes, Daddy,' said Lady Mary with a meekness that would have deceived nobody who knew her.

Having thus carefully dispatched his two young daughters to places where they were least likely to find the missing man, the earl deployed the others there who had been waiting on his word according to practices engrained in him in his military training years before. At the same time, he kept the lad Toby by his side. The long-ago lecture on what to do if the colonel was killed had always gone down well with young subalterns, and Cremond had never forgotten it. 'Four of you to each landing, please. Mind you open all wardrobes, look under the beds and behind the doors. Don't forget either to draw back the curtains in each room.'

He then turned to Toby. 'You come with me whilst we check the ground floor. We'll start with the dining room.'

But that elegant room had been swept clean and order completely restored by the caterers before they had left soon after the party had been declared well and truly over the night before. What they had been truly grateful for, though, was that the next day being a Sunday, there was no hunt breakfast to then prepare for the following morning.

'Nothing here, sir,' said Toby after a quick glance under the dining table.

The drawing room was in a less tidy condition, the carpet having been taken up at some late stage of the evening for dancing. 'Rolled-up carpets can conceal bodies,' observed the earl in a hortative manner, another lesson well learnt.

His assistant obediently peered in it from both ends. 'Nothing in there, sir, either.'

'We'll try the library next. People don't go in there much as a rule, but it was where my book was on show last night if anyone had happened to want to take a look at it.' His great literary endeavour had momentarily slipped the Earl of Ornum's mind. 'Not everybody did, I'm afraid.'

Toby put his head round the library door and scanned the long, narrow, book-lined room. 'Can't see anyone in here either, sir,' he said.

'Go in and have a better look,' said the earl, coming up right behind him. 'If a job's worth doing, it's worth doing well.' If you didn't do it well when you were in the army, the consequences could be dire.

The young man obediently advanced further into the room, turned to his right and then came to a sudden halt. He pointed with a shaking finger at a winged library chair with its high back facing the open door and gave a breathless gasp. 'Here, sir. Look over here. He's in this chair there, sir.'

The figure that they came upon in the library was not behind a door, nor under a bed, nor in a wardrobe – not even behind a curtain – but was simply slumped sideways in a high wing chair. The chair was beside the fireplace, facing towards the inside of the room, and someone sitting in it would have been to all intents and purposes invisible to anyone standing in the doorway behind it. They – whoever they were – would only be seen when someone came right inside the room and turned and looked back as Cremond's assistant had done.

The figure in the chair was that of a young man, his head wedged against the back of the chair at an angle that didn't bode at all well for the health of its owner.

Jonas Cremond bent over him, noted that some blood was still oozing out over the chintz upholstery and then felt his skin. It was warm. 'He's still alive,' he said, trying to find a pulse. 'Get an ambulance, boy,' he ordered, adding, 'And tell them to get a move on.'

CHAPTER TWENTY-FIVE

'Say that again, Sloan,' barked Superintendent Leeyes down the telephone.

'We've identified the murder victim at Ornum, sir,' repeated Sloan. 'He's an employee of Forres and Wakefield, the printers – an apprentice there, actually.'

'Is he anything to do with the missing cash over there?' the superintendent wanted to know at once. Following the money was a long-standing mantra of the superintendent's in his approach to all crime.

'Too soon to say, sir,' said Sloan. 'All I know is that Malcolm Forres couldn't have done it because the first thing we did was put a watch on all incoming flights and ferries just in case he or his wife came back.'

Lenny Datchet might have been the victim of murder, but he had obviously intended to have victims on his own account at Ornum House. Wearing pyjamas over your clothes in a country house party whilst you robbed it was as good a disguise as any burglar could ask for. Sloan decided that this conclusion could wait for later. There was other, more important news for his superior officer to be given first. 'And the missing young man has been found,' he said.

'Jason Fixby?'

'Injured but alive still,' said Sloan pithily.

'How injured?'

'We can't get anything definite out the doctors yet, sir, especially as he seems to have lost quite a lot of blood.' Jonas Cremond had described Jason Fixby as being 'boltered in blood', which seemed to him as graphic as words came. He added, 'You know what hospitals are like, sir. They won't say.'

'Too tight-lipped by half,' agreed Leeyes, never given to disclosing anything himself if he could possibly get away with it.

'They told us that they were only doctors, not Old Testament prophets, but they reckoned his chances were only as good as fifty-fifty.' Whether Jason Fixby, an admitted racing aficionado, would have been cheered or depressed by knowing that his chances were only rated as evens, Sloan didn't know. And as Jason Fixby was still unconscious, he wasn't in a position to know either.

'Bookies at heart, those doctors, only speaking in odds,' concluded Leeyes. 'Just like everyone else.' He sniffed. 'Only they will call them percentages.'

'They did say, though, that the patient had been hit very hard on the occiput,' he offered. Sloan thought that Jason Fixby would have been the first to agree that his injuries would have increased the ante.

'And pray tell me, Sloan, where on earth in the human body is the occiput.'

'The back of the head,' said Sloan, omitting to mention that he'd had to look this up himself.

'Showing off, that's what the doctors are doing,' said Leeyes, not above doing it himself sometimes.

'Yes, sir.'

'Thus demonstrating their superiority over all other mortals,' declared Leeyes, not revealing either that he was actually putty in the hands of his own doctor and didn't much relish having injections.

'Staying on top, sir,' agreed Sloan. 'That's what that's all about.'

The superintendent audibly relaxed and became reminiscent. 'Did I ever tell you, Sloan, my theory about the importance of staying on top, which, incidentally, is what doctors always do?'

'I don't think you did, sir,' he responded cautiously. Whatever it was, it had probably as usual been the outcome of the most recent evening course of lectures Superintendent Leeyes had attended. That, Sloan knew from canteen gossip, had been about *On the Origin of Species*. The superintendent had been asked to leave after insisting that the course should have been called Sons of Satan instead.

'I think that all the peoples on earth are just organisms – different ones, naturally – in a great big Petri dish, all fighting to stay on top of each other.'

'Really, sir?' The betting in the canteen had been that either the superintendent or the lecturer wouldn't stay the course for long. One or the other of them would throw in the towel.

'And it's when you have different colonies of organisms in the same Petri dish, by which I mean the world, of course, that you have trouble.'

'Of course,' agreed Sloan weakly.

'And it explains wars.'

'I afraid you've lost me there, sir.' What Detective Inspector Sloan, head of the Criminal Investigation Department of the Berebury Police Force, was losing as well was time. If ever there was a minute when he should have been able to get on with finding out who it was who had killed Lenny Datchet and who had tried to kill Jason Fixby, it was very much in the here and now.

And not in any Petri dish.

Leeyes said, 'When you have two competing organisms in the same Petri dish, one of them always attacks the other. It's human nature. We all know that.'

Sloan didn't, for one. But now he came to think about it, his superior officer's well-known xenophobia might have been explained by it.

'That fellow Clausewitz got it all wrong about the causes of war,' insisted the superintendent.

Detective Inspector Sloan couldn't place the name. The name he himself wanted very badly was that of the killer of Lenny Datchet and he wanted it soon. And for a bonus, the name of whoever it was who had knocked Jason Fixby into deep unconsciousness. Finding what it was that Jason had been hit with was yet something else on his to-do list. He hoped that the trouble over at Kinnisport would be resolved soon enough for him to have some support.

He needed it.

Leeyes hadn't stopped talking. 'All you have to do, Sloan, if you don't believe me, is to put your Petri dish under a microscope and you can see for yourself them going at it hammer and tongs. Bacteria versus antibiotic sometimes, too.'

'I believe you, sir,' he said hastily.

'I say that it's human nature to attack all strangers,' declared Leeyes, although he never allowed this defence to be put forward when this happened on his own patch. 'Put two differing microbes in the same dish and one will come out top. Like rats in a sack. Bound to. That's why doctors take specimens to see which wins before they prescribe treatment.'

Sloan wanted to say something about it not being human nature surely if we were all microbes in the same Petri dish – whatever that was – but thought better of it. He did say that he wasn't quite so sure it explained wars.

'Wars are a way of cutting down the population of

spare young men,' declared Leeyes didactically. 'Bees do it better, of course.'

'Bees?' echoed Sloan in spite of himself.

'They kill off the drones when they are finished with them.'

Since there was no answer to this, he said instead that whilst he was keeping in close touch with the hospital, he really needed to get back to Michael Wakefield because whatever had been going on at Ornum, it must in some way have to do with his printing firm since it was their Lenny Datchet who had been killed.

'And, sir, we also need to start looking pretty quickly for where all the firm's money that was taken from it has gone. I understand that there was rather a lot of it.' Sloan sighed and hoped it was too big a sum to hide easily but you never knew in these days of the easy money laundering of eye-watering sums. Drugs money was big, too . . . And that had to be done by the police, as well as searching for whoever had killed Lenny Datchet and hit Jason Fixby; it was going to take some time.

And all the help he had at this moment was in the shape of Detective Constable Crosby, young, inexperienced and cack-handed. He'd left him with the body in the bedroom awaiting the arrival of PC Ted York, the coroner's officer, and the black police ambulance that didn't have any windows or markings to arouse the curiosity of those who saw it on the road.

Mention of stolen money always caught the

superintendent's wayward attention. 'That partner of his who absconded must be involved in this some way or another, too, Sloan.'

'Part and parcel of the murder, I shouldn't wonder, sir. Perhaps the attack on the Fixby boy is too, but for the life of me I don't know how or why.'

'Then find out, man. Soonest,' said Leeyes, ringing off.

Free at last, like the Berebury hunt, to cut to the chase, Sloan duly went once again in search of his first witness, Lady Victoria Cremond.

CHAPTER TWENTY-SIX

It had been a very long time indeed since Michael Wakefield had been startled by anything as commonplace as the ringing of a front doorbell but even so he had given an involuntary jump when it did ring in the middle of that Sunday morning. It happened whilst he was contemplating without enthusiasm the stir-fry meal that he had been in the process of assembling. This was at the same time as trying to coax his wife into making more normal responses. At one point he felt so low that just to save his sanity he had been drawn back to an auction catalogue that he had sent for in what he now considered to be his former life.

In it was a description of one of the lots that he had once upon a time wanted so much to buy. A working 1820 Columbian printing press had come on the market and Wakefield had already worked out where he could show it off to best advantage in the entrance lobby of the printing works of Forres and Wakefield.

That, though, had been then.

This was now.

He was snapped out of this dream world by the doorbell ringing once again. For longer and more peremptorily this time. He lumbered through from the kitchen to the front door to answer it. Standing on the doorstep was the Rector of St Peter's Church at Little Missal, the Reverend Jeremy Bostles.

'I had already been planning to look in on you both on my way back from taking the service this morning,' began the clergyman, 'to see how you and Steph were getting along anyway and then . . . '

'We're just about managing all right, thank you,' Mike interrupted him swiftly before the man had finished, not being in the mood this morning for talking let alone for being at the receiving end of sympathy, however kindly meant.

'And then,' repeated the Rector, undeterred by the import of this, 'I noticed your car.'

'My car?' Wakefield looked at him blankly. 'Oh, yes, I didn't put it away in the garage last night, did I? To be quite truthful, Jeremy, I was a bit too tired. It had been a bad day, what with Steph breaking down like she has and everything.'

'I know,' said the Rector. 'Well, if you haven't seen it before then I suggest that you'd better come and take a look at it now.'

Michael Wakefield stepped outside his front door and walked towards his car. 'Good God!' he gasped. 'All four tyres slashed to absolute ribbons.' He edged his way all round the car for the second time. 'At least they – whoever they are – haven't touched the paintwork, which is something, I suppose.'

'I'm afraid, Mike,' said Jeremy Bostles, 'that the obvious conclusion with this is that someone somewhere must be harbouring some very uncharitable, not to say unchristian, feelings towards you.'

'Well, it can't be my former partner Malcolm Forres who did this because as far as I know he's not in England.'

'Someone a bit nearer home then perhaps,' said the Rector, whose sermons sometimes were based on the importance of facing facts, good and bad.

'They're all out to get me,' said Wakefield, tight-lipped now. 'I just wish I knew who.'

'Someone is, anyway,' agreed Bostles matter-of-factly. 'Time will tell who,' he forecast, taking the long view of the bystander.

'The only thing, Jeremy, is that I haven't the faintest idea who they are or what they are on about. I didn't know until now that I had any enemies, and that included Malcolm Forres. We'd always gone on all right.'

'We prayed for Steph in church this morning,' said the Rector, taking a long, considering look at Michael Wakefield's worn and worried face, and adding in a quite matter of fact manner, 'and that was only after seeing the local paper on Thursday. And now this.'

Michael Wakefield grunted. 'Kind of you, I'm sure.'

The Rector went on quite seriously, 'And I think therefore we should be praying for you too, Mike.'

'I can tell you one thing, Jeremy,' his parishioner said heatedly, 'and that's that whoever did this to me, my wife and my car is past praying for and if I ever get my hands on whoever did any of it, then all I can say is that they'd better watch out.'

The Reverend Jeremy Bostles, the absolute epitome of an eighteenth-century antiquarian country clergyman in appearance – he only lacked the shovel hat – shook his head and said seriously that no one, however evil, was past praying for.

'If you say so, Jeremy. If you say so,' said Michael Wakefield. Once upon a time – at a Little Missal dinner party, perhaps – Michael Wakefield would have enjoyed arguing the toss with the clergyman. Without rancour, naturally, and knowing that there was something about all true art and craft that, though not specifically religious, amounted to this feeling which he couldn't put into words.

But not this morning.

'The worrying thing, Jeremy, is,' he said, finding that he was quite glad to talk about it all at last and well out of Steph's hearing, 'is that your guess is as good as mine about who's responsible for this nightmare. And absolute nightmare it is,' he added. 'I know it must be something to do with Forres and Wakefield,' said Mike, 'but I'm dammed if I can think what.'

CHAPTER TWENTY-SEVEN

There was another matter that was also now engaging the attention of Detective Inspector Sloan. He went back to the kitchen of Ornum House and dispatched Toby and the other young men to search for a large motorcycle, not in the car park at Ornum House but further afield, although not too far away either. This was since he presumed Lenny Datchet would have had to walk there in the dark burdened by loot – if indeed that had been his game plan.

'And mind you look carefully, Toby, because it might be hidden under bushes or in a bothy or anywhere else not too far away.' He'd been joined in the big kitchen by Crosby, who managed to convey to him quietly that the body of the murder victim, Lenny Datchet, had now been taken to the police mortuary by the coroner's officer, who had just got back from Kinnisport. 'And, sir,' the constable whispered, 'Ted York says that the tanker's now just outside of our territorial waters three miles beyond Kinnisport.'

The inspector nodded and then turned to Lady Victoria Cremond, who was once again sitting opposite him at the vast kitchen table, where she was flanked by her twin. By way of beginning the interview again, at last he asked her why she had opened that particular second-floor bedroom door this morning.

The advice in his training manual on the interviewing of both witnesses and suspects had included what to do if they were crying. This amounted to doing nothing at all until they stopped crying, however long that took. Crocodile tears, the good book had said, were notably difficult to sustain for long. And they didn't always lead to genuine, blotched red patches on the face or the damp and swollen eyelids of someone truly upset.

Lady Victoria Cremond was not crying. Nor was her sister. She was, on the contrary, quite composed. 'I was just looking for Sheep's Eyes,' she said. 'We all were and for anyone else who hadn't come down to breakfast by then. Mummy and Mrs Bennett wanted to get on with doing lunch, you see.'

'Sheep's Eyes would be Jason Fixby, I take it,' said Sloan, making a note.

Lady Victoria lowered her head. 'We shouldn't have been making fun of him, Inspector, I know, but he was absolutely besotted. It was nice but a bit scary, if you know what I mean.'

Detective Inspector Sloan, highly experienced police officer that he was, knew what she meant only too well and had several unhappy case histories on stalkers and their victims on record to prove it. The fact that a great many crimes had been committed over the years because of this very feeling he did not think was something to say to an attractive young woman just at this moment.

'He was head over heels in love with her,' contributed Lady Mary. 'Mind you, she is very beautiful.'

Detective Inspector Sloan, in his capacity as mentor to Crosby, noted with some concern that Jason Fixby was not the only young man to be smitten by Lady Victoria's beauty. His constable seemed quite bemused by her, too.

Victoria had accepted her sister's compliment without demur.

'So, you weren't looking for the dead boy, Lenny Datchet, at all, then,' said Sloan, trying to keep the witness to the point.

She shook her head. 'No, Inspector.'

'Or know why he should have been in a bedroom here in the first place?'

'Dead,' put in Crosby superfluously.

'No idea at all.' She shook her head again. 'It's a complete mystery to me.'

Her sister, Mary, added, 'And we've no idea either why someone – anyone – would want to kill him, poor lad.'

Unfortunately, the police themselves had no idea

either. At this stage of the investigation, the reason for this death wasn't so much unknown as imponderable.

'I'm sure he hadn't done anything to deserve it,' said Lady Mary.

The history of Lenny Datchet was something the police would be working on as soon as they could. Sloan hoped they would find it out and very soon. And discover what bearing it had, if any, on the events at the ill-fated firm of Forres and Wakefield, master printers of Berebury, let alone on a party at one of Calleshire's oldest stately homes.

'He was too young for that sort of thing,' pronounced Victoria, already wise beyond her years in the ways of erring young men.

It was a sentiment, thought Sloan, that wouldn't have gone down well with the chairman of the Berebury Juvenile Court. It didn't with Detective Constable Crosby either, he having had several injuries sustained in the course of trying to break up fights in a school playground.

With knives.

'He was very ordinary,' offered Lady Mary Cremond, as if this explained everything.

It didn't explain why, Sloan reminded himself, that if anyone had wanted to kill Lenny Datchet, they would want to have done so in the far from ordinary surroundings of Ornum House. Ordinary didn't rank high here at Ornum. For one fleeting moment Sloan wondered if once upon a time the normal reaction to catching a burglar red-handed in this house might have been just to run him through with a sword but not now, surely not in today's world.

'Asking him to the party seemed all right at the time,' said Lady Victoria sadly, 'although of course I wish now we hadn't done.'

'Of course.' Crosby blinked as if he was gazing into the sun.

Which perhaps he was, thought Sloan, noting that Lady Victoria's was a sentiment he'd heard time and time again, but putting the clock back was never an option here or anywhere else – something that sooner or later everyone had to learn for themselves, each successive generation having to get its own feet wet, so to speak. Trying to teach them otherwise was a work of supererogation.

'Tell me what Lenny did during the evening,' he said.

'Never set eyes on him at all,' declared Victoria at once. 'Let alone spoke to him.'

'Nor me,' said Mary. She frowned. 'Or should I have said "nor I"? Mummy's very anxious about how badly we speak.'

'It doesn't matter,' uttered Crosby involuntarily.

'What matters,' said Detective Inspective Sloan, feeling suddenly middle-aged, 'is that neither of you can remember seeing or speaking to him all evening. That's so, isn't it?'

'There were a lot of people here,' said Lady Victoria obliquely. 'Daddy wanted everyone to know about his book.'

'Anyone could have been here,' agreed her sister.

'Anyone at all,' said Victoria. She turned a dazzling gaze on Crosby as one young and therefore likely to understand. 'But it was a really beautiful bike. Lenny was ever such a good driver, too. We had a lovely run round the estate when he brought Daddy's book round the day before the party. He rode really well and fast.'

'Me too. I had a turn riding pillion with him after Victoria,' said Lady Mary. She bestowed a charming smile on Crosby. 'You'll understand how exciting it was, won't you?'

'I want to go into Traffic Division one day,' he stammered. 'They have big bikes there.'

It crossed Sloan's mind again to wonder how an apprentice on a nominal wage came to own such a big machine. He mentally listed this question as yet something else he needed to look into. When he had time to think, that is.

'So you weren't even looking for the boy you found when you opened the bedroom door,' said Crosby, anxious to demonstrate that Lady Victoria was innocent of any wrongdoing.

Lady Victoria Cremond shook her head, her hair tumbling down over her ears in a way calculated to bring any passing young male to his knees, let alone an inexperienced police constable.

'We asked him to the launch party for Daddy's book, but we didn't ask him to stay the night,' pointed out her sister.

Sloan made a note that that didn't jibe with his being found dead in pyjamas and switched his questioning to being about Jason Fixby. 'Did you see much of Jason at the party?'

'Rather,' exclaimed Lady Victoria enthusiastically. 'He was trying hard to be the life and soul of it.'

'I bumped into him all the time,' said Mary. 'Mostly when he was looking for Vicky. She was hiding from him, of course.'

'I wasn't.'

'Yes, you were,' said her sister.

'Besides, he couldn't always tell us apart.' Victoria grinned. 'So sometimes I pretended I was Mary and acted up a bit.'

Detective Inspector Sloan, no innocent, said, 'And sometimes I suppose you pretended to be Victoria, Mary?'

'Rather!' said Mary. 'We always have a lot of fun when we do that. You can get away with such a lot when you do.'

That someone had so far got away with murder, Sloan had no reason to remind her.

Detective Constable Crosby, a complete innocent in the tantalising ways of young women, looked thoroughly shocked.

'I pretended to be Vicky when her Roderick came looking for her,' said Lady Mary, her eyes dancing with delight.

'Beast,' exploded her sister. 'And he's not my Roderick.'

'Yet,' said Lady Mary.

Sloan said firmly, 'Tell us how well you knew Jason.'

'He's been around for a bit,' said the object of Jason Fixby's affections casually. 'You know, we kept bumping into him at things.'

'The races, mostly,' said Lady Mary. 'Daddy always takes us over to Calleford to watch the Ornum Stakes.'

'Jason's really into horse-racing,' said Victoria. 'And that's the trouble. He bets a lot. He said that he was trying to get rich enough to be able to get married, you see.'

Detective Inspector Sloan, more mature now, could still remember when this had been his own youthful ambition, too. That was before he met his future wife, Margaret, and was persuaded into a steady job and to open a savings account.

'You don't get rich betting, though,' pronounced Mary.

'It's a mug's game,' declared Crosby stoutly. 'Everybody knows that.'

'Not Jason,' said Victoria. 'He didn't know it yet. He'd put a lot of his money on an accumulator, hoping to recoup his losses.'

This wasn't the moment, decided Sloan, to say that only the bookies made any money at racing.

'Jason didn't get rich on the horses,' said Mary. 'In fact, he told me he'd been losing quite a lot of money at the races lately.'

Even Detective Constable Crosby, jejune policeman

that he was, sat up at this, whilst Sloan made a note.

'He said it was an arm and a leg, he'd lost,' put in Mary. 'But he was afraid to tell his father.'

It was ever thus, thought Sloan, feeling older still but making a thoughtful note even so.

'Jason told me that he'd been looking into some other ways of making a fast buck, too,' said Victoria.

'Had he, now?' said an interested Sloan, scribbling a more significant note in his burgeoning notebook.

'I think he was working on a new scheme to get himself out of a hole,' said Mary naively, 'but he wouldn't tell us what it was.'

Lady Victoria Cremond looked Sloan in the eye and said forthrightly, 'But then someone else had other ideas, didn't they, Inspector?'

'And got there first,' said Crosby, the one who had supervised the removal of a different body by hearse and heard about the urgent collection of an injured one by ambulance.

Detective Inspector Sloan, investigating officer, was about to ask about any known enemies of the two victims when the door to the kitchen from the outside world opened suddenly and a tall, grey-haired man came in.

'Neville!' exclaimed the Countess of Ornum, advancing towards the visitor and being kissed lightly on both cheeks. 'How very kind of you to come. You'll stay to lunch, won't you?'

'Letitia, my dear,' the tall man murmured as Detective

Inspector Sloan, head of the tiny Criminal Investigation Department of 'F' Division, scrambled hastily to his feet, prodding Crosby to do the same as he did.

And then stood to attention as the assistant chief constable of the Calleshire County Constabulary made his way across the kitchen towards the two policemen.

CHAPTER TWENTY-EIGHT

'It's Detective Inspector Sloan, isn't it?' The assistant chief constable settled himself down at the kitchen table in the vacant chair on Sloan's right. At the far end of the kitchen, the countess and her henchwoman were beginning to load vast chargers of cold food onto the bare wood in preparation for a buffet lunch for all and sundry.

'Yes, sir. From 'F' Division at Berebury.' From where he was placed, Sloan could smell something simmering on the stove, too.

'A pretty pickle this, isn't it, Inspector, for poor Jonas and Letitia,' began the ACC, 'let alone for the dead and the injured.'

'A pretty pickle' wasn't quite how Sloan would have put it himself – a murder and a vicious attack on a youth weren't exactly petty misdemeanours in the eyes of the law – but perhaps in the long perspective of the Ornum family they might have seemed so. He would have to think about that.

But not now.

'From what I gathered from your superintendent, Sloan, you've had both a murder and an assault and battery here overnight.'

'Yes, sir,' agreed Sloan, the ACC being inclined to use old-fashioned terms. He couldn't any longer remember exactly what constituted 'battery' in present-day police speak. 'Aggravated assault' was what he thought of it as these days and that was certainly what had happened to both victims, with fatal consequences to one and serious injury to the other. He assumed the ACC's use of the word went with having had a classical education. For his part, Sloan wouldn't have described last night's events at Ornum House quite so lightly, either. Understatement was all very well in certain circumstances, but murder was murder whatever way you looked at it.

The ACC looked round. 'And where's Jonas got to now?'

'The earl decided to go with the casualty to the hospital in the ambulance, sir.'

'Very wise of him. The boy might very well still have been in danger.'

Detective Inspector Sloan gave himself a metaphorical kicking for not thinking of that himself, conceding that perhaps a classical education might have something to be said for it after all. Knowing what the Greeks and the Romans had got up to in lurid detail must broaden the mind.

'And I suppose, for all that we know, his assailant might still be here in the Ornums' home,' went on the ACC logically. 'Is that the case, Inspector?'

That was something else that Sloan hadn't given as much attention to as perhaps he should have done but without back-up to deploy over the great house, it would have been difficult to do. 'All we were able to do, sir,' he said by way of exculpation, 'was to have a cursory search here. We rather assumed that his assailant, that is whoever carried out both the attacks, left the building as soon as he could.' He promptly qualified this by saying, 'If indeed both assaults were committed by the same person.'

'I am sure you would agree that two different killers in the same house on the same night seems unlikely,' said the ACC, his attention momentarily diverted by the sight of an increasingly anxious search being carried out by those preparing the lunch at the far end of the cavernous kitchen.

'Yes, sir.'

'And the assailant leaving the scenes of the crimes as soon as he could makes sense, Inspector, but not so soon as to cause comment should he have been seen doing so. Hostesses, I'm told, tend to notice things such as that.'

Detective Inspector Sloan nodded, giving an inward

sigh. Perhaps it was the countess he should have been interviewing all along and not her elusive daughter.

'As I am sure you would be the first to agree, Sloan, what really matters is what the killer was wearing.'

Until now, Sloan had always been quite happy with his own grammar-school education. Exposed to the mindset of the ACC, he wasn't quite so sure any longer. A classical education obviously had something to be said for it after all because he, a working detective inspector, hadn't yet got round to giving any real thought to what the killer might having been wearing being so important.

'Perhaps, sir, just as the deceased, who was wearing pyjamas over his outdoor kit, the killer was dressed to pass in the crowd.'

'Black tie,' said the ACC promptly, 'if he was over a certain age, that is.'

'There would seem to have been so many people wandering all over the place in the evening that he wouldn't have wanted to have been seen in something that showed him up as a stranger,' offered Sloan.

'Good point, Inspector. Though, my goodness, there was such a good crowd there you couldn't be sure that you had seen everybody.'

Sloan made a mental note to ask the countess this – she had struck him as someone who would notice a sartorial lapse quickly enough. Among the no-longer-young, anyway, the clothes of the current young defying convention.

'And if so,' carried on the ACC, 'the killer could have made good his escape in the general exodus at the end of the party – that's if he had the nerve to stay that long.'

Sloan nodded and agreed that anyone dressed as a guest could have left with the majority of the other guests without being noticed as a killer, mentally adding to himself that whoever had been planning to murder usually would have had the nerve to stay for the right moment to take his leave.

'All the same, I do wonder what he was wearing,' mused the ACC. 'I don't remember any man that I saw sticking out in the crowd myself but, as I said, I might not have seen everybody there.'

'Surely, sir,' the inspector ventured, 'that would suggest the perpetrator was one of the guests.'

'And I also wonder,' murmured the ACC, 'whether coming here disguised as a house guest constitutes "going equipped" within the meaning of the Act.'

'I couldn't say, sir, I'm sure,' said Sloan, this being something else to which he hadn't ever given any thought either. It was the sort of academic hair-splitting that he customarily left to those with more time and less to do than he had. There was the cheese-cutter, though, a weapon that would have sat easily in a pocket.

'He might have come from the caterers,' said the ACC. 'There were plenty of them about until after the supper was served and tidied away but they all cleared off pretty smartly after that.'

'I've already asked for a list of their names and of the guests, sir.'

'Good man,' said the ACC absently, his attention now wholly engaged at the other end of the kitchen where the countess and Mrs Bennett appeared to be looking for something – and not finding it. 'This head injury – Jason Fixby, I think you said was his name – is there any news of him yet?'

'The doctors think that he's probably had a subdural haemorrhage as a consequence of the blow to his head and that, if so, it will need an emergency operation. We've alerted his father, Herbert Fixby – his mother's dead.' He coughed and added, 'I am given to understand that the earl knew Jason slightly anyway in that it was his daughters who had asked him to come to the party.'

'The Double Troubles,' said the ACC immediately.

'Them,' said Sloan feelingly. His failure to pin Lady Victoria down to interview properly still rankled.

'The boy's still unconscious, I take it?'

'Yes, sir.'

'And on bed watch?'

'I'm afraid there's no one available – they're all over at Kinnisport, sir.'

'Your enquiries are all very redolent of taking part in a TEWT, aren't they, Sloan?'

'Beg pardon, sir?'

'A tactical exercise without troops.'

'I'm sorry, sir,' Sloan began warily. He didn't know what 'redolent' meant either, but he didn't want to say so. He understood what it was like to be without troops, well enough.

'A paper exercise, no actual people being involved, I mean, as all the manpower is defending our shores over at Kinnisport today. Including the chief constable.'

'It hasn't helped, sir,' admitted Sloan. 'But the people at the hospital have been warned not to let anyone near him. Unfortunately, it is now apparent that he had been hit from behind and so might not have seen who hit him anyway.'

'Or ever be fit enough to tell you if he had,' said the ACC realistically. 'What was he hit with?'

'Too soon to say, sir. We're still looking for a weapon.'

The ACC wasn't listening. Instead, his attention was engaged by the increasingly anxious searching by Letitia Cremond and Mrs Bennett of every drawer and cupboard in sight. 'I think, Sloan, I'll just drift over that way and see what's wrong,' he said, rising to his feet. As he did so, he cast his eye along the table to Sloan's left and said, 'I think your constable could be in some danger, Inspector, and that you should do something about it before ill befalls him.'

Sloan stood up at once. 'My constable, sir?' he said, spinning his head round to his left, where Crosby had been seated beside him. But Detective Constable Crosby was no longer sitting there. His chair was empty. Sloan quickly looked round the room, his eyes alighting on Crosby much further down the table to his left and thus previously out of his range of vision. He was being firmly pinned down between the Cremond twins, one on either side of him.

All policemen get used to the sight of fear on the faces of those with whom they have dealings. Sloan himself had witnessed it many times before now. He'd seen the countenances of women drained to an ethereal whiteness when they saw him approach and were afraid of bad news. He'd noticed, too, a fear they'd never expected to experience on the faces of villains caught in an illegal act beyond excuse and even seen it on the faces of shocked men clambering out of a fatal car crash with an expression set in a determined rictus of silent despair. But he had never seen it on Crosby's face before.

The constable was well and truly pinned down, as surely as a specimen moth, between the twins and obviously wasn't enjoying the experience one little bit. His whole being was rigid with alarm, his face an unbecoming shade of puce.

'What's your name?' Victoria was asking him.

'Crosby,' he croaked.

'Not that one, silly. Your Christian name.'

'William,' he said. 'William Edward.'

'Willy,' cried Victoria gleefully. 'He's called Willy.'

Crosby blushed.

'That's a nice name,' said Mary, starting to toy with his left ear. Victoria was playing with the top buttons on his shirt. He shied away from them both like a nervous horse.

'Who's a pretty boy, then?' asked Victoria in a sing-song voice that was new to the constable.

It was no consolation to Crosby that this was the same expression and tone used by his landlady when addressing her budgerigar.

Or that the words 'pretty boy' usually cropped up in quite a different – and risible – connection in the police station canteen.

Crosby started to wriggle as Lady Mary turned her attention to his hair, ruffling through it in a way altogether too familiar for his liking.

Lurking dimly somewhere at the back of Detective Inspector Sloan's memory now was an ordinance from the police authority about the importance of not bullying junior officers by those who outranked them. Pushing this instruction even further to the back of his mind, he bellowed, 'Crosby, come here at once.'

'Yes, sir,' came a muffled response as the constable broke free from the attentions of the twins and scrambled to his feet. 'Coming, sir. At once, sir.'

The instructions on the interviewing of witnesses had been no less specific and included an admonition against the intimidation of them by the interviewing officer. Sloan proceeded to ignore this, too.

'Lady Victoria,' he said with unusual firmness. 'I want to talk to you in the dining room now. Alone.'

CHAPTER TWENTY-NINE

'Pelion upon Ossa,' pronounced Kay Harris down the telephone line from her cottage in the wilds of the countryside out beyond Capstan Purlieu.

After seeing the rector on his way, Michael Wakefield had remained standing outside his front doorstep whilst he took a long look at the tyres of his car. Whoever had savaged them had done so quite comprehensively, all four of them being clearly beyond repair. With grim humour, he decided that none of them were even worth kicking any more. He'd shaken his head in bewilderment, too, at seeing them, unable to begin to comprehend who it was who might have done this amount of damage during the night. It would have needed a sharp Stanley knife at the very least.

Who or why.

But there came no answer.

Dismissing the notion that it might have been some drunk-fuelled random yobbos who resented other people's good cars and nice houses and had nothing better to do on a Saturday night, he found himself agreeing with a favourite sentiment – a sermon he delivered on occasion – of the rector's: that actions taken in malice should never prosper.

That was the point at which he had telephoned Kay.

'Pelion upon what?' he said now.

'Ossa. In other words, piling on the agony,' she said.

That he had more than one enemy, he was in no doubt about at all by now. But the fact that he couldn't think of anyone other than the absent Forres only added to his discomfiture. Whatever harm his former partner had done him surely couldn't be associated with slashed tyres at Little Missal. Especially not since the Forres couple were thought to be still in France. The police had assured him that in the event of either of them so much as setting foot in the United Kingdom the authorities would soon know about it.

The police had already asked him if his firm had business rivals capable of causing Forres and Wakefield aggravation. Whilst they had appeared to accept his assurance that profitable jobs for firms such as theirs were not thick enough on the ground to invite much competition, he didn't know whether they believed him or not. He couldn't tell.

'Misery upon misery,' she said.

'You can say that again,' he responded grimly. 'I've

half a mind to start wearing my fool's cap in earnest until I know what it's all about.'

'Your what?'

'My fool's cap. The one I wear at our annual wayzgoose.'

'Your jollification with much beer, you mean,' she said.

'The printers' outing customarily given by a master printer to his men,' he said with some dignity. 'In memory of Sir John Spilman, an Elizabethan papermaker so keen on keeping his monopoly that he had part of his coat of arms – a fool's cap – watermark put on every page.'

'Hence the page-size foolscap, I take it,' she said, as quick on the uptake as ever.

'Yes, but I don't know where they got the double elephant paper size from,' said Wakefield.

'And it doesn't matter,' she said crisply. 'What matters is finding out what's been going on at the firm. And how long for. That's very important.'

'If you say so.'

'I do say so, Mike. And I mean it. It must be something to do with that new girl at the accountants'. Nothing happened until she came on the scene. Had you thought of that? Or why Malcolm and Christine have taken off?'

He was saved from saying that he had thought of nothing else since they'd gone by becoming aware of the smell of burning coming from the kitchen. Hastily making his farewells to Kay and ringing off, he hurried back to the kitchen to find the charred remains of the stir-fry he'd left heating up on the stove when the rector had arrived. He had plunged the frying pan and its contents into the sink before he noticed that Stephanie was beginning to stir. Just as the burnt cork and feathers with which the Victorians used to bring swooning young ladies with eighteen-inch waistlines back to their senses had done, so the acrid smell of the blackened food seemed somehow to have got through to her when nothing else had done.

'Michael,' she pleaded slowly and painfully, 'you must tell me what's going on.'

'I only wish I knew,' he said, dropping into a chair beside her and deciding they'd have to have baked beans for their Sunday lunch.

'Jeremy told me he'd prayed for me in church this morning,' she said, child-like.

'He promised to pray for me, too,' he said, adding with unconscious irony, 'God only knows we need it.'

'Mike.' She plucked at his sleeve. 'About Kay . . .'

'What about Kay?'

'I'm sure she knows something that we don't but I don't know what it is.'

CHAPTER THIRTY

Michael Wakefield picked up the telephone at the Old Rectory at Little Missal with some misgiving, eyeing it when it rang as if the machine itself could be of a malevolent disposition. He'd been trying to cobble some lunch together for the pair of them and had not been making a particularly good fist of it.

'That you, Mike? It's Gilbert here.'

'What's up with you, Gilbert?' he answered wearily. The firm of Forres and Wakefield had always had a policy of keeping to office hours as well as respecting their workers' peace on Sundays. Besides which he himself was very tired, not having had much sleep the night before.

'It's not up with me,' said the production manager. 'It's with Lenny Datchet.'

Wakefield emitted a long-drawn-out and audible sigh. 'Strewth, what's he done now?'

'It's not what he's done, Mike. It's what someone's done to him.' Gilbert Hull took a deep breath and said, 'He's been killed.'

'Lenny? For heaven's sake, how?'

'I don't know how but it was over at Ornum House. You know, where we did that book for the earl . . .'

'Of course I know,' said Wakefield impatiently. 'When? How?'

'Overnight, they think.' Hull stumbled a bit as the words came tumbling out. 'Last night, I mean.'

'Killed at Ornum House? Good God, what in heaven's name was Lenny doing over there at night?'

'It's his mother who's just been on to me and she says he was at the launch party for the earl's book that we did for him,' said Hull. 'She'd been sitting up for him, waiting for him to come home and tell her about the party.'

'And then he didn't come home, you mean?' Wakefield said, more as a statement than a question.

'And no, Mike, before you ask, I didn't know what he was doing over there either until she told me. Apparently one of those Ornum twins had invited him to the big "do" there. You know what those two girls are like with any young fool in trousers.'

'Don't I just? And so does everyone else in the county. They're man-eaters, the pair of them. So how did he get killed then and there, and why? I always thought he would come to grief one day on that blasted motorbike of his.'

'So did I.'

'His pride and joy, he kept on telling me it was, but it was much too powerful for him to handle safely. So what did happen to him, then, if it wasn't on his bike?'

'That I don't know and I don't think his mother does either yet, but she says the police are on their way to take her to the mortuary to identify the lad.'

'Poor woman,' said Wakefield, as he riffled through his memory. 'If I remember rightly, Lenny didn't have a father, did he?'

'Never, at least never one who would own up to him,' said Hull. 'Actually, I think the father left home.'

Wakefield nodded to himself. The firm had been trying to be helpful in offering Lenny the apprenticeship. He looked now in the direction of Stephanie, sitting at the kitchen table as still and as motionless as a shop window mannequin. She would have been the first to offer to accompany Lenny's mother to the mortuary if she had been herself. That she wasn't herself today was patently obvious.

'Poor Mrs Datchet,' he said, genuinely compassionate. He wondered en passant what it was that Dr Browne had given Steph, poor woman, too. The general practitioner had said it was just something to help her through the next few days, explaining that the ancients had called it 'temple sleep', which they, too, had applied after mental trauma, to give the brain a rest from what it didn't want to have to process. 'I'm very sorry but . . .'

'That's not the whole of it, Mike.' Hull gave a gulp. 'They've told her that someone had killed him.'

'On purpose, you mean?' he responded blankly, not thinking straight himself now. 'Whatever for?'

'Your guess is as good as mine. Not an accident was what the police said to her.'

'At Ornum? Good God, man, what sort of parties do they have over there?'

'Search me. I wasn't there and I don't move in those exalted circles. I don't know anything more than that, but I thought I'd better let you know pronto.'

'Right.' For a moment Wakefield thought about how to help Lenny's mother and then remembered that he hadn't got any money now to do it with. He sighed. If only Steph had not been in such a state of inanition and had been sitting by his side, her usual alert and helpful self instead, she would have known what to say, but he wasn't sure that he did. In the end, though, he formed the words, right ones or not.

'His mother said she thought it was funny that she hadn't heard his bike coming back late last night but she imagined he'd been caught up with one of those girls, which I for one wouldn't have put it past them.'

'Poor woman,' said Wakefield again.

'It means, Mike, that that great big motorbike will still be over there somewhere, too.'

CHAPTER THIRTY-ONE

Detective Inspector Sloan took up his position at the head of the Ornum dining table with Lady Victoria sitting on his left and began his long-overdue interview with her again with a certain degree of formality.

'Now, Lady Victoria . . .'

'You can call me Vicky, if you like, Inspector.' She smiled winningly; her cheeks dimpled. 'Everyone else does.'

'Thank you,' he said gravely. The advice on the conducting of interviews had as it happened been silent on this point. He started again. 'What I need you to confirm, Lady Victoria, is that you had invited the deceased to the party.'

'Yes,' she said simply. 'Lenny gave me this absolutely divine ride on his bike when he came over on Friday . . . his motorbike, that is – all round the park. It was a big bike and it went like a bomb.' She gave Sloan an anxious glance. 'He didn't go too fast or anything, Inspector, I promise you.'

Sloan didn't think that this was the moment to say that Lenny's speed wasn't of the essence and so kept silent.

'He was a really good biker and he took Mary for a lovely run, too, after me. We both liked him a lot and he seemed good fun, so we asked him to come last night.'

'Did you know him?'

'Oh, no. We didn't actually know him at all.' There was a world of meaning in what she said and how she said it. 'He only came here to bring Daddy the first copy of his book off the press. We'd never seen him before then.'

As invitations to a death went, decided Sloan, that was in a league all of its own. On second thoughts, perhaps not. The Borgias had had their victims to dinner before they were murdered, hadn't they? It was the sort of thing that the ACC would know.

'Did you see him much during the evening?' asked Sloan once more, turning over a page in his notebook.

Lady Victoria wrinkled her nose. 'Now that you come to mention it, Inspector, I don't think I did, but there were so many people milling about that I could easily have missed him.'

'But you definitely saw him in the bedroom this morning?'

Her colour rose. 'Yes, but I didn't know at first that

it was him. Truly, Inspector, I didn't.' She looked at him earnestly and said, 'His face was all white and red and blotchy – besides, he didn't move when I went into the room, so I knew something was wrong.' Her voice trembled a little then. 'I'd never seen anyone dead before, you see, but I was quite sure whoever was in that bed wasn't breathing so I went to find Daddy.'

'Quite so,' said Sloan, changing tack. 'And Jason Fixby? Did you see much of him during the evening?'

She brightened immediately. 'All the time, Inspector. He was hanging about near me most of the evening.'

'Until when?'

Her voice sounded rather unsure again now. 'I don't know exactly. After supper, probably. Mary says she didn't remember seeing him after that, either. There were a lot of people milling about by then, and some of them spilt out into other rooms. And then we started dancing in the drawing room. He was there for some of the time because I danced with him myself – not too often, though, in case he got funny ideas, you know. You can't keep track of everyone, anyway – you know what it's like at a big party.'

Sloan wasn't sure that he did. Not at that sort of a party, anyway. 'And after that?'

'Jason hadn't been invited to stay the night, I do know.' She sniffed. 'So I'm afraid I rather assumed that in the end he had gone home even though he hadn't come to say goodnight to me or to Mummy, which wasn't like him at all. I would have thought he would have known better than that, but he had had rather a lot to drink in the evening and might not have wanted us to notice.'

Detective Inspector Sloan wouldn't have known better than that either. Working detectives didn't usually have to say their thanks, goodnights or their farewells to anyone when they left the scene of a crime. There were plenty of times, as well, when people were only too thankful that they had left at all.

Lady Victoria was still talking. 'You know there's always a moment at a party when someone decides to leave and so everyone else decides to go as well. The older ones, anyway. People can be like lemmings sometimes.'

That was something that Detective Inspector Sloan certainly hadn't known. You didn't leave the superintendent's office until told to do so.

'It's all right if it isn't too soon and so doesn't spoil the party, of course,' said that experienced young socialite.

He gave way to temptation and asked Lady Victoria what happened if the moment came too late for the host and hostess.

'You accidentally leave the front door open, of course, Inspector.'

He tucked this nugget of good practice away for when his garrulous next-door neighbour outstayed his welcome, and then went back to the matter in hand. 'Jason Fixby . . .'

'So,' she carried on, 'I thought that he must have gone home then.' She took a deep breath and gamely carried on. 'Mary wondered at first if he might have started talking to someone else or given another girl a lift home.' She gave another sigh and did seem near to tears now. 'That's until they found his car was still here. And that's when I knew he hadn't left.'

'I'll be interviewing Lady Mary presently,' was all Sloan said.

She suddenly sparkled and said, 'Give my love to Inspector Harpe, will you, please? And tell him that I'm still keeping the pedal on the metal in spite of everything.'

Since Inspector Harold Harpe of Traffic Division was known throughout the force as Happy Harry because he had never been known to smile, maintaining that in Traffic Division there was never anything at which to smile about, Sloan decided against doing any such thing.

The advice on how to bring witness interviews to an end had been quite specific, too. It included, as well as the ostentatious shutting of a notebook, the putting away of the pen. And if it was being recorded, the need to announce the time and date when the interview ended. This usually led to a palpable relaxation in the atmosphere. This was no accident. The timing of the end of the interview was, of course, usually the prerogative of the officer concerned, but carried with it an especial emphasis on noting and remembering what was said by the interviewee immediately after the shutting of the notebook by who was supposedly by then off guard.

It wasn't like that today.

When the low-pitched boom of a beaten dinner-gong reached them, Lady Victoria immediately got to her feet and set off for the kitchen and lunch.

CHAPTER THIRTY-TWO

'That you, Seedy? Bill Matthews here.'

'Hi, Bill,' said Sloan, who was always known to his friends at the police station as Seedy on account of his initials being C. D. 'What's up now?' Having got a murder and a murderous attack on his plate already, Sloan couldn't think of anything else to add to the morning's tally of crime that could matter now.

'Not important, Seedy, just odd,' said the station sergeant at Berebury. 'I only came on at twelve – all our shifts have gone haywire this morning on account of that wayward tanker outside Kinnisport. I wasn't meant to be on duty at all today.'

'I thought not,' Sloan teased him, 'seeing as you usually take such good care to have your Sundays off.'

'Don't you start, Seedy. The wife's bad enough. She says it's because I'm always out drinking with friends late Saturday nights just so that I can't take her to church early Sunday mornings.'

'I can see her line of thinking,' said Sloan.

'And I can tell you that nearly all uniform who were supposed to be around here are over at the coast playing war games.'

'Go on.'

'So I thought I'd better get myself up to speed by looking at the report book, an activity known in more exalted circles, I understand, as "reading oneself in".'

'And?' asked Sloan, hoping his impatience didn't show to an old friend.

'And I came across a mention of one Michael Wakefield of Little Missal. He's someone you've been having trouble with, isn't he?'

'Him being in a load of trouble might be a better way of putting it,' said Sloan. 'Poor bloke. But go on.'

'Whatever,' said Bill Matthews amiably. 'Anyway, there was this message quite early this morning from a member of the public who didn't want to leave his name . . .'

Sloan pricked up his ears. Anonymous reports were a pain in the neck at the police station because they couldn't be checked out and either verified or disregarded. But even the fact of anonymity was not without interest.

'He – it was a "he", all right,' went on Matthews, 'told the desk sergeant that he'd been walking past the Old Rectory at Little Missal on his way to work this morning.'

'Early on a Sunday morning?' said Sloan sceptically.

'Presumably on a farm,' said Matthews, 'since the sarge noted that he could hear cows lowing in the background or whatever it is cows do.'

'Moo,' said Sloan. Unlike their superintendent, he wasn't worried about the invasion of the countryside by the well-off.

'If you say so, Seedy. Anyway, he told the desk sergeant he could hear it, whatever animal it was.'

'Did he, indeed?' said Sloan.

'He did try to get a name out of the caller, but he wasn't lucky there.'

'Go on.' There were always those who thought that any connection with the police had its dangers. It wasn't only the superintendent who held that the more the government knew about a subject, the greater danger that person was in. And that that held in every regime the world over.

'Anyway,' went on Matthews, 'this guy – the member of the public, that is – said he happened to be walking past the Old Rectory at Little Missal and spotted that the car standing outside its front door had had all its tyres slashed. He thought it was a bit odd as he knew the guy who lived there . . .'

'Michael Wakefield,' supplied Sloan.

'That's the name, and he was sure that he wasn't the sort of man to have a rival in love or to have done anything likely to warrant a revenge attack, which that sort of thing usually is, although you never can tell.'

'True,' agreed Sloan, an open mind being important in all detective work.

'I asked around here and the man Wakefield seems to have been in good standing out there,' said Matthews.

This sentiment took Sloan's mind straight back to something that the superintendent, with his magpie tendency, had picked up on one of his evening classes. It had been an early method of determining guilt or innocence well before the country had settled on the idea of twelve good men and true doing the deciding based on the evidence before them – if, sighed Sloan to himself, that was in fact what they did do. He often wondered about that.

He searched his memory now for the name of the practice – compurgation or something like that with the word 'detecta' cropping up for good measure from time to time. The decision in those days hung on statements of innocence given by those who knew the accused under oath who swore to the veracity and innocence of the said accused. Trial by oath, it was, 'oath-helping' another name for it.

'Carry on, Bill,' he said, conscious of time passing.

'It wasn't so much this guy Wakefield having had all his tyres slashed as the fact that he hasn't reported it,' said Matthews, 'Odd, that, don't you think?'

CHAPTER THIRTY-THREE

After Kay Harris had rung off, Michael Wakefield had simply gone on thinking.

Whatever harm Malcolm Forres had presumably done him, surely the man didn't come into the picture here and now since the Forres couple were presumably still in France? The police had again assured him that should either of the pair of them even so much as to try to set foot in the United Kingdom, they would soon know about it. What neither he nor the police knew was whether he had been orchestrating damage from afar.

And, if he had, why?

And if not, who?

The police had already asked him if his firm had business rivals. Whilst they had appeared to accept his assurance that specialist high-quality printers were not thick enough on the ground to invite much competition, he didn't know whether they believed him or not. Unfortunately, with the police, what they knew or didn't know was something that one never could tell: until matters came to trial, that is. They would never say before then.

There was one thing that seeing the slashed tyres had done for Wakefield, and that was to convince him beyond doubt that he hadn't been – wasn't being – a fool. That thought immediately brought what he had told Kay Harris to mind. A fool's cap was something he literally used to wear at the annual wayzgoose, better known as the printers' outing, customarily given by a master printer to his workers. The whole firm would go by coach, always excepting Mrs Kay Harris, of course, to whom such junketings were an anathema.

They would finish up at a good pub and he, Michael, would put a fool's cap on his head before launching into his customary tale of how it had descended from the heraldic symbol of Sir John Spilman, an Elizabethan papermaker so determined to hang on to his monopoly that he put a watermark of a fool's cap, part of his coat of arms, on every page. Hence the paper size before metrification of foolscap. The staff all knew the story inside out and would end up chanting it with him and mocking him if he got so much as a word wrong from the year before.

No, he wasn't being a fool now. This was all too real – it was concrete evidence that someone, somewhere –

and not only Malcolm Forres – was gunning for him. Whether they were gunning for the firm, too, or just him and Steph with the nightmare mixture of theft and malice that had befallen them, he couldn't decide.

It was then that the telephone rang again. Wakefield picked it up to find Gilbert Hull back on the line. 'Mike,' he said tersely, 'I've just had Lenny's mother on the blower for the second time this morning.'

'And?' he asked warily.

'The police have now been back on to her asking if she knew someone called Jason Fixby, which of course she said she didn't.'

'No,' agreed Wakefield, 'she wouldn't have done. I'm not even sure if Lenny himself would have done, either, so there's no reason for her to have known the name. Jason usually only turned up with us from time to time when old Herbert didn't. And that was usually at audit time.'

'That's not it, Mike,' Hull hastened on. 'Apparently, someone clobbered Jason Fixby on the head so badly last night at Ornum House that he's now unconscious in hospital.'

'Strewth,' exploded Wakefield. 'Him, too?'

'Sounds like it.' Hull paused and then said seriously, 'It sounded to me, from what the police told her, as if he's at death's door in hospital now.'

'Poor chap. What on earth is going on over there, Gilbert? One death and one attack.'

'Search me,' Hull said. 'I must say, from what she

said the police told her, it seems as if the attack on the Fixby boy might have been meant to kill him, too. Mike, have you any idea at all what's up at Ornum? And for God's sake, why?'

'None whatsoever.' He shook his head even though Gilbert couldn't see him doing so. 'It's all a complete mystery to me. I can't begin to imagine why anyone would want to kill Lenny either.'

'And in such a beautiful house, too.'

'I didn't know you knew it. I don't.'

'It was open to the public last year in aid of some Calleshire charity or other. Muriel and I went over to see it – she was a bit disappointed.'

'How come, if it was so beautiful?' He was only talking to put off the moment when he had to think of Jason Fixby lying unconscious from a head wound, a Jason Fixby whom he knew and who, too, was connected however slightly with the embattled firm of Forres and Wakefield.

'You know what Muriel's like. All she wanted to see were the family's private apartments. Which she didn't get to do, by the way.'

Wakefield did know what Gilbert's wife, Muriel, was like. She was always keen to see how the other half lived and would have liked to have been one of them herself. She had ideas of the high life founded on certain society magazines and well above the reality of suburban Berebury, where she lived.

'Fortunately,' said her husband, 'the countess was

serving the teas in the old stables and so she got a good look at her, apron and all, which kept her happy.'

'I'm glad to hear it,' said Wakefield, adding drily, 'I expect the earl was being a car park attendant that day.'

'Could be.' Hull paused before he said, 'Mike, do you suppose that any of this could have something to do with us?'

'I wish to high heaven that I knew myself, Gilbert, but I don't. As far as I know, until last week everything at the firm was hunky-dory and now . . .' Speech failed him for a moment. He started again. 'And now we're talking murder, brutal attacks and bankruptcy. If you can explain any of it to me, you're a better man than I am.'

'And from what Mrs Datchet has just told me, Jason's life is hanging in the balance,' contributed Hull. 'The police are coming soon, she said, to collect her and take her to identify Lenny, poor woman.'

'Poor woman,' echoed Wakefield. 'First Lenny and now Jason . . .' he murmured. 'Is that the end of it, do you think?'

'Just what I was thinking, Mike. Who next?'

Wakefield said it didn't bear thinking about but what he wanted to know more than anything else was why.

There was an unnatural pause before the production manager ventured to speak again. He couldn't have sounded more tentative. 'Mike, what about tomorrow?'

'Tomorrow?' asked Wakefield, caught off balance.

'Tomorrow's Monday.'

'What about it?' With an almost visible effort, he brought his mind round to considering the fact.

'The works. Do we open as usual?'

'What's that? Oh, I suppose so.' There had been a slogan going about that came to mind now. He searched his memory until it came back to him. 'Keep Calm and Carry On' – that was it. He repeated it now to Hull.

'If you say so, Mike,' said Hull. 'If you say so. Easier said than done, though, in the circumstances.'

Wakefield stiffened his shoulders and quoted someone else – actually, it was his own late father. 'If there's work to be done, then well done it should be and without delay.'

'There's that little book of verse for our local poet,' responded the production manager, taking this literally, 'and this year's Christmas card for the Mayor of Berebury. There's still estimates to be done for the Calleford Calligraphic Society, too.'

'I hadn't forgotten.' The printer grimaced. 'And they're bound to want artwork of their usual high standard. They always do.'

'Kay calls it challenging,' said Hull. 'And then there's the university, Mike. They always want some different fancy design for their graduation ceremony each year.'

'True.' Wakefield didn't know whether to laugh or cry that there was work and aplenty waiting to be done by the sadly defunct firm of Forres and Wakefield. Instead, he said, 'Good. By the way, Gilbert, I may be rather late in tomorrow morning. I've had a little trouble with the car, and I'll have to wait here for the garage to turn up.' He scowled. 'I had my tyres slashed last night.'

Hull said, 'That's odd. I wasn't going to mention it seeing as you've got so much on your plate, but I had a brick through my window.'

'Last night, too?'

'About midnight, I should say. I was asleep and fortunately Muriel was staying with her mother.'

CHAPTER THIRTY-FOUR

Detective Inspector Sloan found that talking to Superintendent Leeyes after interviewing Lady Victoria Cremond wasn't so much a refreshing change as a coming back down to earth with a bump.

It transpired that the superintendent was still at the Berebury Golf Club and moreover had no intention whatsoever of coming over to Ornum House any time soon, murder and mayhem notwithstanding. 'We're all waiting for some of the younger fellows who've done thirty-six holes to come in,' he explained. 'To find out how they've got on.'

Detective Inspector Sloan translated this as telling him that the superintendent was having his lunch there at the club, come what may. 'Of course, sir.'

'And you, Sloan, how have you got on?'

'We've located the deceased's motorcycle, sir,' he

said. 'It was propped up behind a wall on some rough ground beyond the car park here. Very much out of sight, naturally.' He really would have to have a chat with the beefy young man called Toby, who had found the machine, about becoming a police cadet. 'It's registered in the name of Leonard Datchet at an address in Berebury and we'll be going round there in due course to talk to his mother.'

'Hidden behind a wall in case anyone noticed it and took the number down, you say,' concluded Leeyes, calling out to someone in the distance that yes, another beer would go down very well, thank you.

'We'll be getting traffic's low-loader out to bring it back to the yard as soon as we can, sir,' said Sloan.

'Not today, you won't,' said the superintendent with spirit. 'Inspector Harpe's over at Kinnisport now with half the county force. Last I heard was that the tanker's entered our territorial waters and is making in the direction of the harbour there at a rate of knots.' He sniffed. 'They tell me that the chief constable's taken charge of our side of things over there.'

'I see, sir.' This might well account for the presence of the assistant chief constable at Ornum House today as a guest and off-duty. He'd heard on the grapevine that the two of them didn't get on, the chief constable having worked his way up through the ranks and his deputy fast-tracked from somewhere.

Or, as it was said by the unkind, nowhere you'd ever have heard of.

'No, you don't see, Sloan,' Leeyes insisted. 'The chief constable isn't sure which embassy to deal with, seeing as it looks as if the vessel is flying the flag of an unknown republic.'

Sloan was tempted to say something about the Jolly Roger and its skull and crossbones but thought better of it.

'And what's the ACC up to now?' asked Leeyes, rather less than respectfully.

'The countess couldn't find the family's silver soup tureen to use at the luncheon they're giving today for everyone who's still around after the party. The ACC couldn't find it either.'

The superintendent sniffed again. 'They're only figureheads at that level, chief constables, not proper coppers. They've forgotten any policing they ever knew.'

'So,' carried on Sloan manfully, 'the ACC suggested that Crosby went back and searched anywhere that Lenny Datchet might have stashed what he'd stolen, and he found a great cache of silver in the housekeeper's cubby hole at the end of the corridor where they found the body.'

'Waiting for the right moment to make his escape with his haul, I suppose,' concluded Leeyes.

'So we supposed, too, sir,' said Sloan. He himself was waiting for the right moment to make his own and Crosby's getaway from Ornum House. He couldn't very well thank the countess for having them there to investigate one murder and one criminal attack in her house, whatever one of her daughters had said was the polite thing to do.

'Having wandered round the house in the night at will in his pyjamas, I suppose,' grunted Leeyes. 'An excellent disguise in the circumstances,' he said. 'Quite clever, really, when you come to think about it.'

'Yes, sir. I daresay if anyone had seen him roaming about up there, they wouldn't have suspected robbery.'

'Or even been surprised,' said the superintendent balefully. 'Not with Lady Victoria and Lady Mary being who they are.' He paused and then went on, 'I understand that it's quite common in country house circles such as this one.'

Sloan coughed and said, 'I've been told, sir, that it's known by those who do move in such circles as "corridor creeping".'

'Good point, man. But it doesn't explain why Datchet was killed in the first place, does it? Tell me that, Sloan. We don't even know where to begin.'

'It's a total mystery at this point, sir,' agreed Sloan. 'And we don't know for sure either whether the attack on the Fixby boy had anything to do with the murder of Datchet.'

'Or everything to do with it, which seems more likely,' pointed out Leeyes. 'First Fixby and then Datchet, I take it?'

'Probably, sir, since Fixby was fully clothed when they found him,' agreed Sloan. He didn't know if that was the actual order of the attacks on the victims' persons, but he didn't see that it mattered anyway at this stage of the investigation.

'Do we know what the two victims had in common?'

'Not exactly, sir.'

'And what is that supposed to mean, might I ask?'

'That we know that Lenny Datchet worked at the printers of the earl's book but as far as we know Jason Fixby's connection with Forres and Wakefield is only tangential.'

'And what exactly does that mean too?' The superintendent sounded quite peppery now.

'Only that the Fixby boy worked for that firm's accountants, which strikes me as a very tenuous a connection to say the least.'

'The very same firm where one of the partners has made off with the takings?'

'Yes, sir.'

'And what in heaven's name had either of them got to do with the Ornums, of all people?'

'I don't know, sir. Not yet. In fact, I can't think of any real connection at all, myself, beyond knowing that Fixby was fixated on Lady Victoria and Datchet had delivered a book there.' Perhaps trying to get some sense out of Lady Victoria was easier after all than parrying the superintendent's questions. He was saved by his superior officer's phone coming to life with an outburst of loud cheering in the background at the golf club.

'A chap's just come in with two birdies and an eagle, Sloan,' explained Leeyes.

'Good for him,' said Sloan absently, his mind momentarily going back to the song 'The Twelve Days of Christmas' and its partridge in a pear tree, which was closely followed by mention of two turtle doves. Perhaps seeing as there was an eagle involved as well as two birdies, he should be thinking about the three French hens as well. The ten drummers drumming had always gone down well – if noisily – on the wooden floorboards of the school hall. The twelve lords a-leaping had occasioned a lot of noise, too, whilst the ten maids a-milking had come in for much schoolboy ribaldry. There were no eagles, though.

Now that Sloan had met a real live lord, he could see why the lords in the song might have leapt. What he couldn't fathom was why either of this weekend's victims should have been attacked in that lord's house. Perhaps they had both stumbled upon some deadly family secret? Hadn't there been a house – a castle, he thought – somewhere – Scotland, perhaps – said to house a monster? Although nobody could prove it, and that had been said in spite of once trying to do so by hanging a towel out of the window of every room in the building they could get to and then looking from the outside for a window without anything hanging from it.

And hoping to burst into that room and find a monster. The owner was thought to have thwarted that particular enterprise and quite right, too.

And hadn't there had been another house in England

somewhere with a real secret room, a stately home, where the skeleton of a Plantagenet knight had been found still sitting at a table after five hundred years? He was thought to have fled the anger of a new king and in locking everyone out had accidentally locked himself in, poor fellow. According to Machiavelli, new kings were more dangerous than old ones, regime change being a dangerous time. They did know that, even at the police station, when a new senior officer took charge and a new broom started to sweep too clean.

And there had been that interview not long after he'd joined the force by some psychologist or other who had asked each of the new recruits in turn how they would have tracked the first Mrs Rochester down in her attic prison. He himself hadn't even known what the man had been talking about, but the brightest spark of their cohort had suggested using a heat-sensitive camera. He'd since heard that that member of the force was doing well these days in the Diplomatic Protection Squad.

Sloan made a mental note and resolved that as soon as there were men and women to spare again on the strength, he would have Ornum House searched from top to bottom.

And sideways, too.

A further burst of cheering erupted down the phone from the golf club and interrupted his train of thought.

'You still there, Sloan?' barked Leeyes.

'Yes, sir. Sorry, sir. I didn't quite catch what you were saying.'

'Old Wilkins had to fork out a bit more than he thought after his hole-in-one,' said Leeyes, practically chortling. 'Cost him a bomb.'

'Bad things happen to good people,' Sloan observed sententiously. He didn't think that applied to Lenny Datchet, though. Young Jason Fixby he didn't know enough about to say.

'I don't mind that,' said Leeyes. 'What I don't like is good things happening to bad people.'

'Quite so,' said Sloan.

'And now,' carried on Leeyes, 'what I would like to know is the connection of both Datchet and Fixby with the Earl of Ornum.'

'So would I,' said Sloan feelingly.

'And you, Sloan, what are you going to do next?' The background noise from the clubhouse was getting louder.

'We're heading for the hospital, sir, and then go back to Little Missal to have another chat with Michael Wakefield since whichever way we turn, his printer's business seems to figure in our enquiries. Besides, there's something else in the picture.'

'What's that?' asked the superintendent.

'The foreman at Forres and Wakefield's works over there – a man by the name of Gilbert Hull – had one of his windows smashed in last night. He found a brick on the bedroom carpet this morning.'

'Check him out soonest, then,' commanded Leeyes.

'Fortunately, the man Hull's wife's away at her

mother's. He was asleep at the time – he said it was just after midnight that it happened – but by the time he'd got to the window, whoever had thrown it had got away in the dark.'

'What on earth's going on at that firm, Sloan? Nothing there seems to make any sense so far.'

'And, sir,' went on Sloan, tacitly agreeing with this, 'Michael Wakefield had all the tyres on his car slashed at some time overnight yesterday, too. He's so worried about his wife that he forgot to put it away in the garage last night.'

'Murder and petty crime don't usually go together,' observed Leeyes.

'No, sir, they don't.' Sloan had already given this anomaly some thought without coming to any conclusion. 'And rather oddly some person unknown went to unusual lengths to see that we knew about the slashed tyres.'

Leeyes grunted.

'I think, sir, that I told you that Michael Wakefield's wife has had to be heavily sedated and so he was having to keep quite a close eye on her?'

'You did.' The noise in the clubhouse rose another decibel.

'Very distressed, she was, about the theft at the works and the looming bankruptcy. Not that anyone could blame her for that. What seems to have really pushed her over the edge was the local newspaper publishing the details of it all on its front page. She had wanted to be gone from the village before the neighbours found out about it.'

'Loss of face being more important than the loss of the money, you mean?'

'Yes, sir. To her, that is.' The distinction between the two events in Stephanie Wakefield's mind was obviously of greater significance to her than it was to the police. He would have to see if his own wife, Margaret, a bellwether in such matters, would have agreed with her. 'But I'm more worried about who it was who told the newspaper about it so out of turn. And why.'

'Not cricket?' said the superintendent sardonically.

'Not if it came from us, sir,' Sloan said seriously, 'or come to that, someone in the printer's, let alone the accountants'.'

'Fixby and Fixby?'

'They certainly know all about it. I couldn't think of who benefited unless that couple who scarpered so quickly wanted it known for reasons of their own.'

'And so stirred the pot.'

'Exactly, sir.'

It was at that moment the sound of a bell being rung came over the telephone from the golf club.

'Lunch,' pronounced Leeyes, 'I'll have to go. Let me know how you get on.'

'Of course, sir,' said Sloan in as neutral tones as he could manage, ending the call with a sigh and going in search of Crosby.

CHAPTER THIRTY-FIVE

Sloan didn't have far to go to find him. He spotted the detective constable as soon as he hung up and turned his head. He was standing in the hall outside the door leading to the kitchen, hopping from one foot to the other in a state of agitation.

'Sir,' he said urgently, pointing to the kitchen door, 'we've been asked to join everyone in there for lunch, but we don't have to, do we, sir? I mean what with the ACC and those two girls being there.'

'No,' said the detective inspector firmly, 'we don't. What we do have to do now, though, is to get over to the hospital at Berebury instead to see how Jason Fixby is doing.'

'Oh, thank you, sir. Thank you.'

'But without burning any rubber on the way, mind you.'

'Of course not, sir,' said Crosby virtuously as if the very thought of driving fast hadn't ever crossed his mind.

'And get something to eat, too,' he added, suddenly becoming aware of time having passed.

'The scenes of crime team have knocked off to have their nosh at the Cremond Inn down in the village, sir, but they said if you want them sooner, they'll come back.'

'I should hope so, too,' said Sloan, feeling hungrier still now.

'And they said to please tell you that they'd found the murder weapon although they don't have high hopes of fingerprints.'

'The putative murder weapon, Crosby.'

'The putat . . . what you just said . . . weapon, sir. A poker, sir.'

'Excellent. That's the first bit of good news that I've had today.'

'Really, sir? How come?'

'It speaks of an unpremeditated attack on Fixby, whereas the garrotting of Datchet suggests something planned very carefully.'

'That's good, then, is it, sir?'

'It means that Jason Fixby's attacker had had no time to plan before he hit his victim. And that, Crosby, is when mistakes are more likely to happen.' He paused and then went on, 'It also means that something quite unexpected had occurred to make the attack on the Fixby boy so necessary. What that was we don't yet know. An immediate attack,' he added for good measure, 'but with its urgency so far unexplained.'

'It couldn't wait, you mean, sir.'

'I do.'

'And afterwards someone would be needing to get away pretty quickly,' concluded Crosby. He looked at inspector for confirmation. 'Wouldn't they?'

'True. That's something else that's interesting.'

Crosby's brow became furrowed. 'What is, sir?'

'That there were no signs of flight on anyone's part last night. None that we've been told about, anyway. Think about it, Crosby.'

Fortified by a good lunch in the hospital's canteen, Detective Inspector Sloan had led the way along a quiet corridor in the hospital and then into an unmarked room. The two policemen were confronted there by the disturbing sight of an anguished old man sitting at the bedside of his only son. He was not alone. Sitting in a chair by his side was the Earl of Ornum.

'I thought it better to stay, Inspector, until we know a little more about what's going on,' explained Jonas Cremond. 'Just in case . . .'

The sentence hung in the air, unfinished.

'Thank you, my lord. Much appreciated, I'm sure, since we're so shorthanded today.'

The earl said modestly that he knew he wasn't the man he had once been any more, but he still thought he could hold his own with an intruder. 'Until help came, that is.'

'Quite so,' said Sloan, starting to take in what he saw of the bandaged back of the head of a totally inert patient. Completely shaven heads were nothing new in today's fashion scene, especially male ones that would be grey should hair be allowed to grow again on them, but this one was different. To begin with it was only one half of Jason's head that had been shaved, leaving some curly locks spattered with blood on the uninjured side. This had the effect of reminding everyone how injured the victim was. Sloan was quite surprised at how disconcerting he found this.

So, it seemed, did Constable Crosby.

'Nasty,' he observed from a distance.

It would have been easier, thought Sloan, if he could have thought of the Fixby boy as a lay figure, not as a human one. A tailor's dummy, perhaps, not as Jason Fixby was now, beset by rubber tubes inserted in every available orifice and wired to equipment resembling a smartphone: a very smart phone indeed. This was making intermittent sounds and sending out flashes of green light from time to time apparently all on its own.

Cremond pointed to the machine. 'The nurses come in pretty pronto when it goes off, Inspector, and adjust something or other and then do something to stop the noise although I don't know what it means when it does start bleeping.'

Herbert Fixby, his face grey with anxiety, took his

gaze off the recumbent figure of his son for a moment and said sadly, 'I don't know what anything means any longer. And nobody will tell me anything – at least, anything that I can understand. All I get from the doctors are words that don't mean anything to me. You know what they're like.'

Detective Inspector Sloan, mature adult that he was by now, did know what they were like and interpreted their behaviour as the medical profession not telling Herbert Fixby anything that he didn't want to hear, which was something quite different. 'I'm not sure that we know anything more than you do either at this stage, Mr Fixby,' he said.

'I don't, for starters,' said Crosby with quite unnecessary frankness.

Herbert Fixby, his head shaking a little now and his voice beginning to quaver, said that he'd never thought the day would ever come when he would be glad the boy's poor mother was no longer alive.

'It's a very nasty injury, Mr Fixby,' said Sloan. Something else that he had also learnt by now was that false comfort never did any good to anyone. The last thing he wanted to do was to give the boy's father any cause for optimism. 'I'm afraid someone hit him very hard indeed,' was what he said now. He had already spotted the precautionary cannula dangling from the boy's left wrist, the traditional quick way into a damaged body for doctors in a hurry.

'What I want to know,' said Fixby *père*, 'is if he'll be

all right when he wakes up.'

What Detective Inspector Sloan wanted to know – needed to know – was whether Jason Fixby was going to wake up ever again.

And whether his assailant was even now waiting in the wings to make quite sure that he didn't.

'You mean, sir,' ventured Crosby with an air of one seeking clarification on a minor point of detail, 'when he wakes up, will he be able to tell us who hit him?'

'Yes,' said Jason's father simply. 'And why. I mean who on earth would want to harm Jason anyway?'

Detective Inspector Sloan wanted to know that, too.

And why.

Especially why.

'And at a party of all things, for heaven's sake.' Fixby looked across at the earl. 'Why there? Tell me that, gentlemen.'

Sloan thought he probably could have helped him answer that. A large party at Ornum House that was full of people, old and young, strangers and friends, in an ancient building full of odd corners and corridors that could have been tailor-made for confusion and movement, let alone noise, was as good a place as any for all manner of nefarious activities. This reminded him of something else.

He turned to the Earl of Ornum. 'It did occur to me, my lord, that in the interests of background study, perhaps I should read your book.'

'Really, Inspector?' He sat up, flushed with pleasure.

'If you're sure, I should be very happy to present you with a signed copy. I'm afraid you'll find it very dull.'

Herbert Fixby was following a different line of thought. 'I could have understood nobody recognising anyone else if it had been a masked ball,' he said plaintively, 'but it wasn't.'

'It was a black-tie affair, Inspector,' responded Cremond quietly. 'Not that the young took any notice of that yesterday.'

In his way, Lenny Datchet had been dressed for his part. Had Jason Fixby's attacker been, too? If so, in what? wondered Sloan to himself.

'It wasn't as if Jason had any enemies,' Herbert Fixby was going on, 'even if he did mix with some funny types at the races.'

Crosby started to say that he must have had at least one enemy but at the last minute thought better of it and kept quiet.

'And it wasn't as if he was in any sort of trouble,' went on his father.

'Not into drugs, you mean,' said Crosby, translating this into current speech.

'Mind you,' admitted Herbert, 'I might not have known if he was, his mother being dead, you see.'

This was something Sloan did see. Boys talked to their mothers when they didn't talk to their fathers.

That was the moment when, accompanied by a loud buzzing noise, the green light turned upon an instant to red. A nurse was in the room in seconds, closely followed by a young doctor, her white coat flapping as she hurried in after her.

The others stood back whilst the doctor attended to the machine. She then turned to Herbert Fixby and sounded calm and reassuring, saying that the patient was all right for the time being. 'Just a blip on the machine. Happens all the time. Nothing to worry about.'

Detective Inspector Sloan could only applaud this example of the profession of medicine being its usual marriage of science and compassion.

He was less happy when the Earl of Ornum said to him in a low voice that he couldn't think why whoever had attacked Jason in the first place hadn't come back yet to finish the job.

Neither could Detective Inspector Sloan.

CHAPTER THIRTY-SIX

As a fledgling young constable, still sporting his prickly new uniform, a then inexperienced Sloan used to think that the worst job in policing was being on point duty – all boredom, abuse and varicose veins. They didn't have police officers on point duty any more, leaving the traffic to sort out its own problems and priorities, thus saving trained men for attending the calamitous accidents on motorways that weren't supposed to have them.

And Sloan had never forgotten how glad he had been then to leave lane markings, road junctions and even sometimes broken traffic lights behind and start to climb up the force's career ladder. What he hadn't realised at the time was that more glorified jobs could be worse than standing, white-gloved, at a crossroads.

He knew something else now, too, and that was where his duty lay. Leaving the unmarked side ward in Berebury District General Hospital and being driven by Crosby through the town to a small, terraced house near the canal, he walked straight into an encounter that was worse, much worse, than any traffic job and that was talking to the newly bereaved.

'May we come in, Mrs Datchet?' he asked as the door was opened a crack and a stricken female countenance looked out at them. The ways in which police could legally enter a property took up several pages of their rule book. Crosby, he knew, favoured what was called 'dynamic entry', with a two-handled battering ram capable of carrying all before it. Asking and receiving permission was by far the quickest.

He was aware that someone else – Sergeant Polly Perkins, probably – would have already visited Mrs Datchet and delivered what at the police station they called their 'death speech'.

'You're not from the press, are you?' she asked suspiciously. Her face was tear-stained and almost as blotched as Lenny's had been.

'Police,' said Crosby inevitably.

The woman nodded, opened the door a fraction wider and waved them in. The two policemen followed as she led the way through to her kitchen. A large brown teapot stood on the table beside a half-empty bottle of milk.

She gestured to it. 'Cuppa tea?'

'Please,' said Sloan in the interests of maintaining good relationships and establishing a rapport with the woman.

'I can't eat nothing, myself,' she said. 'Not since they told me that Lenny's gone.' Tears started to well up again in her eyes. 'Not that I'm that hungry any more.'

Detective Inspector Sloan, human being as well as policeman, made what he hoped was a sympathetic noise in his throat and said, 'It's all been very difficult for you, I know.'

Her hands had been lying lightly clasped together but she soon started to twist and untwist them. 'He was only going to a party.'

'I know,' said Sloan.

'Some party,' she said.

'Some chicken, some neck,' quoted Crosby, who had picked up the expression from someone somewhere but couldn't now remember where.

She put her hand on the teapot and asked Crosby if he wanted some tea, too. Crosby, having seen the colour of what came out of the stewed pot, declined with more speed than he should have done.

'I always thought it was that big new bike of his that would kill him, not a party.' She gave a gulp. 'He loved that bike.'

'Saved up for it, did he?' asked Crosby, out of turn.

She shook her head. 'He could never have done that

on what he earned. No, he did a job for someone off the record, he said.'

'Over at Ornum?' asked Sloan.

'No, no, well before then. He wouldn't tell me who for, though. Said it was private.'

'So what was he doing there?'

'It was one of those young girls that asked him. The daughters there. I'd read about them in that flashy magazine that my lady passes on to me.'

'Your lady?'

'I clean for her,' said Mrs Datchet. 'She showed it to me.' She sniffed. 'No better than they ought to be, if you was to ask me.'

'Quite so,' said Sloan diplomatically.

'And I didn't like it when Lenny asked if he could borrow his granddad's pyjamas to take with him.'

'Not his dad's?' asked Crosby involuntarily.

Mrs Datchet favoured Crosby with a long, considering look before she said, 'His dad didn't wear them.'

'What else did he take with him?' intervened Sloan swiftly.

'Just the big holdall his dad used to use before he got ill. Oh, and his best shoes. Lenny didn't think his old ones would do.'

At this further mention of Lenny's name, his mother broke down completely. Her frame racked with sobs, she seemed beyond speech. Detective Inspector Sloan sat beside her in silence whilst Detective Constable Crosby, not exactly the hero of the hour, muttered something about making sure the car was all right and fled.

Detective Inspector Sloan waited until her sobs subsided and then continued with his questioning, asking first who had been in touch with her today.

'That nice Mr Wakefield rung me,' she said, dabbing her eyes. 'And Mrs Harris. Lenny didn't like her. Much too sharp, she was, for his liking. Nothing got past her, he told me.'

Sloan would have dearly liked to know what hadn't got past her. He would have to get out to Capstan Purlieu as soon as he could and find out.

'What about Mr Forres?' he asked. 'Did Lenny like him, too?'

'I think he was all right, although Lenny never said much about him.' She looked at him. 'He's disappeared, Lenny said. Did you know?'

Sloan nodded. 'There was something else I needed to ask you. Did Lenny ever speak you about a young lad called Jason Fixby?'

She paused for thought and then shook her head. 'Not that I remember. There was a crowd of them with motorbikes that went around together, showing them off and upsetting everybody with their noise but I don't remember that name.'

'He had a car,' offered Crosby. 'Jason did.'

'Then I wouldn't have known him,' she said immediately, 'and Lenny wouldn't have neither. Not to speak to, anyways.'

'Right,' agreed Sloan tacitly.

Mrs Datchet dried her eyes and looked at him with a straight face. 'You'll tell me what happened one day, Mr Sloan, won't you?'

'When we know ourselves,' he promised her.

CHAPTER THIRTY-SEVEN

It had been with a genuine concern that Michael Wakefield had watched his wife eat, a concern he hadn't experienced since their children had been babies long ago. Giving up on the burnt saucepan on the stove, he had somehow conjured up some beans on toast ready for their Sunday lunch.

Stephanie had eaten, if not well, then at least adequately. As the effects of the doctor's sedative had started to wear off, so she had slowly begun to thaw out not unlike some melting ice maiden.

'What did the policeman who rang this time want, Mike?' she asked. She was still sitting in the same place at the kitchen table, her movements still mannered, her voice still trembling a little, but she was visibly more awake and aware now.

'To know why on earth someone would want to slash

all the tyres on my car,' he said evenly. He had produced another mug of coffee for each of them and he pushed his wife's one across the table to her now. 'So I told them that I wasn't the only one. That Gilbert Hull, our production manager, had had a brick thrown through his bedroom window last night and he works for the firm, too.'

'And so does Kay Harris,' she said. 'Did you tell them that?'

He shook his head. 'Kay hasn't said anything.'

'And why did Gilbert have a brick thrown through his window, then?'

He shrugged his shoulders. 'I don't really know. Gunning for Forres and Wakefield, I suppose, like everyone else seems to be. But don't ask me why because I don't know.' The loss of four car tyres and a broken window seemed relatively unimportant in the vast scheme of things, especially in a week that had seen him lose his all, but he knew it wasn't, that there would be a reason and that the reason would somehow or other be connected to everything else ghastly that had happened that week. It had been soon apparent that was what the police had thought, too.

'Damaging all four tyres, Mr Wakefield, smacks of something personal,' Detective Inspector Sloan had said, his open notebook splayed unseen across his knees in his office.

'As if you'd gone and upset somebody big time,' his constable had supplemented.

Wakefield had told the police all he knew and now

his wife wanted to know even more. Such as what had they done to deserve everything that had happened since Malcom Forres and his wife had disappeared with all the firm's money.

'I only wish I knew, my dear,' he said wearily. 'But first of all, they need to know why poor Lenny was killed and we don't have any idea at all about that and if you ask me, they don't have either.'

'Perhaps Lenny knew something that we didn't,' she murmured.

'That was one of the things the inspector said that they would be looking into. Not that I can think of anything myself. Even if . . .' He stopped, a new thought coming into his mind.

'Even if?' she asked.

'Even if he'd been in touch with Malcolm Forres.' Wakefield picked up his own coffee cup and took a drink from it although he felt the need for something stronger, much stronger. 'Don't let your coffee get cold, Steph. It'll buck you up a bit.'

She suddenly started to sing, warbling uncertainly, '*Nobody knows the trouble we're in*. But they do know, Mike,' she said, tightening her lips. 'It was all in the paper.'

'Not all of it,' he said. 'Not yet, anyway. Someone clouted Jason Fixby quite badly at Ornum last night, too. The papers don't know that yet.'

'Jason? What's Jason got to do with us?'

'That was something else the police wanted to know,

and for the life of me, I couldn't tell them.'

'I don't know that I can take any more,' she said. 'That was where we were meant to be last night, too, wasn't it? At the party.'

He nodded.

'Don't say, I beg you, that anything so awful can't happen again to us or them.'

A week ago, he would have dismissed her fears with light – even with amused – reassurance but not today. That was then, this was now. Today he said carefully that he didn't know and that nobody seemed to know anything.

'I hope to God that it doesn't but there's no denying that it could. Think back, my dear. Who else knew that Lenny would be at Ornum House last night? Apart from his mother, that is.'

'Are they thinking about mistaken identity, then?'

'Heaven only knows what they're thinking. The police never say. And if you're talking about that constable of theirs, if he's thinking at all.'

'You said that Lenny wasn't such a bad boy,' she said, setting her cup back down on the table with exaggerated care.

'He was no timekeeper, according to Gilbert. He was always bellyaching about him for that.'

'It's not a reason for murder, Mike.'

'No.' He carried the used coffee cups back to the kitchen worktop, pleased that Steph was beginning to come back to life again.

'And would something terrible have happened to us, as well, if we'd been there?'

'That's what the inspector wanted to know. Would we have been in danger, too, if we had been. And that young constable with him,' he growled, 'had the cheek to ask me why we'd been asked to a party at Ornum House in the first place. I told him why and then he wanted to know who else knew that and then he wanted to know who else knew that Lenny would be there, too.'

'Gilbert knew because Lenny boasted about it.'

'But you didn't know that he would be there, did you?'

'I told him that, too. And then he asked about the Fixby boy but I couldn't tell him anything about him being there either because I didn't even know he'd been asked.'

'Questions, questions,' she said, 'and no answers at all.'

'And then he wanted to know the names of everyone who knew we weren't going there after all.'

'And who did?'

He screwed up his face in recollection. 'I said that I had come out of my office and told Gilbert and Kay Harris. She and Gilbert were having a proper stand-off about a comma, or was it a full stop?' He managed a smile. 'And if it hadn't been that it would have been something to do with a semi-colon. That's how they tell at uni if an essay has been bought, not written. Did you know that?'

'That's Kay all over.' Steph essayed her first smile in days. 'At least she wasn't quoting Oscar Wilde and his spending the morning putting a comma in and the afternoon taking it out like she usually does.'

'Then Gilbert reminded me that I had ordered a car to take us to Ornum in style, so that I could have a drink, and so I went in search of our typist and got her to ring the car hire people to cancel the booking.'

She screwed up her eyes the better to concentrate. 'Meg next door knew we were supposed to be going but I don't remember telling her we weren't. It's all a bit of a blur in my mind now.'

He sat by his wife's side in silence for a whilst waiting for her to reach any more unpalatable conclusions on her own. 'So, it's not just us, then, is it, Mike? Not if Lenny and Jason Fixby have been targeted. What about Kay? Has anything happened to her?'

He shook his head. 'As she lives so far out in the sticks, even beyond Capstan Purlieu, it would have been a bit risky for any assailant to drive out there in the middle of the night without being seen on one of those little country lanes to throw a brick through her window. More coffee?'

'Please.'

As he came back carefully carrying a couple of steaming mugs, he found himself standing on the remains of two crushed lemon drizzle cakes still on the kitchen floor.

Never had Thursday seemed such a long time ago.

CHAPTER THIRTY-EIGHT

The car park at Ornum House was much emptier now than it had been when the police had first arrived that morning – a time that Detective Inspector Sloan was beginning to think was what Crosby would have called 'forever ago'. In the space in the car park that had then been occupied by the Ford Ka with the broken rear light, owned by Mrs Bennett of Ornum village, was presently parked the van of 'F' Division of the Berebury Police Force's forensic team, presently extracting every last drop of useful detail in the library.

Sloan knew without being told that the car in the farthest corner of the car park, now covered all over with waterproof sheeting and festooned with police black and yellow evidence tape, would be that belonging to Jason Fixby. And no doubt somewhere out of sight beyond the car park would be a motorcycle owned by Lenny Datchet, similarly shrouded and awaiting collection for further examination by specialists.

He was at a loss to know what evidence they could provide but finding even that much out would have to wait for later, things being what they were.

There was much to be done before then and as far as Sloan was concerned there was no one on the force's strength available to help with doing it. Not until the demands of a foreign tanker in the sea lane outside Kinnisport were resolved. There had once been a Dutch admiral who had made it too far up the Thames for England's comfort but that had been a long time ago.

The two policemen were immediately welcomed by the countess. 'Come along in, both of you, and tell us how Jason, poor boy, is doing.'

'I'm sorry to say, Your Ladyship, that he's only just holding his own,' reported Sloan. 'His father is with him but he's not talking yet.' He was conscious that his use of the word 'yet' displayed quite unwarranted optimism. Whether Jason Fixby would ever talk sensibly again was open to question.

'No more than that, Inspector?' The assistant chief constable was sitting with the Countess of Ornum at the worn kitchen table at Ornum House, two empty coffee cups now pushed to one side. Of the Ladies Victoria and Mary there was nothing to be seen.

'I'm afraid not, sir.'

'Sit down and tell us exactly what the doctors say,' said the ACC.

'Very little, sir.'

'Always a bad sign,' commented the ACC.

'Except, sir, they do confirm that the patient had clearly received a very heavy blow to the back of his head.' Detective Inspector Sloan, aware of his obligations as a sworn police officer, was nevertheless also aware that the assistant chief constable was thus giving him tacit permission to talk police business in front of the countess. He didn't know whether this came under the umbrella of noblesse oblige or not. He knew it meant, though, that they weren't to be considered suspects. Who could be considered suspects was something he would dearly like to know: there weren't many possible ones in view at this particular moment.

'I suppose,' said the countess, lifting her head from the piece of paper on the table before her that she had been studying, 'that only means, Inspector, that you won't be looking for a woman in connection with the attack on Jason.'

'Don't you believe it, Letitia.' The ACC was shaking his head. 'It doesn't follow these days, my dear, and you'd know it for sure if you'd ever played mixed hockey. Hero's hockey, we used to call it.' He turned to the inspector. 'So, Sloan, where do matters stand now?'

'I had a message from our scenes of crime people, sir,' said Sloan, who had never played any game that involved holding an implement, let alone with women, 'to the effect that they thought they'd found a weapon in connection to the attack on Jason Fixby.'

'You could call it a very close connection indeed,' muttered Crosby, who in the absence of the twins appeared to have recovered some of his *amour-propre*. 'Seeing as he was hit with it.'

'So, sir,' said Sloan hastily, 'we came back to look into it.'

'Look at it, I hope,' murmured Crosby under his breath, not used to standing silently by and beginning to show signs of boredom.

Mercifully, the ACC carried on without giving any sign of having heard the constable speak. 'Sounds promising,' he said, also being a policeman and thus with his mind firmly fixed on what mattered. 'Go on, Inspector.'

'Scenes of crime are primarily searching the library where it is presumed the attack took place. In the first instance, that is.'

'Beginning at the beginning,' said the ACC approvingly. 'Quite right, too.'

'That's why we had to have our coffee after lunch here in the kitchen,' explained the countess, waving her hand in the direction of the used coffee cups beside them. 'We usually have it in the library, but we weren't allowed in there today by your people.'

Sloan said, 'We already knew that Jason had been hit very hard indeed last night with something fairly heavy – the doctors told us that – but we didn't know what it was to start with.'

'The weapon,' amplified Crosby, sotto voce.

'And you do now?' asked the countess.

'We do, milady. A poker. We're on our way back there now.'

The countess winced. 'That would have given anyone a nasty crack on the head.'

'Found still in the fireplace there among the fire dogs and the logs.' In Sloan's domestic circle, the collection of fireside implements standing in a hearth was known as a companion set. He didn't suppose they were in Ornum House. There they were twice the usual size of such things and were gun-metal grey. And so were the fireplace in which they stood and its fender.

'The proverbial blunt instrument hidden in plain sight,' observed the ACC. 'What about fingerprints?'

'I'm afraid not, sir, although the suspected item has now been taken away for forensic examination,' said Sloan, taking refuge in police speak.

The ACC stirred. 'Talking of which, I'm afraid, Inspector, that the news from Kinnisport can only be called unhelpful. I'm advised that you're going to be very shorthanded for quite a whilst still.'

'Sir?'

'The tanker crew can't speak English and so the harbourmaster doesn't know what they're asking for. He isn't prepared to let the crew ashore and they're quite prepared to wait in the harbour until he does.'

'A stand-off,' muttered Crosby gleefully to himself, wishing he was there.

'I thought English was the language of the sea, sir,'

hurried on Sloan. 'Like in the air.'

'I understand that only the captain and the first mate speak it,' said the ACC. 'And I am also told that they have both been clapped in irons and are now somewhere in the bowels of the ship.'

'The scuppers,' said Crosby, dangerously audible now.

'Thank you, Constable,' said the ACC frostily. 'I am quite aware of what you do with drunken sailors.'

Detective Inspector Sloan rushed into speech once more. 'So, sir, we've gone back to examining the question of motive.'

'In both cases?'

'Yes, sir.' He thought he heard Crosby whisper, 'And how,' but wasn't quite sure.

'Are there any connections between the two assaults? The victims don't seem to have a great deal in common.'

'None that we have been able to establish so far, sir, but we're working on it.'

'Who benefits?' asked the ACC, nobody's fool.

If Detective Inspector Sloan had been asked the same question among friends in the police canteen, he would have said, 'Search me.' Here and now he simply said that he didn't know yet, sir, but he would be finding out as soon as he could.

The ACC stroked his chin. 'I know I'm a bit out of touch with the young these days, Inspector . . .'

'Who isn't?' said the countess.

'But I suppose as far as the boy in the library is

concerned, there can't be any question of another suitor having a go at him, can there? I understand that he is quite fixated on Victoria, and it is no accident that he was known as Sheep's Eyes by the twins because of his devotion to her. Juvenile passions can run very high, you know.'

Detective Inspector Sloan, himself a seasoned husband and father now, did know. His mind went straight back to the days of his own callow youth, memories of calf love flooding painfully back. He didn't need to try too hard to remember the strength of feeling engendered in his circle then by one pert young lady or another in those confused days of adolescence.

He had never forgotten how jealous he had felt when one of his own mates had tried to chat up his squeeze of the hour – Jane, was it? Or had it been the busty Penelope? Or even for a whilst Marcella of the wide blue eyes? And all the time the Margaret whom he was one day to marry had stayed quietly on the far fringes of their group. There and not there, waiting until he'd grown up.

'Girls can be heartless creatures,' the ACC was saying. 'But not heartless enough to commit murder, surely.'

'That's the trouble, sir,' said Sloan. 'We lack motives for murder in both cases. All we can assume so far is that the first attack was planned, cheese-cutters not being in your pocket every day, and the second by someone taken by surprise.' This was something else Sloan had already been thinking about. 'I've seen the poker.'

'And he can't have hit himself on the head with it,' pointed out Detective Constable Crosby under his breath.

'I know it's not relevant,' said the countess, shuffling the lists in front of her, 'but although Vicky is smitten with Roderick, he certainly isn't in love with her.'

'Really?' said the ACC with interest. 'How do you know that, Letitia?'

'I'm her mother,' said the countess, whose daughters would have been surprised at her insight. 'And I noticed that Roderick spent a great deal of the evening with the bishop's daughter. Not with Vicky. She didn't like that. The young do get so worked up about such things,' she added, still studying the list in front of her. 'They grow out of it in the end.'

She turned to Sloan. 'I don't see anyone on these invitation lists, Inspector, likely to have done murder.'

The two senior policemen there said almost in concert that you never knew, whilst Sloan sighed as it was borne in on him that he would have to interview Lady Victoria yet again and soon. He asked her mother where he could find her.

'The twins have taken Toby outside and are showing him round the park,' she said.

Sloan hoped that he had imagined it, but he thought – he could have sworn – he had caught sight of Crosby drawing his finger across his throat in an unmistakable gesture known the world over.

He hurried into speech. 'It's the question of motive that's worrying me most, sir,' he said to the ACC. 'Granted that Lenny Datchet was almost certainly on a burglary spree, but he wouldn't have been killed for that. As for Jason Fixby, we have no idea why he should have been a victim of anything other than his unrequited love for the Lady Victoria.' He started to rise to his feet.

'Where to next?' asked the ACC, although Sloan wouldn't have been too surprised if he had said, '*Quo vadis*?'

'There's just one more loose end to tie up,' said Sloan, 'and then I think we can call it a day. It's been a long one.'

CHAPTER THIRTY-NINE

'Must we, sir?' said Crosby, sighing heavily. 'Same old, same old.'

'We must,' said Sloan. He didn't want to work any longer today either, but he knew that before going home he would have to report to Superintendent Leeyes on how the day had gone. And perhaps find out for himself how matters stood at Kinnisport and thus whether he could count on more effective assistance than was forthcoming from Detective Constable Crosby the next day. He said nearly as much to the constable, adding piously, 'And remember, Crosby, the superintendent will want to know everything he can.'

Crosby slid into the driving seat of the unmarked police car standing outside Ornum House, slamming the door behind him with quite unnecessary vigour. Barely waiting for Sloan to fasten his seat belt, he set off with a handbrake turn and a noisy flourish of skidding tyres. 'Back to Berebury, I think you said, sir,' he said.

'In one piece, if you don't mind.' Sloan fished the address he had been given by Michael Wakefield out of his pocket and spelt it out. 'It's a semi-detached house in Quay Street, near the river. I've got the number here.'

The two policemen drove back from Ornum to Berebury in a loaded silence.

There was no need for dynamic entry when they got to Gilbert Hull's home. Not only was the front door already open but as they approached the house two young women came out, both clutching large bundles of clothes in their arms.

'Sorry,' called out the leading one, hurrying on, 'but we can't stop. We're off to the dress rehearsal at the theatre and the stage manager'll kill us if we're late. We can't keep the cast waiting either.' She looked back over her shoulder. 'Dad's just coming if it's him you want.'

They were followed almost immediately by Gilbert Hull himself. He was staggering along behind the two women, carrying a great pile of hat boxes, each one perched insecurely above the next. As he saw the two policemen, the man almost lost his footing, the top three boxes then cascading down onto the garden path. One of boxes burst open and a grey top hat tumbled out.

'Do be careful, Daddy,' called out the leading

woman. 'These clothes have all got to go back to the costumier's after the play. We won't be back here now until next Sunday, remember, but you and Mum had better be in the audience on Saturday night or else.' She helped her father scoop up the escaped topper and then the two women hurried on their way as Sloan and Crosby advanced towards Hull, now relieved of his burden of hat boxes.

It was as he walked up the path towards the house and the man standing in front of it that Detective Inspector Sloan had what he was for ever afterwards to think of as his domino moment. He stood stock still by the bottom step of the little flight leading up to the front door for a long moment, considering the enormity of the thought that he had just had.

'We've come to talk to you about Lenny Datchet's death, Mr Hull,' announced Sloan briskly, regaining his senses.

'Then you'd better come in, Inspector,' said Hull.

'But among other things, we've also heard you had a brick thrown through your window last night.'

'Been talking to my guv'nor, have you?' Hull said, leading the way into his front room. Pushing empty boxes and a lot of tissue paper out of the way, he indicated a couple of chairs.

'And been talking to your guv'nor's wife, as well,' lied Sloan, visualising another domino as he spoke – this one being nudged by the first. Or was it the other way round?

'She's not been her usual self lately, hasn't Steph, I'm afraid.' Hull waved a hand round the disordered room. 'Sorry about the muddle in here but my wife's away at her mother's.'

'Quite so.' Sloan nodded. Life wasn't the same in the Sloan household either when his wife, Margaret, was away. Sardines was a good enough game for a children's party but no substitute – even on toast – for meat and two vegetables for dinner.

Hull was still looking round the room. 'My wife'll have this straight again in no time.'

'I'm sure,' said Sloan. 'No, your guv'nor's wife's convinced that the lady who works with you – the one who was there the other day when Mrs Wakefield cut up rough like she did . . .'

'Our Mrs Harris?'

'That's the one. She's convinced Mrs Harris knows something we don't about Lenny's death, and we wondered if you had any idea what it could have been.'

'And do you?' supplemented Crosby, keen to hurry matters along and get home.

The production manager shook his head.

'Mind you,' said Sloan largely, 'I can see Mrs Wakefield isn't quite back to normal yet.'

'So the guv'nor told me,' murmured Hull, sinking his head between his hands. 'God, whatever's going on with the firm? Lenny killed and that boy from the accountants' bashed and Malcolm Forres nowhere to be seen.' He raised his head and said to Sloan, 'And where do slashed tyres and a brick through a window come in, for heaven's sake? Tell me that, Inspector.'

'I couldn't say, sir. Mrs Harris might have had some damage too, since she's a member of the firm, but that'll have to wait until tomorrow now,' said Sloane mendaciously.

'We're on our way back to the police station, you see,' said Crosby, the wish being father to the thought.

'But not until we've seen your damage, for the record,' said Sloan. 'Then we'll be gone.'

'The brick's still upstairs.' Hull led the way to the front bedroom on the first floor, opening a door to reveal a smashed window and shards of glass spattered all over the carpet. 'It was lucky I'd left my bedroom slippers beside the bed, or I'd have cut my feet when I got up.'

'Very lucky,' agreed Sloan, instructing Crosby to test the brick for fingerprints. 'I take it that you've checked that there was no note wrapped round the brick when you found it on the floor?'

'You mean a message?' Hull shook his head. 'Not that I've seen, Inspector. Not that I've even looked,' he admitted. 'Perhaps I should have done but I was only half awake when it happened.'

'And you've left everything as it was, like you should,' said Crosby, peering across the room. 'Good boy.'

Detective Inspector Sloan swallowed hard and with a considerable effort said nothing. It was all very well being made to act as an exemplar to Crosby, but it wasn't an easy role to play especially when you never knew what he was going to say next. Rebuking the constable would have to wait until they were in the privacy of the police car. Middle-aged men were not meant to be called good boys by junior police officers.

Hull hadn't appeared to have noticed the verbal lapse on Crosby's part. He was concentrating on what he feared the police would think of as a lapse on his own part. 'I'm afraid,' he said, looking sheepish, 'that I've left all the clearing up to my wife. As I said she's due back tomorrow and she'll see to it all right. I just shut the door and slept in the spare room.'

'Good thinking,' Sloan said hastily before Crosby could applaud this behaviour too. 'No other message for you anywhere else?' There had been no message on Michael Wakefield's car either, but it hadn't needed one: the inference was clear enough. Someone somewhere was gunning for Wakefield. That someone was also gunning for Hull would seem to be clear enough now, too.

And in view of the death of their apprentice Lenny Datchet, perhaps it was the whole firm of Forres and Wakefield that was a target.

Although, Sloan reminded himself, Jason Fixby wasn't a member of it and he, too, had come to grief last night. He would like to have time to think about this.

And the domino effect.

'Not that I've seen one anywhere myself although you could say that a brick through your window was a clear enough one.'

'Quite so,' said Sloan again.

'There was nothing else anywhere that I could see, Inspector. Mind you, I was more than half asleep at the time and didn't think to look that closely when I woke up – was woken up – that is.'

'Someone, somewhere, doesn't like you, sir,' pronounced Crosby.

'Nobody ever likes a production manager,' Hull said grimly. 'You could say it goes with the territory.'

Sloan told Crosby to get on and check the brick for fingerprints, taking care where he trod.

'It's not natural not to have picked it up,' muttered that worthy almost under his breath, 'and swept up the glass, let alone not bring it downstairs.'

'If Mr Wakefield sent you here to me' – Hull almost visibly worked this out – 'then you'll know about his slashed tyres, too, Inspector, won't you?'

'We regard it as important, sir, that actions seemingly taken in malice don't succeed.' This wasn't so much police dogma as something laid down by Sloan's church-going mother, but he didn't enlighten the man on the point. 'Besides, I understand you are aware there have been other developments.'

'Unwelcome ones,' added Crosby.

Hull's face cleared. 'I'm sorry, I understand your concern about the brick now, Inspector. I should have realised that myself. All I could think of when the guv'nor told me about his tyres was how thankful I was that I'd put my own car in the garage.'

'And about Lenny Datchet,' said Sloan heavily. 'Your apprentice.'

'Too young to die,' interposed Crosby. 'A bit younger than me, he was.'

'His mother let me know, poor woman,' said Hull, nodding. 'Lenny was all right up to a point, Inspector, if that's what you want to know. In fact, he was no different from any other apprentice of his age. The only thing he really cared about was that big motorbike of his and careering around the countryside on it, certainly not his work. It's a wonder that he wasn't killed on that machine and not at Ornum House.'

'They go to their heads, do fast bikes,' opined Crosby censoriously. He would have liked to own one himself but couldn't afford to on a constable's pay.

Detective Inspector Sloan, policeman first, last and all the time, soon got back to business – police business. 'What I would very much like to know, Mr Hull, was how Lenny came to be at the party at Ornum House in the first place.'

'Not his usual social circle, I should say.' Crosby sniffed. 'More than a bit above his pay grade, that lot.'

The man grimaced. 'Believe it or not, he'd been invited to the launch party there. He was quite cocky about it, too.'

'He'd only told you he'd been invited, you mean,'

put in Crosby, taught never to take anything at its face value. 'You didn't get to prove it, I suppose?'

'It wasn't like that, gentlemen.' Gilbert Hull shook his head. 'No, he really had been. He told me so himself and that it was one of those terrible twins who had asked him to the party.'

'Luring him to his doom, was she?' asked Crosby, only just beginning to explore the wilder side of some popular fiction.

'In the event, it would seem so,' said Hull neatly. 'Apparently he'd made a great impression on the two of them when he delivered their father's book out to Ornum. At least,' he qualified this, 'that's what he told me.'

'And your guv'nor? He'd been going to go there in place of the publisher of the earl's book, I'm told.'

Another domino appeared in Sloan's mind alongside the last one, this one at an angle ready to knock its neighbour down.

'Him, too,' agreed Hull. 'But he'd called off attending on account of his wife not wanting to go after . . .' He paused and then diplomatically qualified this by saying, 'He told me that there have been what you might call some problems on the home front.'

'So we have been given to understand,' said Sloan. 'And you, Mr Hull, what do you yourself understand about what's going on?'

'I'm afraid I understand very little. Why anyone should want to kill our Lenny beats me. At least' – he gave a weak smile – 'unless it's the earl, because Lenny was having it off with one of his daughters. And that's not very likely in this day and age, times being what they are now.'

'But didn't all earls used to do that sort of thing once upon a time?' asked Crosby naively. 'I thought they had ancient rights over their tenants or something.'

'I think, Constable, that you may have something called *droit du seigneur* in mind,' said Hull. 'That used to crop up in some of the older books we published for the last Duke of Calleshire but two. You had to watch him.'

'So what's that, then?' asked Crosby, whose historical knowledge was sketchy and his French non-existent.

'Crosby,' intervened Sloan swiftly, unwilling to spell out exactly what these ancient rights amounted to, 'I can assure you that life was very different then.' Anxious as he was not to have to explain to his constable at just this moment the particular ancient custom practised by the landowner on his tenantry, he hurried on, 'But, Mr Hull, you need to know that the earl isn't at the top of our list of suspects for the murder of your apprentice.'

'Not in the frame,' amplified Crosby.

'Definitely not. Now, sir,' Sloan said speedily, turning back to Hull, 'tell me about Jason Fixby. What do you know about him?'

'Not a lot, Inspector. He used to come to the works

a couple of times a year as bag-carrier for his father as the old boy got a bit behind with things, but we never saw a lot of him.'

'Would he have known Lenny Datchet?'

'I shouldn't imagine so. Not outside of work, anyway, and not even there. Lenny's only connection with racing was going too fast on his bike and it's general knowledge in the town that Jason's interests are with the horses.'

'Perhaps, then,' suggested Sloan, 'you would like to tell me a little bit about Malcolm Forres.'

It soon became apparent that Gilbert Hull did not like to do any such thing. That partner, he responded, had very little to do with the actual printing side of the business, leaving it all to Mike Wakefield whilst Malcolm Forres saw to the paperwork and the money side of things.

'Not that he didn't understand printing, mind you, Inspector,' said Hull. 'It was just that he wasn't as interested in it as Mike is.'

And no, he had no idea where Forres was now. There had been no messages from him that he, Gilbert Hull, was aware of and yes, there were indeed a lot of rumours flying around at the works, but he couldn't answer to any of them. Mr Wakefield would be the one for the police to speak to about that.

Not him.

Detective Inspector Sloan and Detective Constable Crosby took their leave, only pausing as they did so to look at the broken bedroom window from the front garden.

What neither Gilbert Hull nor Detective Constable Crosby saw was the growing row of dominos in Sloan's mind, each leaning just a little bit further over than the one before.

CHAPTER FORTY

'You did what yesterday, Sloan?' spluttered Superintendent Leeyes. He was never at his best first thing on a Monday morning.

'Hid down the road from Hull's house, and then followed his car when he left there shortly after we'd left him,' said Sloan.

'Followed him to where?'

'The home of Mrs Kay Harris.'

'Who's she?'

'The firm of Forres and Wakefield's grammatical guru. We got there just in time, thanks to a bit of nifty driving on Crosby's part.'

'In time for what?'

'To stop Hull attacking her. He told her he'd just driven over to see if she'd had a brick thrown through her window too, or her tyres slashed like Wakefield had, but she hadn't.' Sloan drew breath. 'I'm afraid, sir, that I had deliberately misled Hull to believe that she knew what was going on.'

'She's not the only one who doesn't know what's going on,' said Leeyes irritably. 'What exactly is it that you're trying to tell me?'

'That everything suddenly fell into place in my mind, sir. Each domino knocks the one next to it down a little bit further, you see. It's the first domino falling against its neighbour that sets them all off, of course.'

'I do know about the domino effect, thank you, Sloan, but I still don't know what it is you're talking about.'

'It's what I saw when I was at Hull's house. It reminded me of something the ACC had said that suddenly made everything clear to me and set the dominos off, one knocking the next one down.'

'It may very well have made everything clear to you, but I must say that what you're talking about now doesn't mean anything at all to me.'

'The ACC asked me what the murderer would have been wearing. I didn't think much about it at the time, but it turned out that it was what really mattered.'

'I take it this man Hull wasn't disguised in pyjamas, too?'

'No, sir. He was wearing a black tie.'

'Some disguise,' pronounced Leeyes disparagingly. 'A black tie.'

Sloan hurried into speech. 'A very good one, sir, as

it happens, since all the other older adult male guests were wearing them and what went with them, too.'

'You mean the grown-up adults, I take it,' interposed Leeyes, no fan of young males of any age.

'Yes, sir. It was very effective, as it happens. It was only when I saw where he'd got his rig-out from that the penny dropped.'

'And where was that, might I ask?'

'The costumes for his daughter's amateur dramatic society's play. One of Oscar Wilde's period pieces. She's the wardrobe mistress for it. As it happens, the countess had spotted that one of the guests was wearing rather an old-fashioned bit of neck gear but there was no reason why she should have made the connection and I'm afraid I didn't make it either at the time.'

Sloan couldn't quite decide if he was watching the superintendent's fingers drumming on his desk or was only imagining the movement.

Leeyes said, 'So you're telling me that the man Hull went to the party with the settled intention of killing someone?'

'Not someone, sir. Just Lenny Datchet. He didn't realise at the time that he'd have to try to kill Jason Fixby as well.'

'Go on.'

'Yes, sir. He knew that Lenny would be there, and that Michael Wakefield wouldn't be so that no one else there would know him, he not normally moving in those highfalutin circles. The Ornum parents couldn't possibly have known everyone since their daughters had been inviting all and sundry to the party.'

'So Hull went wearing a black tie like everyone else. But why did he want to kill Lenny Datchet?'

'Because he knew too much, that's why,' said Sloan succinctly.

Leeyes sounded quite plaintive for him. 'Do you think you could possibly begin at the beginning, Sloan?'

'There are two beginnings, sir.'

'One of them will do,' rasped Leeyes.

Detective Inspector Sloan paused to marshal his thoughts. 'It all started with Hull's daughter, sir.'

'More dominos, I suppose,' asked Leeyes acidly, 'or just fancy clothes?'

'Neither, sir. She's a real enthusiast for whatever she does. Before she took up with amateur dramatics, his daughter was well and truly into researching family history.'

'Never a wise thing to do if you ask me, but all the same, it doesn't usually lead to murder.'

'If we'd known about that in the beginning, sir, we'd have known where to look later.'

'Keep going.'

'Hull's daughter quite innocently researched her own family history, which they all do first, and then in the way of enthusiasts went on to look up that of other people whom she knew.'

'Found something nasty in that man Wakefield's woodshed, did she?'

'No, not in Wakefield's.'

'His partner, then? The one who's taken off with all the funds?'

'Not Forres exactly but in his wife's.'

'Tell me.'

'Christine Forres had changed her name before she married Malcolm Forres.'

'Not illegal.'

'Before then she'd been called something quite different and very well-known indeed. Naturally, she didn't want anyone to know what it was.'

'What was natural about that?'

'It was a notorious one. She'd been in prison for killing two small children whilst she was babysitting them.'

The superintendent, a long-serving police officer, whistled gently at hearing the name. 'Her?'

'Her,' agreed Sloan.

'How come she was living in our patch without my being told?' Leeyes demanded, territorial to the last.

'Do you think, sir, it might be something to do with the rehabilitation of the offender?' offered Sloan, conscious that he might be on shaky ground with his superior officer. 'Having a new name and starting a new life and all that?'

'And did her husband know, do you suppose?' said Leeyes, for a moment not railing about the rehabilitation of the offender regulations as was his usual wont.

'If he didn't then Hull must have told him, because

Hull had been blackmailing Forres for years to keep it quiet. In my report, sir, you'll see that the new accountant at Fixby's had picked up that a little bit of money had been going walkabout every year for a long time.'

'But not a lot?'

'That's what was so interesting.'

'That's one way of looking at it, I suppose,' grumbled Leeyes. 'Explain yourself, man.'

'For starters, blackmailers don't usually bleed people to death,' said Sloan, 'but Hull had another agenda altogether. It looked at first as if everything was going to go on in the same low-key fashion until it suited Hull, and then two things happened.'

'And what might they have been?'

'Lenny Datchet spotted that something was going on that shouldn't have been and had to be placated with a new bike and was getting more demanding.'

'The price of silence is usually high.' Leeyes nodded.

'And Michael Wakefield started to talk about retirement.'

'He is getting on a bit,' said Leeyes patronisingly.

'That upset Hull's long-term plans.'

'Which were?'

'To have the firm put into the hands of the official receiver and then buy it back at a knockdown price with the stolen money. Don't forget he had the whip hand as far as Malcolm Forres was concerned.'

'I said to follow the money,' declared Leeyes

complacently. 'If you hear hoof beats, think horses, not unicorns.'

Detective Inspective Sloan rose to his feet and said, 'But Kate Booth will be able to explain it much better than I can, sir. I'll send her report round for you as soon as I can.'

'And the attack on Jason Fixby?' Leeyes reminded him. 'Or have you run out of dominos?'

'A bit of bad luck all round. It turned out that there was someone else there who recognised Hull after all.'

'Tough,' observed Leeyes, waving him away.

Detective Constable Crosby was waiting for Sloan when he came out of the superintendent's office. 'Where to now, sir? Newhaven?' he added hopefully. He liked long journeys.

'I'm afraid not, Crosby. We can't prove anything yet, but we think that the Forres pair caught a ferry there the other night. All the same, we've got search warrants for their house at Peverton and Hull's home to be enacted when we've got officers around again.'

'Hull had Forres by the short and curlies, didn't he, sir?'

'He did indeed, Crosby. I doubt if the pair of them will ever come back to England now. I reckon that rather than be charged with complicity to embezzlement they'll be like the *Flying Dutchman* and spend the rest of their lives without safe harbour.' Sloan had another thought. 'And without a lot of money either.'

'Tough,' said Detective Constable Crosby.

CHAPTER FORTY-ONE

'One of the cleverest pieces of chicanery I've ever come across,' declared Kate Booth, as she regarded the two policemen across her desk at Fixby and Fixby's offices that morning, as bright-eyed and bushy-tailed as ever.

'Like in motor racing, you mean, miss?' asked Detective Constable Crosby, clearly puzzled. 'Chicanes can make the track very difficult.'

'No, Constable, that's something quite different,' the young accountant said kindly, 'and I daresay you haven't come across the word before.'

Detective Inspector Sloan wasn't sure he had either so remained silent.

'It means to use deception as a way of getting what you want.' Kate spelt out a definition for their benefit.

'Like a doctor saying it won't hurt so that you keep still and then it does, you mean?' suggested Crosby, who hadn't forgotten his childhood immunisations. Or, for that matter, forgiven the perpetrators, either.

'You could put it like that, Constable,' said the woman, keeping a straight face. 'Even the clear intention to deceive might be an offence. I wouldn't know that for sure.'

Detective Inspector Sloan, feeling himself to be in uncharted financial waters, did not respond to the implied query. He studied the ceiling instead.

Kate Booth straightened out the papers on her desk and carried on. 'To make a business bankrupt by theft purely in order to bring about a fire sale was clever enough, but to plan to use the money stolen from it to go towards buying it back at a knockdown price takes some doing. I don't think anyone's ever thought of that one before.'

'They will now,' forecast Crosby.

'And also to leave Malcolm Forres temporarily out of the picture,' went on Kate, 'is pretty good going, too. In theory he could have come back and carried on when the dust had settled and the stolen money in full view.'

'How come?' asked Crosby.

'I think' – Sloan nodded – 'that he'll be now saying he knows nothing about any robbery. He and his wife will be saying that she saw that her mother was fit to leave – false alarm and all that – and that they went off to France for a bit of a break. They'll say they knew nothing about anything as they were so out of touch without his mobile.'

'He forgot his phone, didn't he?' said Kate.

'Sort of,' said Crosby.

Sloan had already told her that Jason Fixby had come round briefly before falling into a deep sleep without saying anything. Herbert, his father, was still by his bed but was now sound asleep in his chair. The Earl of Ornum was insisting on staying in the room until Jason was able to tell them what had happened, not even a formidable ward sister being able to persuade him otherwise.

'We reckon, miss, that all Jason had done to get himself clobbered was to recognise Gilbert Hull, black-tie rig-out notwithstanding,' said Sloan.

Crosby leant forward and put his oar in. 'He couldn't have known anything then about Lenny Datchet being killed, you see, but he did know Hull.' The production manager was a common criminal in Crosby's eyes now and as such had already lost his Christian name.

'We knew that the money for Datchet's motorcycle had come from someone else, but we didn't know who at the time,' said Sloan, a certain guilt already creeping into his thinking. 'We certainly didn't know why.'

'The price of silence,' deduced Kate Booth.

'The temporary price of silence,' insisted Sloan. 'It wouldn't have lasted. It never does.'

'A dangerous game, Inspector, blackmail,' said the woman, still lost in wonder at the complexity of the crime.

'Indeed, miss,' said Sloan.

'And they were playing an even more risky one with wrecking the business and hoping to buy it back at a knockdown price.' She picked up a sheet of paper. 'It wouldn't have been worth much on paper, anyway, after all the shenanigans that had been going on – not with their class of clients.'

CHAPTER FORTY-TWO

'Kay! What on earth brings you here so early?' exclaimed Michael Wakefield, who had opened his front door to find Kay Harris standing on the doorstep of the Old Rectory at Little Missal well before breakfast time.

'In a word, Michael, since you ask, "perfidy".'

'You'd better come in and explain,' he said, opening the door wider to let her in. He then stood at the foot of the stairs and called out to Steph that they had a visitor. 'We've been told about Gilbert, Kay, but the police haven't really explained anything except to say that Jason Fixby is still holding his own and that Lady Victoria has promised to visit him when he comes round properly.'

'Long may his recovery continue,' said Kay fervently, looking up as Steph came into the kitchen.

The Stephanie Wakefield who had come down the

stairs that morning bore no relation to the mental wreck of the previous days. She was a woman restored.

Kay sat herself down at the kitchen table and recounted the events of the previous evening. 'Apparently the police inspector had let slip to Gilbert – only he hadn't let it slip; he'd done it on purpose – that I knew something about what had been going at the firm.'

'Steph was sure you did,' put in Mike.

'But he wouldn't believe me,' said his wife.

'And I did know something,' Kay said calmly. 'The only thing was I didn't know who it was who was up to no good. From where I stood it could have been any of you.'

'Could it, indeed?' said Wakefield drily. 'And?'

'And so the police followed Gilbert out to my house. Just as well, as it happened.'

'What happened?'

'It was more of a case of what didn't happen but might have done.'

'Go on.'

'First of all, Gilbert tried to say that he'd only come out my way to check that I hadn't had my tyres slashed or a brick through my window like you and himself.'

'Which you said you hadn't.'

'Which I said I hadn't.'

'Then?' he asked.

'Then I noticed that he'd brought a pair of those thick gardening gloves with him.'

'You need them for pruning roses,' Mike said.

'That's just what the police inspector said, but only if you're a gardener, which I'm not, and which I knew Gilbert wasn't either. Good enough, though, to threaten to strangle someone with without leaving any fingerprints or that stuff that says who you are anywhere on anything.'

'DNA,' supplied Wakefield.

'DNA either if they didn't promise to keep quiet about what they'd found.'

'He didn't . . .'

'He didn't even try because that young constable burst in before he could so much as lift a finger against me, let alone leave DNA or a fingerprint.'

'Gilbert? Are you quite sure about all this, Kay?'

'Quite sure,' said Kay.

'Steph couldn't believe it when I told her what the police had said.'

'I wasn't as sure as that police inspector was. He arrested Gilbert on the spot for the murder of Leonard Datchet and the attempted murder of Jason Fixby, saying something I didn't quite grasp about the domino effect and not needing to go back to the boneyard for more tiles any more, whatever that might mean.'

'But why Gilbert, of all people?' Wakefield looked stunned. 'I know about playing the game of dominos all right, but I couldn't work out what on earth he had to gain by killing Lenny.'

'The entire business,' replied Kay seriously. 'That's

what Gilbert was after all along.'

'And how was killing Lenny going to bring that about, might I ask?'

'Datchet must have found something out that let him get his motorbike out of Hull. I don't know what but the police'll find out soon enough. That meant the lad had to be silenced or their whole plan would come to nothing.'

'Whose whole plan and what was the plan anyway?'

'Can't you see, Mike? It was Hull and Forres all along who were in cahoots to take control of the firm.'

He shook his head. 'No, I can't see that.'

Kay said, 'I'm sure that what had been planned was that Malcolm took all the money – everything, in fact – out of the business, hid it up somewhere that Gilbert could get his hands on it and then high-tailed it to France with Christine, leaving everyone to think they were the guilty ones.'

Stephanie shuddered. 'It doesn't bear thinking of.'

'They had to do it more quickly than they'd bargained for because of that bright new young accountant girl finding that money had been going out that shouldn't have been for quite a while.'

'I agree she must have spotted that everything wasn't hunky-dory quite early on,' admitted Wakefield.

'An informal way of putting it,' said their English specialist, 'but no matter.'

'I reckoned something was wrong, too,' said Stephanie, now busying herself with a coffeepot. 'The trouble was I didn't know what.'

'With me so far, Mike?' asked Kay.

Wakefield looked from one woman to the other and nodded silently.

Kay said, 'Malcolm stashes the money and papers away somewhere safe where Gilbert can get his hands on them and then removes himself and the notorious Christine from the scene – you never knew his wife's history or who she really was, did you?'

Wakefield shook his head. 'Not then.'

'Malcolm's obviously aware that he will be suspected of the robbery but he's not going to be available for questioning and can't have known about the murder. The business goes into liquidation and you with it, and Gilbert uses the money to buy the Forres and Wakefield business at a rock-bottom price after you've gone bankrupt and are out of the picture. With me so far?'

He nodded his head again.

'When Gilbert learns that neither you nor Les Moran will be at the party at Ornum House but that Lenny will be there, he sees this as the ideal venue for a murder that no one has any reason to connect with him. He thinks that no one there will know him except Datchet, who will be dead. It was sheer bad luck on his part that Jason Fixby had been invited there, too, and recognised him so, poor lad, he had to be silenced as well.' She paused and looked at the two Wakefields. 'And now it's all over, bar the shouting.'

'Not until I get my share of the money back, it isn't,' growled Mike.

Kay Harris looked at him and said, 'You still haven't got it yet, Mike, have you? It's still the firm's money. Malcolm isn't going to come back to claim it and be charged with complicity.'

'I've still got to find it,' he said, a man still shaken by what had happened.

Kay Harris said, 'Try the very back of the cabinet under the perfect binding finishing machine. Look behind rows and rows of lever-arch files. Safer there than taking it home where his wife might find it.'

'They're full of old invoices,' he protested.

'Not quite full of them,' said Kay. 'If you make the effort to get behind them, you'll find all you want there. That's where I found everything. It was whilst I was looking for details of that book we did on the runic alphabet, remember?'

The printer stirred. 'Now that was a lovely job.'

'But what I didn't know was who'd hidden them there,' said Kay. 'It could have been anyone.'

'But it wasn't anyone, was it?' said a happily restored Steph. 'It was Gilbert and Malcolm. Coffee, Kay?'

CHAPTER FORTY-THREE

Breakfast at Ornum House that Monday morning was very much as usual, the earl having come back from the hospital and had some sleep.

'Neville left you a note, Jonas, before he went home last night,' The countess pointed in the direction of the sideboard, where there was an envelope propped up against the coffeepot.

The earl reached for it, opened it and read it before setting it down on the breakfast table with a smile playing on his lips. 'Good old Tony,' he said.

'Tony who, Daddy?' asked his daughter Victoria, who was tackling a dish of prunes jostling with sliced peaches.

'Tony Heber-Hibbs – the best batsman the school's ever had.' Jonas Cremond's mind went back over the years, and he became suddenly misty-eyed. 'We used to call him Sticky Wicket, you know.'

'Don't prunes and peaches look pretty together?' said Victoria. 'Black and orange.' She was counting the prune stones at the edge of her plate and muttering, 'Tinker, tailor, soldier, sailor . . .' to herself.

Lady Mary was munching toast. 'But where is this Tony now?' she asked, as always interested in the whereabouts of any male mentioned.

'He's our man in Lasserta, Mary.'

'What?' she said.

The countess winced. 'You mean who, dear, not what.'

'Who, then,' she said impatiently.

'He's Her Britannic Majesty's ambassador to the Kingdom of Lasserta and, before you ask, it's a remote island in the Indian Ocean with an unlimited supply of oil. It appears that he rang the police yesterday.'

Victoria lifted her gaze from her dish of prunes and peaches and asked what he had been talking to Uncle Neville about.

'This tanker lying just outside Kinnisport,' said her father. 'He says it's from Lasserta. Apparently, Tony can speak the crew's lingo and he's had a word with them. They say if they don't get what they want, they'll spill all their oil in the harbour and then open the sea cocks.'

'Nice,' said Victoria.

'Not nice,' protested the countess reprovingly.

'Oh, all right, then, not nice,' agreed Victoria,

selecting a prune. 'So? Go on, Daddy.'

'Tony says we're going to let a deputation ashore and he's flying over here to sort it all out.' The earl, looking up from the letter, was clearly delighted. 'That means he'll still be here for Saturday's match. I'm sure the captain would fit old Sticky Wicket in the team.' He started to get to his feet. 'I'll ask him first thing.'

'No, you won't, Jonas,' said his wife firmly. 'What you're doing first thing, all of you, is taking the silver back to the bank. It's safer there.'

CHAPTER FORTY-FOUR

Detective Inspector Sloan finished his preliminary narrative account of the actions taken by the police following the murder of Leonard Datchet and the attempted murder of Jason Fixby with a feeling of relief. He signed and dated the report and, laying his pen down, he shuffled the pages into a neat pile, laid this on his desk and decided it was high time he headed for the police station's canteen.

He heard the noise before he got there, a raucous cacophony of shouting and jeering accompanied by the stamping of feet. It became louder as he opened the door of the canteen only to behold Constable Crosby and his friend Constable Fleetwood standing sheepishly in the middle of the floor with everyone else around them grinning.

Inspector Harry Harpe of Traffic Division, he who

had never been known to smile, fetching up beside Sloan on his way in, was almost cheerful for once. 'Caught again, Seedy,' he said. 'It always works.'

'What was it this time?' asked Sloan.

'Letsby Avenue,' said Harpe.

'And where did our duplicitous station sergeant send them on this occasion?'

'Bill told them that he had had a report of a disturbance in Letsby Avenue, a turning off Railway Terrace, and would the pair of them go and investigate pronto.'

'Credible,' agreed Sloan.

'He warned them it might involve a bit of a punch-up, which obviously made them dead keen to get going.'

'It would,' agreed Sloan again. 'What's the betting that they'd switched their body cameras off before they left the station?'

'No takers,' said Inspector Harpe. 'Just what the pair of them would want – a punch-up with no sergeants around to remind them of the rules of engagement and no cameras on to record it.'

'And?' asked Sloan, although he knew what the answer would be by now.

Harpe grinned. 'They couldn't find any such place, let alone any punch-up.'

'How far did they get?' Sloan asked Happy Harry.

'Practically quartered that end of the town.'

'Looking for a bit of action,' said Sloan, not unsympathetically. 'And?'

'And, of course, they couldn't find it.'

'Because it isn't there,' said Sloan. 'So?'

'So they rang Bill Matthews and told him they couldn't find any Letsby Avenue anywhere. It wasn't even on their map, they said.'

'Did they? That should have told them something was going on.'

'It should have done but it didn't. So Bill told them to go on looking.'

'Rotten of him.'

'I'll say.'

'And in the end, they had to come back to the station and say so.'

'Hence the jollification,' concluded Sloan.

'Too right. And now look at 'em. No fight left in either of them.'

The remark was justified. The two police constables clearly didn't know what to do or say – they just stood there, not unlike animals awaiting the auctioneer at a livestock sale.

Detective Inspector Sloan, personally always in favour of animal rights even after a protestor in their cause had fetched him a nasty whack behind his knees with a placard, felt that the pair of them had had enough by now. He bellowed, 'Crosby, Fleetwood, over here. This minute.'

Crosby had seen him come in and couldn't have got to Sloan's side more quickly. 'Sir,' he pleaded, 'we don't know what's going on.'

Fleetwood, sturdier than most, growled that someone was taking the mickey out of them and when he found out who it was, he'd make them sorry.

'No, you won't,' said Sloan. 'You'll man up and grin and bear it.'

Fleetwood's scowl still boded ill for someone when he caught them.

'Sir,' pleaded Crosby, 'what did we do wrong?'

'You fell for the oldest trick in the book, Crosby. "Letsby Avenue" is a pun on the policeman's favourite sentence, which is "Let's be having you, chummy." Don't let it happen again.'

ACKNOWLEDGEMENTS

With many thanks to Roderick Watson, sometime practitioner in insolvency, and Thelma Rolfe, printer and bibliophile.

Catherine Aird is the author of more than twenty crime novels and story collections, most of which feature Detective Inspector Sloan. She was awarded the CWA Diamond Dagger for her lifetime contributions to crime fiction. She holds an honorary MA from the University of Kent and was made an MBE. Apart from writing the successful Chronicles of Calleshire, she has also written and edited a series of village histories. She lives in Kent.